TETRALOGY OF THE TIMES

STORIES OF CYPRUS

G. Philippou Pierides

G. PHILIPPOU PIERIDES

Tetralogy of the Times
Stories of Cyprus

TRANSLATED FROM GREEK BY

DONALD E. MARTIN

AND

SOTERIOS G. STAVROU

WITH A PREFACE BY

THEOFANIS G. STAVROU

A NOSTOS BOOK
1998

This volume is number twenty-one in a series of publications dealing with modern Greek history and culture, under the auspices of Nostos, the Society for the Study of Greek Life and Thought, Minneapolis, Minnesota, and in collaboration with the Modern Greek Studies Program at the University of Minnesota.

Theofanis G. Stavrou, *general editor*

Cover and frontispiece: Portrait of G. Philippou Pierides (1957) by Andreas Charalambous, courtesy of the artist

Technical and editorial assistance for this volume was provided by Elizabeth Harry.

This translation is dedicated
to all people whose lives, like the lives of the Cypriot
people, have been altered by the act of war.

TABLE OF CONTENTS

TIMES OF SUFFERING (1978)

ADDENDUM

PREFACE

G. PHILIPPOU PIERIDES belongs to the category of Cypriot writers, poets, and artists who devoted a great part of their creative work to portraying the dramatic developments in Cyprus during the last half century. He has certainly captured the political and social transformation on the island and nowhere does he do it better than in the four collections of stories entitled *Η Τετραλογία των καιρών* (*Tetralogy of the Times*), published in one volume by the Bank of Cyprus Cultural Foundation in 1989. The result is a major accomplishment by both author and publisher. For although the four collections had already been published separately, it is in this edition that they assume their place in a meaningful chronology rendering the volume a powerful historical and artistic document, a monument, one should add, capturing the mood of the Cypriot people, in an almost Chekhovian sensibility, from the years of their British colonial status to their present predicament. As the author points out in a prefatory note to the Greek edition, "The shocking events of 1955–1959 in Cyprus moved me— as they moved other writers, too—to attempt to express the events and the climate of that era. Of course, I did so in my own way and from my own spiritual and sentimental vantage point. At the time this was my sole intention."

The first section of the *Tetralogy*, "Times Immovable," portrays the period before 1955 when Cyprus was a British colony. It is followed by "Times of Difficulty," which canvasses the struggle of the Cypriot people for independence and concentrates on the years 1955-1959. "The skimpy independence of 1960," to use the author's words, was gained or granted as a result of the Zurich and London agreements, which established the Republic of Cyprus. The first years of independent Cyprus are captured in the third collection of stories called "Times of Affluence." It brings the story to 1974 when the coup d'etat against Archbishop Makarios took place, an incident which gave Turkey the opportunity and excuse to invade Cyprus. The Turkish invasion and its consequences—political, social, and moral—are dealt with in the fourth section, "Times of Suffering."

G. Philippou Pierides wrote the *Tetralogy of the Times* when he was at his peak as a writer and as a social observer (1963-1975). Born in Cyprus in 1904, the author moved to Egypt where he worked for many years as an employee in the cotton industry. Since the middle of the nineteenth century, Egypt had attracted a great number of enterprising Greeks from mainland Greece, Cyprus, and other diaspora centers of the Levant. Many of these Greeks of Egypt excelled in business, education, and letters. Pierides took an active part in the intellectual life of Alexandria and his first work, *The Cotton Growers*, was published in 1945. Soon thereafter, he returned to Cyprus where he settled and became active in the island's intellectual life. Among other things, he served as director of the Public Library and Gallery in Famagusta (1955-71) and worked in the Phaneromeni Library in Nicosia (1971-79). The return to Cyprus gave him the opportunity to become an eyewitness to the events he so admirably describes in his *Tetralogy of the Times*.

An old wish to meet the author, whom I had held in high esteem for many years, was realized through the good offices of Dr. Maria Iacovou in the summer of 1993. It was on this occasion that he presented me with a copy of his *Tetralogy*. The brief visit with the author and the reading of the *Tetralogy* later that summer enhanced the image I had of the man and his work: a person as old as the century, of small but determined frame, integrity written all over his face, and master of wise words with which he managed to articulate the spirit of Cyprus in a profound and beautiful way. I read the *Tetralogy* reflectively during the month of August 1993. In fact it proved to be the reading event of the summer for me. As a Greek Cypriot, I experienced through this reading a rare reacquaintance with my native island. All the characters of my village and the island with whom I grew up and whom I later watched go their own way as they watched me go mine, all the places, the spirit of the place, all the smells and noises, the customs and colors of a gentle, beautiful people—conquered but invincible, compromised in some areas but with sufficient integrity left in them to guarantee the survival and hoped-for revival of the island—all these realities and images dominated my thinking during the reading of the *Tetralogy* and beyond.

The third part of the *Tetralogy*, "Times of Affluence," was first translated and published in the *Modern Greek Studies Yearbook* volume 10/11 (1994/95), which was devoted to Cyprus. But it was always the intention of the translators and the publisher that the *Tetralogy* appear as an independent volume in the Nostos series in order to make the work accessible to a wider audience through an English translation. The translation and publication of the *Tetralogy* were planned to coincide with the Twenty-first Annual Celebration of Greek Letters at the University of Minnesota held on May 15, 1998, devoted to "Aspects of Cypriot Culture." During this event emphasis was placed on Cypriot culture, above all literature, and special homage was paid to G. Philippou Pierides. It is hoped that the publication of this important work will direct attention to other deserving works of literature which deal with universal concerns even though set against the Cypriot landscape. It is fair to state that the *Tetralogy* could be useful to students of history, political science, sociology, and anthropology, as well as to those interested primarily in literature. It is an impressive saga chronicled through successful storytelling of an island and its people.

July 13, 1998   Theofanis G. Stavrou
                                                 Minneapolis

ACKNOWLEDGEMENTS

THE GROUNDWORK for the present translation was done in Nicosia, 1994, during a semester of teaching English at the University of Cyprus. The book itself is a treasure beyond price from which I learned much more about Cyprus and about people than I did from a six-month sojourn on the island. My debts of gratitude for this are far greater than I shall ever be able to repay: to Theofanis G. Stavrou especially, who handed me the book and then arranged a visiting professorship for me at the University of Cyprus; to my wife Sherrilyn, who was there with me the while and who typed a great deal of the first draft; to the members of the Department of Foreign Languages and Literatures, especially Stephanos Stephanides, Jim Davy, Yannis Ioannou, Joanna Byles, and Maria Margaroni, for their splendid hospitality; to Yannis Ioannou again for introducing me to Mr. Pierides; to Agni Zaverda, who also typed many, many pages of text; and to Mary Kay Rubey of Rockford, Illinois, who performed her usual Word-Perfect magic. Thanks also to the Rockford College administration for granting me a leave of absence to do the work.

I feel particularly privileged to have been able to collaborate with Soterios Stavrou, from whom I have learned much English, more Greek, and some useful humility! I will always value the many discussions we had, especially the numerous long sessions we had in Rockford and Minneapolis as we sought to advance the manuscript from the original rough rendition to its present status.

On behalf of Soterios and myself I would also like to thank the following individuals who proved helpful to the completion of the project: first and foremost Soterios's wife Elizabeth, who read the manuscript through and through several times and offered valuable suggestions; Stavros Stavrou and Themis Stavrou, whose understanding of Cypriot culture and idiom came to our rescue more than once; and finally, Father Anthony Coniaris and John and Ingrid Larson for their willingness to support the project along the way.

Donald E. Martin

TIMES IMMOVABLE

THE LAST JEWEL

THE OLD NEIGHBORHOOD stretches in the morning, attempting to shake off its torpor, until the sun is high. Then it livens up with the commotion in the market which spreads its tentacles all around: sounds reach like a distant rumble from the center of the small town; gangs of kids start off for school, scattering an iridescence of color and voices onto the streets; housewives open windows and shake out bedding; young maids run errands barefooted . . . Right up till noon. Then the neighborhood falls back into its lethargy.

The two or three hours right after noon are the most inert. The deserted streets, the closed house windows, the few small trees, rising hopelessly behind courtyard walls, sink into silence and abandonment.

And only late in the afternoon does a weak pulse again reveal the dull presence of life, a pulse set by isolated cries and events that come and go in the same monotonous daily sequence.

About five o'clock the paper vendor will hawk the *Herald*, which has circulated very early in Nicosia, but has just arrived around here. ("The *Herald* is here," Kyria Eulalia Kaneli will say to herself. She sits in her drawing-room and awaits she knows not what. She will wag her head meaningfully as if only now realizing that precisely what she expected has happened. And she will send her maid out to fetch her a paper, so she can read the society section. She must see which of her countless friends and relatives, scattered all over the island, must be sent a letter of congratulation or condolence, suitably formulated according to the circumstances and the position or degree of relationship of the recipient.)

3

Then in turn, and at long intervals of silence, will come the ice cream man's horn . . . the *koulouras* with his afternoon batch . . . and, finally, at dusk, Salih the Turk will fill the neighborhoods with his resounding cry, which he has repeated identically for twenty years now at exactly the same time, as if he were sending a final message to the sun, which has set. *"Ayrann!"* he will cry out, in clipped fashion at first, as if he were rehearsing, then repeat it in a long-drawn-out melody, his voice breaking into an ascending chromatic scale, as if the notes were steps which his voice climbs one by one to reach a bell-like performance all his own: *"A-a-y-y-ra-a-a-nnn!"*

As if Salih had given them the sign they had been waiting for, two of the three shops, the corner grocer and the notions store, will close up.

The third, the Smyrna General Store and Winery, is a small *taverna*. But if you are a stranger and tired of looking at the uniform, corrosive bad taste of the province, you will find relief inside here. Three little tables, spread with square, red and white locally made cotton, the shiny counter, the colorfully striped curtains in the entryway, the huge, bright green philodendron in the corner, the loaded shelves, and the tasteful arrangement of everything create a pleasant and friendly atmosphere.

§

Following the strange roads laid out by the human lot, Liza of Smyrna ended up at this shop in the shadow of run-down mansions in the most forgotten little town in Cyprus.

This is how it happened: when she was passing through town with a theater company, Haritos upped and fell in love with her and married her. He was a musician, a dreamy fellow from another world, who made his living with music lessons—violin, mandolin, piano—but he spent most of his time circulating around the villages listening to and copying out local tunes played by the fiddlers. He lived poorly, having only this house for support, all that was left of the substantial property which he inherited from his parents and which dissolved in his hands without his knowing how.

Liza, who was beginning to show her age a bit, accepted the lowly situation fortune offered. Besides, she felt compelled to take under her protecting wings this vulnerable child with the spare frame, the faded black suit, and the thoughtful eyes which looked trustingly upon everything. When you tried to point out to him the shifty characters hiding behind their disguises, he would smile awkwardly as though it were all his fault. Haritos, of course, was not a child. He was older than she: forty years old when they met. But that's how Liza looked upon him—as a child.

She rolled up her sleeves and set her household in order without bending the knee to any of the important ladies of the area, who looked down their noses and kept the actress at a proper distance. But she was not so stupid as to let all these inflated geese know how much she despised them. She had instinctive discernment and was at ease with the way they behaved, the way they dressed, the way she herself remained indifferent to the stupidities that tyrannized their lives. The important ladies finally realized that this devil-woman was unscathed by their attempts to put her down; moreover, she had a sharp tongue in reserve when she really needed it. With two razor-sharp and true words she was capable of putting the most uppity lady in her place. They understood and tacitly agreed to a compromise. They did not concede to Liza the rights of equality, but she retained the right not to put up with insults, the right to go to the bishopric on the annual holy days to pay her respects along with the rest to His Grace, the right to sit in the Club with her legs crossed and to smoke (a right accorded to her alone) without the others considering it indispensable to pretend that they were horrified by her behavior.

However, what they did recognize unreservedly, to her face and behind her back, was the competence she showed in managing Haritos's finances. This respect for money and the ability to hang on to it and find ways to increase it was a self-evident virtue which spoke directly to their souls. On that subject, then, Liza earned their complete respect. From the very first months after their wedding, she found a way to jar the memories of several parents of Haritos's students who kept forgetting to pay for their instruction. She mercilessly monitored the weights and the charges of the grocer, and if she shopped now and then for clothing for herself or Haritos, she shopped with open eyes and tight fists.

In time she took a loan from the Bank and succeeded in converting Haritos's deserted patriarchal mansion into a small, tidy apartment with a courtyard in the back and a shop out front to rent out.

And when Markos, the corner grocer, uneasy about some rumors that were circulating—that supposedly Liza would rent the shop to someone intending to open a grocery store—offered her three pounds a month to take it himself, she demanded eight! Markos tore his hair and howled that he was being ruined, but he upped his offer every so often till he reached five pounds. But the woman of Smyrna held out well, and as things proved, they would agree on six. Well, it was at that time that all the women admired her.

But she did not get the shop rented because in the meantime Haritos fell ill and before they realized the seriousness of his condition, he died.

The troubles came like a summer squall: sudden, wild, short-lived.

Liza and Haritos's few friends, who had run to help, took his sickness rather lightly at first. But suddenly they found themselves struggling within a nightmare: restless, upset, hopelessly helpless, inconsolable. Only Haritos endured calmly until he died with that patient smile still on his lips, the abiding expression of his entire life.

Liza closed his eyes, gathered up all his notebooks and papers, down to the last shred, preserved them devoutly, and began to think about what to do now.

She kept the shop.

And after a few months, when she had run about here and there laying in the supplies she needed, she opened the Smyrna General Store and Winery.

Markos was furious. Some ladies pretended to be scandalized. But most of the neighbors understood. How else was the poor woman to earn her bread? How pay off the debt? Besides, they had grown used to accepting Liza as an exception in their midst, untrammeled by what was appropriate and what wasn't, the considerations that dominated their own lives. Some of the women even secretly admired her. They, the defeated ones, felt intuitively that this devil-woman, an actress or not, had in her own way brought to them, amid the slavery that oppressed everything about them, a message of personal independence and daring. They supported her. And they came off the better for it, because Liza did not try to cheat them.

There were also some householders, such as the merchant Nikitaides; Mr. Loukias, a retired judge; the director of land registry; Dr. Kanelis; Mr. Zoulios, the photographer, all appreciators of the fine *meze*, an art in which they found that the Smyrnian woman was unrivaled. She always had something choice to serve, sometimes octopus on the embers, sometimes mackerel salad, sometimes *lountza* or smoked ham with freshly fried crispy new potatoes, always something different which evoked the same encouraging flattery.

"Liza, you are, after all, a genuine master of the *meze*."

And the same complacent response:

"That's the way we Smyrnians are."

They would come in the evening to sip a small glass, tell a joke, and dispel their boredom for a while before going home to dinner.

Her most regular customers were Zoulios, and the doctor. Zoulios, would have more than one drink, and Liza would grow tired of him, because, in spite of his lavaliere and the thick gray hair which gave him the appearance of an artist, he was a non-stop talker. The doctor was drawn to Liza's by nostalgia for his homeland. He was Anatolian, too, and was here as a refugee.

But the doctor was different, different from everyone: the good person who passed among us like a blessing in order to leave engraved on our hearts a seal of humanity.

Of all who met him, there is no one in our small town and the surrounding villages who would not remember Stathis Kanelis with affection, the doctor with his domed head groomed, his brown gold-flecked laughing eyes and his hands with the long fingers, which could—both eyes and hands—touch all pains gently and consolingly.

He never drank more than a glass of wine, "white and dry." But he liked the fine *meze* and expressed his joy like a young child when Liza offered something from Anatolia.

"Soutzoukakia a la Smyrne! Mmm! . . ."* he would say, rubbing his hands together so that you would think he was going to eat a plateful.

He would nip one up, then another, drink two swallows of wine and stop.

"Help yourself, doctor, since you like them," Liza would say.

"They're splendid," he would say, but he would not take another.

He knew that Liza took this particular delicacy from the plate she had prepared for her own supper. And besides, he thought it would hurt the feelings of his wife, Eulalia, if he arrived home having already eaten.

Kyria Eulalia belonged to one of the first families of the country. She was no longer young when her family married her to the newly-arrived refugee doctor; they had carefully weighed his worth.

She had aristocratic notions and habits and did not sympathize with the popular tendencies of her husband. She was polite to Liza because that's the way she thought a lady of high society should behave "in such circumstances." Though he did not deign to talk about the matter, Kanelis realized what suspicions his wife had got into her head about his relationship with Liza. He found the situation humorous. He was sure that it caused Kyria Eulalia no pain. Why, her romantic soul even enjoyed the role of melancholy superiority which her imagination had created for her.

"What's she to do, poor woman?" he would say to himself. "She plays out roles in fairy tales she creates for herself out of boredom."

But who can measure up to the stature of his imaginary self? Kyria Eulalia would soon come down again to the level of her real self, in the midst of prosaic everydayness and trifling cares, to grumble and to chatter non-stop. And the doctor suffered patiently.

"My wife, young sir, is not Euthalia," he said once to a young man, who made an error on her name while asking him to convey his respects to Kyria Euthalia. "She is not Euthalia. Unfortunately, she is Eulalia."

8

If only she had at least presented him with a son! But no. Their only child was a girl.

But even this ceased to matter, because as Marietta grew up and filled the doctor's house and heart, his grievance vanished.

When Marietta finished grade school, Kanelis was sure that in this age a girl could go on and even surpass her father as well as a boy could. And when she finished high school he sent her to Athens to study medicine.

How pleased Liza was then, and how she cut short those who found Kanelis's decision too daring for the patriarchal traditions of our country!

"You people are asleep," she told them. "Why, in Europe women have even become ministers of state."

And what say, by any chance, did Liza have in this matter? None. But she could not leave unanswered every owl who thought that only the darkness was good and who dared to call the doctor's judgment and the rights of a girl like Marietta into question. Couldn't they see how much this decision was costing him?

"You'll miss your little girl, doctor, when she's gone," she told him one day, the words slipping out by accident.

"I know, Kyria Liza, I know," he said, as if talking to himself, and sank again into his silence.

Whenever she saw him fall silent that way, Liza knew how genuinely unapproachable this affable man was in his solitude. But it was not a silence that grew heavy. It only spread out between them like an expanse of calm filled with the fluttering of good intentions. One could sit in silence for hours with Kanelis without getting uncomfortable. Liza stopped her coming and going in the shop and sat quietly in a corner.

But with the war and the occupation of Greece by the Germans, Marietta found herself confined to Athens, and months passed without word from her. Then Kanelis's bouts of silence became heavy, because his solitude surpassed the bounds of his endurance. For all that, he tried to struggle against the surge of his personal pain, taking with clear eye the measure of human pain and continuing to

9

dedicate himself to his patients and to the suffering people who had come to depend upon him.

He felt sorry for his wife, but how could he help her when he saw her confronting the same pain in a manner totally contrary to his own. Kyria Eulalia now became inquisitive about everything; she would read all the news and articles in the *Herald*; she followed the vicissitudes of military operations and political ferment. But all these matters she successfully brought into focus upon herself and her fluctuating hopes for Marietta's return.

§

But that is an old story.

After the liberation, when she was finally able to return to her country, Marietta did not find her father alive. Nor was she herself the same old rosy-cheeked girl who lit up a thousand colorful certainties with her laughing eyes. Those blossoms have now formed into an unripe fruit. Her sunken cheeks and pinched lips and eyes often half-closed to focus on some distant point, showed all the marks of the difficult passage from the kiln of an ordeal to spiritual maturity.

All the women who went to her house to welcome her back were disappointed with her disinclination to satisfy their inexhaustible curiosity.

"I can imagine, my dear Marietta, what all you went through after being so used to better things," each one began in her turn.

But Marietta did not say much; she only smiled good-naturedly as if her mind were elsewhere. And the little she did say related to the drama of the occupation in a general and impersonal way.

"Heaven help us!" the ladies whispered among themselves. Some found Marietta naive, others found her pretentious.

Even Liza, who ran eagerly to see her, returned to the store deep in thought.

"Something is on her mind," she said to herself about Marietta.

She came one morning unexpectedly and found Liza in the store.

She was wearing a brown skirt and a light sweater of the same shade, but a little lighter, with a small white linen collar. Except for that small collar, which was shining white and freshly ironed, nothing revealed any particular care in her way of dressing. Nevertheless, her appearance testified to her good taste and natural charm.

She sat down and, as she crossed her legs, Liza stopped to admire the well-shaped limb, the slight, wiry ankle, the arch of the foot proudly outlined.

"A queen!" she said to herself as she fussed over the girl.

But Marietta did not appear to notice anything. She just sat comfortably concentrated, as if she were by herself, and looked out beyond the deserted square towards the sea, which could not be seen from there.

Liza remembered the doctor. That was the way he would sit silently, except that he would not have had his teeth clenched.

She sat next to the young woman and waited.

"Tell me about yourself, Kyria Liza. How is it going for you?" said Marietta finally and looked at her affectionately.

Liza jumped.

"O.K., my child. Yes, we're getting along."

"Have you paid off your debts?" she asked in the manner of a person who sees no sense in vagaries.

Liza responded in detail: how much she had paid off, how much was left, not much.

"In general how did you all get along down here all this time?"

Liza was pleased by her interest and described the economic luxury that the country knew throughout the war. Mobilization, military bases, the English army, which was well-paid and spendthrift . . .

"We didn't have to go without down here. We got along quite well."

The other listened attentively.

"It's the dirty gifts of war," she said finally, wrinkling up her lips.

On the other side of the square a fat woman came out onto a balcony dragging a rug. She struggled to get it hung

11

on the railing and then began pounding on it furiously with a stick, as if she were sounding an alarm. The emptiness of the neighborhood, startled, urgently echoed the blows.

"How loaded with emotions all these ruins were in my dreams back there," said Marietta, her manner revealing her perplexity in finding it all so indifferent now.

"But it's your country, Marietta," said Liza. "And besides, right here you are the best among the foremost people. You can make of your life whatever you like."

"Do you, too, believe, Kyria Liza, that securing comfort is enough to fill a person's life? Or . . ." But she did not feel like continuing. How can one explain to someone else the questions that torment one's thoughts: all that the eyes have seen, the roads that one has traveled to realize how distant the times are since these ramshackle mansions have brought joy and pain to living people!

Liza's hint at preeminence led Marietta's thought, by some curious association, to the photograph of her grandfather, which hung fading away in the Conference Room of the Town Hall, along with two other "departed mayors." Hadji Pieras, fierce-looking with his fez and thick, joined eyebrows gazed out, as if he pitied the sorry state of his descendants. How well she understood Hadji Pieras, his heavy, hopeless shadow which obstinately refused to admit that it no longer amounted to anything. He wasn't even a shadow. She wondered whether Liza could possibly believe that in our age the family archives could have any meaning.

Liza wavered. One moment she was content with the thought that this Marietta was in no way different from the one she expected, except that she was tired. The next moment she found that, no, the Marietta of her imagination was nonexistent just as she herself was nonexistent to the distant and closed-up girl right here.

"Besides, as a doctor, you will be walking in your father's footsteps," she said temptingly, as if she were opening a golden door.

Marietta jumped.

"Nothing around here is as dear to me as the memory of my father," she said.

But immediately she drew up her brows. Her own words were sounding like so many sentimental commonplaces. They were destroying the magic in everything she felt touched by the love that she saw joining the hearts of so many simple folks around the memory of the doctor. That which shone within her was so tender, so touching, so beyond the conventionality of words . . .

Liza understood. But this time, too, her expectation was in vain. The girl did not open her heart to her, but again only remained motionless, her gaze fixed on her own thoughts.

She has the severity of Hadji Pieras, Liza said to herself. But how she resembles the doctor, my God. The same great forehead. The same eyes.

§

What else can they do who find themselves living in a sleepy little town? They coil themselves around the worries, the arrogance, the self-respect they have always had and occupy their lives with such trifles. The annual school celebration, the prices of lots, worries about each season's new stitchery, rivalry over the luxury of the buffet at every reception, card-playing, the Philoptochos fund-raiser, the complicated maneuvers in the settling of girls who wait around and sit at the piano, playing the same Chopin nocturne over and over. What are they to do? Without those things, without their serene faith in the solidity of this primitive self-sufficiency of the conventional, they would be in fear of losing the very basis of their lives; they would dissolve into nothing. So they make do. They make do very well by relying on the customary, where all human propensities will finally find some way of being castrated and put to rest. Even the most restless—even those tortured by the necessity to stand out from the crowd—will find in some harmless deviation the way to fool themselves into feeling that they have a calling or that they are unique: one will cling like an oyster to theosophy, the other to philanthropic works, yet another to the expensive keeping of rare breeds of dogs, and another in his decision to hold everything in contempt.

Kyria Eulalia found two props to keep head and shoulders above the crowd: her aristocratic lineage, symbolized by her large house, and her rich collection of rare plants and flowers, which secured her first place among the flower fanciers of the entire island, not excepting a group of lofty English ladies who were fanatical on this subject.

The house was built for Hadji Pieras when he was at the height of his great power. Spacious and imposing, with its archways, its chambers, and the tiled indoor courtyard, the shelters, the stables, the storage areas, the heavy oaken gate. It preserved in its silence the recollection of the good old days when the courtyard was full of share-croppers and servants, when cars, carts, and teams of horses came and went all day. Eulalia received it as her dowry, her only share in her father's property. All the rest went to the two sons, to keep up the name. Such was the wish of Hadji Pieras and Eulalia found it right.

A rich growth of vegetation has now taken over the courtyard, the apsidal shelters, the terrace on the second floor, and lent its character to the entire place, which became a refreshing spot, full of shade and foliage of a thousand different shapes and all the shades of green, with small flashes of yellow, red, pink, orange, that barely lent it warmth: rubber plants, palm trees, bourbon palms, amaryllis, begonias, *kykas*, crow-foot, and a range of others with exotic names, from the most abundant with gigantic proud leaves to the most delicate.

Fitting in with the verdant peace and inseparable from it, the memories of the old times lie in wait everywhere.

In the salon the cherry-red upholstery and curtains faded to the indefinite color of watered-down wine. Behind its dulled and mottled surface the huge Venetian mirror hides a depth of mystery. Opposite, on a large, dark background in a gold frame, a finely drawn nude, conventionally melancholic, holds in rosy fingers an elegant death's head. On the console two plump, half-nude bronze ladies, allegorical figures from the intellectual pantheon of last century, lean indolently on a stopped clock. Their identities, Order and Precision, are for lack of other means of identification engraved in French beneath their bare feet.

"He studied to be an artist," said Marietta.

"An artist?" said Kyria Eulalia, surprised. "That's not a profession. And his family?"

14

"His name is Panos Armanis. His father was a tailor in Nicosia," answered Marietta, and her curtness shut the door on any further discussion.

Kyria Eulalia realized there was nothing left for her but to give her conventional and needless consent. She wrapped herself sumptuously in the veil of lost expectations and fell silent for a long while, her head bowed.

Finally she said with a sigh, "Since you've made up your mind to it, what can I do?"

She got up from the armchair, went over to the jardinière, which was in the middle of the salon and filled with pots of colorful caladium, carefully picked off three wilted leaves, and added:

"But it isn't the wedding I dreamed of for you, my child."

Marietta was standing in front of the window looking out. She could not help but be upset by her mother's melodramatic manner, but she controlled herself with the thought that her annoyance was egotistical and unfair.

She turned to her mother and spoke gently.

"He is a man with heart and merit, mother. When you get to know him, you will be pleased, I'm sure."

Moved by these words, Kyria Eulalia opened her arms; Marietta responded so as not to hurt her feelings.

§

The lighthouse at the entrance to the harbor is awake all alone in the night, and its thoughts become a circle of light playing on the water, making perceptible the unseen jubilation of the sea.

Out in the open sea, in the middle of the dark uncertainty, the *pyrofani* rocks at its mooring, a spot of light that scatters on the blue waters, bunches up, and scatters again uninterruptedly the liquid sheaf of its phosphorescence.

Small lighted presences. Infinitely small flames of will, which resist the blandishments of sleep.

The lighted window high on the second floor stayed up to keep vigil tonight also, over the pitch black neighborhood.

A small room, its walls covered with close-packed rows of books on shelves and, next to the window, the desk. The doctor's office. His cell, as he used to call it. His beloved

15

books. Not the heavy, leatherbound tomes containing the wisdom of doctors; these are in the book cases of his big office on the ground floor. In the silence of these books live voices of another order: poets, prose writers, thinkers, our own and foreign, from the blind master singer to the beginning of our century.

Everything stayed the same as the doctor had left it, down to the small silver-framed photograph on his desk: Marietta when she was in high school, and there is the present-day Marietta sitting opposite without noticing her, absorbed as she is in her book.

Lately she has been riveted in her attempt to solve some problems of timeliness which have shaken up her existence by going back to the basic causes. She draws a vertical line in the margin with her pencil, then lifts her eyes from the book and stares off into the distance. Her mind is on the wing. So it is. We will alter the face of the world.

Out of habit Liza goes to bed late.

She swept out the shop before closing, tidied up the house and sat down at the table, where she had put down a basket with some clothes taken from the line. They smelled clean. She wiped her glasses on a white piece of underclothing from the basket and began looking through the clothes item by item to separate out those which needed mending. She was in no hurry, as if this job had no other purpose than to occupy her hands at a time when her thoughts, saturated with the aroma which everything here puts forth for her alone, would turn to the past.

This was no nostalgic daydreaming. It had nothing of the languid attachment to former times which shrivels up sentimentalists. No, no. Liza walked solidly upon the earth. It was not, then, melancholic reminiscences that wrapped around her on these tranquil nighttime hours, when she was surrounded by the reminders of her turbulent youth. Those hours of night were fine and companionable. The memories had the substance of a living presence, and Liza would turn back among them and relive the moments of reality in the most natural way—the same natural way that she first lived them.

Two colored posters on the walls continued to advertise in muted voices the variety program which Rosalia Manet's Light Theater Troupe would present—how many years ago?—in Constantinople, Alexandria, Smyrna. Spread across the pillows on the couch, a bright red shawl with gold embroidery and long tassels looks like an exotic bird with wings widespread speaking strangely to and receiving from the opposite wall replies from a large open fan of white ostrich feathers, which had over the years taken on the hue of old ivory. From among the framed photos, which were everywhere and completed the image of a dressing-room, a large one stood out on the chest of drawers: a young Liza wearing a dark knee-length suit, light stockings, and a heavy felt beret, which covered her hair and imparted a devilishly attractive little-boy look to her lovely face, her almond-shaped eyes, accented in black, and her provocative lips, half-open in a street-urchin smile. Her legs cut a dance step, a light cane held high in her right hand. This was her great success, her favorite role.

> *I am the new woman*
> *who will smoke*
> *and vote*
> *each one of us is worth ten*
> *I don't give a nickel . . . for a man.*

From all she had scattered to the four winds, these few items remained to remind her of an era of triumph, luxury, and lavishness. These things, along with a batch of yellowed newspaper clippings in the chest of drawers. And in the same drawer under the carefully stored clothes, a small cherry-colored box lined with white silk on the folds of which shone a ruby artfully set in a gold ring. Liza opened the box but rarely. But she loved it and she often remembered it, the last jewel remaining to her.

She took off her glasses, rubbed her tired eyes, and began getting ready for bed.

Later, before she went to bed, she turned out the light, opened the window, and leaned on the sill.

Behind the redolent jasmine that adorned the courtyard, she could see slantwise a part of the small square and, beyond, the dark mass of the houses. And above their low

17

roofs in the background Marietta's lighted window beckoned to her in the dark like a sign of victory.

"She'll stay up all night again," she murmured. And a wave of affection for Marietta flooded over her, a feeling generated from her innermost being.

§

She was sitting in the doorway of the shop and saw them emerge from the narrow street and cross the square in conversation. They saw her, too, and Marietta said something to her companion. They turned in her direction. When they arrived, Liza arose and Marietta took the man's hand, saying:

"Kyria Liza, I'd like you to meet Panos."

He must have been a year or two older than Marietta. Of medium height, he seemed to have a strong build with his square shoulders. But the pallor of his face, the drawn features, and a gleam deep in his blue-gray eyes showed a person just beginning to emerge from harsh suffering. The roomy sport jacket he was wearing, the carelessly knotted purple tie, his tousled blond hair, his way of looking one squarely in the eye, gave the impression of unaffected cordiality, in contrast to Marietta's focused expression.

He extended his hand to Liza, smiling.

She found him likable, but certainly not worthy of a girl like Marietta.

Would they sit and have something? No, they thanked her; Uncle Iraklis was waiting for them. They would come back another time just to see her.

Liza cupped Marietta's hand in hers.

"I wish you happiness."

Marietta seemed happy.

They met Aunt Elpinice in front of the church of St. Mamas.

The image of her drawing room returned to Panos. There the redoubtable old maid, seated on a rocking chair, created her imaginary illnesses among her photographs: those of her living relations lined up on the console; those of the dead ones hanging opposite the console.

18

As soon as Aunt Elpinice saw them she let out a screech of happy surprise and insisted on kissing her children, the well-matched couple, again and again right there in the road.

Yes. She had come to light a candle to St. Mamas, our patron, and was on her way home to change because she had been sweating. Greetings to little Eulalia. I'll come one of these days to congratulate her. And Panos shouldn't forget that she by all means wants a photograph of him. He promised her one, didn't he? And wouldn't they be taking pictures at the wedding? Ha! Ha! Ha! . . .

And she set out on her way in her quick little steps.

"How old would you say she is?" asked Marietta.

"Around sixty?"

"Seventy and beyond . . ."

"Unbelievable!"

"She still looks on my mother as her little cousin. That is how I remember her ever since I came to this world. She has always been grumbling that she was about to die."

Mr. Loukias caught up with them under the pines of their park. He slowed his pace and continued along the way with them. He, too, was going to the Club.

"How do you like our little town, Mr. Armanis?" he asked, then answered his own question, "Provincial, eh? Athens it isn't! When I was a law student . . . ," and he moved his cane as though he were stirring egg-lemon soup to show how much he had enjoyed Athens when he was a law student.

Then he took from his pocket a large handkerchief with a blue border, took off his homburg, and mopped his bald head.

"And what plans do you have after the wedding, Mr. Armanis?"

Panos didn't answer. Besides, they had arrived at the Club, and some of those seated outside rose to welcome the guests.

Uncle Iraklis was awaiting them in the reading room drinking cognac. His huge frame barely fit in his armchair.

19

"Welcome," he said. And without getting up he pointed to them the two armchairs next to him.

"Cognac, Panos?" he asked with a familiarity that surprised Panos.

"Thanks, but I'd prefer a little vermouth."

"Vermouth, Andreas, and another cognac for me," he called to the waiter. "And what'll you have, Marietta?"

"A lemonade," answered Marietta and looked at Panos with an imperceptible smile.

Uncle Iraklis, who considered himself head of the family, had his own notions about the place of women in society and could never accept the doctor's decision to send Marietta to school—especially medical school. So he would regard it as an unacceptable affront to his authority if his niece now asked to have a drink with him in the Club. Well, let him be.

On the second day after Panos arrived, Marietta, to please her mother, took him to visit Uncle Iraklis. Iraklis assumed the role of patron before them, but he asked no questions. His position said, all I ask is that you show me the required respect. Beyond that, I will not meddle in your affairs. And he allowed twice the time—four days—before he returned the visit one morning, just happening to be passing by, as he said, and invited them for lunch on the following day at his house.

"Come by for me at the Club at around eleven so we can go together."

It was his official recognition of his niece's engagement. And he thought this the best occasion to put aside formality and stop calling Panos Mr. Armanis.

He spoke without looking Panos in the eye. He would only look at him sidelong with his small, cunning, deeply set eyes.

"Since you're an artist, what do you think of the picture Eulalia has hanging in her salon? Good art, eh? And what meaning! Where can you find such work these days? The old man brought it from Marseilles one year that he took a load of silkworm cocoons there."

Panos kept silent. He was beginning to lose patience.

In a little while they were surrounded by some of the most important people of the small club—as many as happened to be there just then: Dr. Kaloyannis, with the gold

20

chain and ruddy face of a corpulent notable, who addressed Marietta as "dear colleague" as though in jest; Mr. Papazinoviou, a bald little old man wearing a stiff collar; Mr. Antidimarchos, who measures the minutes, tick-tock, with the massive amber beads of his *koboloyi*; and Mr. Loukias as well as one or two others.

Without stirring from his place—just an attempt at motion as though he were trying to get up—Uncle Iraklis made the introductions to each one: our son-in-law . . . exceptional artist. The others were very glad to meet him and looked curiously at Panos as if they were trying to guess how much he weighed.

A discussion came up about drawing and art in general, and Mr. Papazinoviou, raising his hand with two fingers joined as if he were taking an oath, gave a weighty disquisition on art in connection with religion and virtue, treating them as tangibles cut to his own personal measurements. Each one gave his opinion. And Panos was worrying all the while that they might ask his opinion. What would he say to them? Fortunately, no one asked. The conversation gradually wandered till it settled upon their cares and concerns and they were back on solid ground.

It was four o'clock when they left Iraklis's house.

Panos seemed tired and out of sorts.

"Are you tired of this?" asked Marietta.

He smiled at her and took her arm.

"I feel a bit like a fish out of water," he said.

"Patience. We had to give this satisfaction to mother. This will console her later when she will be alone again. The poor soul thinks protocol is so important."

"I understand, Marietta. You're right."

They walked in silence for a while in the quiet of the afternoon.

"It'll be different in Nicosia. We'll get to work," said Marietta at last. "Your family will not have so many prejudices."

"What 'family'?" laughed Panos. "You know I'm not of good family. My mother is just a simple woman who will only love us."

There was not a soul in the narrow streets. A hush weighed upon the town, and the shadows of the houses had scarcely begun to lengthen. Their footsteps resounded in the glare of the sun. Behind a fence they heard a pig grunting.

When they reached the street corner, they saw Uncle Tassos coming down the nearby road. He was wearing an open shirt, a linen jacket, gray gabardine pants, and had a large fragrant jonquil in his buttonhole. His white, wavy hair and bony face gave him a delicate look, almost spiritual, but his ruddy, pock-marked nose betrayed the tippler. In contrast to Iraklis, he was tall, wiry, and agile for his age. He was genuinely happy to see the youngsters.

"Did you make it through that ceremony, too?" he asked, laughing. "You seem weighted down with food and drink. Or are you just blown up with formalities?"

He stepped between them and took each one by the arm.

"Come on and let me buy you a coffee at Liza's, so you can recover your good mood."

Uncle Tassos had not married. He had traveled much in his youth and now lived quite alone. Only rarely did he go to the Club or the coffee shop. The others thought him eccentric and gossiped about him because he did not take seriously anything that they concerned themselves with.

From his first conversation with him at Eulalia's, where he came and found them every day, Panos found this much-traveled, unpretentious man to be lacking in neither culture nor judgment.

"Coffee at the wine shop?" asked Panos, bewildered.

"My good man, Liza is a sophisticated tavern keeper."

§

Kyria Eulalia objected, but at last gave her consent to a wedding for a small circle, without invitations, without reception, since she had their promise that she would be free to send announcements after the wedding to whomever she thought appropriate. This, too, is customary nowadays in good society.

The ceremony would take place at the monastery of Prophet Elias, where three automobiles would go carrying the bride and groom, Eulalia, Uncle Iraklis and family,

Uncle Tassos, and Aunt Elpinice, who was also Marietta's godmother. From Panos's side, his mother and brother would come from Nicosia. The Holy Abbot sent word that he himself would officiate.

"I like your mother," said Panos. "She is strong, equal to living alone in her imaginary world. Down deep you're very like her. You two share a desire to make things happen."

Marietta smiled.

"But I don't live in imaginary worlds."

"That's another matter," said Panos, and, lifting his glass, he turned to Kyria Liza, "To your health, Kyria Liza."

"To your health, Kyria Liza," Marietta said also. "But come, sit with us."

She had served them *ouzo* and was busy behind the counter preparing hors d'oeuvres.

It was Friday, close to noon. The wedding was to be on Sunday.

She brought over the tray of hors d'oeuvres and sat with them.

"To your health. May you live happily," she said with emotion.

She wanted to add good wishes for their future plans but did not know how. As if she even knew what they had in mind! Yet her instincts did not play her false. She felt that they were eager to get back on the boat and set sail.

"And good luck in your plans," she added.

Marietta and Panos looked at one another.

Clever woman, Panos said to himself.

They clinked glasses.

When she closed the shop that night Liza turned and looked upward. The window was not lighted tonight. Naturally. The wedding is tomorrow and they will have matters to tend to.

She did her housekeeping, ate supper, but all the time a thought was niggling at the back of her mind.

She opened the wardrobe, took out a blue silk dress, examined it carefully, holding it by the yoke, arms stretched

23

out, and decided that, in order to get it ready, she needed to adjust the collar a little before she ironed it. Tomorrow she would go congratulate the young couple. She sat down, put on her glasses and threaded the needle. But she could not relax.

Within her a golden light shone, playing with the shadows around evasive shapes. The remote and haughty expression on Marietta's face, which had in an unexplainable but definite way the sign of a promise. The calm, fine, sorrowful countenance of the doctor. The innocent, childlike eyes of Haritos. The recent and trusting face of Panos. And the living are not to part from the dead. They are just to seek, as partners, and at the same time separately, the secret path which leads beyond the marsh waters. And herself bound to them with the ties of a common expectation.

A long drawn-out roar was heard from the direction of the sea. One of the freighters that occasionally dock at the harbor was setting sail with its load of carobs.

Liza smiled. She figured it out! She found the gift that would suit Kanelis's daughter. What else? Could she go empty-handed to congratulate the bride?

She got up, went to the chest of drawers, opened the drawer and took out from under the pile of clothes the little cherry-red box. She opened it and gazed for a long time at the ruby glittering under the light. Then she shut the box, put it on the corner of the table and resumed her sewing.

Her mind was at peace. This way she would live in their memory. She felt no hesitation, only pleasure in the decision she had made.

BOREDOM

ON THE EVENING they said goodbye to one another, Zenios, who was leaving, was silent.   Pierretis, who was thinking about how much he would miss his young friend and admirer, was moved to the point of reciting verse in his deep, imposing voice.

The two of them were strolling along the shore, the sea was sighing serenely; listening silently, Pierretis was reciting.

Then he took his friend by the arm and said, "Never mind about it. The main thing is to keep your true self separate from your other self which is a plaything of circumstances."

But Zenios kept quiet.

Months went by. Pierretis received a letter from his friend saying that he had got a job at a restaurant in Sidney.

He imagined then the great, bustling city pitching about like an exotic ship on Conrad's oceans and filled with the mystery of people of every sort, and reflected on the sensitiveness of his friend now adjusting to other ways of thinking, and feeling homesick for "the green shores of the homeland."

Pierretis is a sentimental soul, who can create in his imagination emotions that arise from circumstances he had not witnessed, since he himself had remained on the island, where conditions were fairly favorable for him, only twenty-eight years old and already a first-class clerk in the land registration office. No matter how much one subordinates, out of intellectual superiority, the practical aspect of life, one does not simply decide to chase after the enticing unknown just for the sake of adventure, when he has a permanent position with good prospects and can consider at leisure the advantages afforded by one or the other of the various good marriages which he would be able to make when that time came.

Therefore he finds a way to keep his deeper self separate from the everydayness of his job as a clerk and from the meaningless things that surround him. Putting on the cloak of intellectuality, he feels distinguished and psychologically isolated, even though he maintains excellent relations with those around him, because he has chosen to be affable, to have his own peace and their esteem.

If they spend their lives in trivialities and stir up suspicions and enmities among themselves without purpose, it is, he thinks, because they have forgotten how to look at the sky.

Some of them had begun to look askance at Pierretis, too, because of his infatuation with the intellectual. But once they were sure that there was nothing to worry about, they found it rather appealing and proper—his infatuation, that is. Why, just the other day, when he gave yet another lecture on poetry at the Areti Club, all the best people in the small town, both men and women, came to listen with the diligence of people who know how to appreciate intellectual trends. Actually it was more as if they owed him gratitude for the self-esteem that he had graced them with.

Oh, if it were not for that little devil that occasionally awakens within him and guffaws, the rascal, and gives him the finger. If it were not for dark times when ennui would seize upon him, and he would feel his shiny robe scatter to the winds, leaving him stark naked before himself with the bitter feeling that he struggles in vain to hide.

Nevertheless, these are complicated issues. You should guard against the temptations of weariness, lest you become a pawn of your anxieties, which lie in ambush inside you. For if you do become a pawn, can your thought processes work clearly when you are in financial uncertainty? . . . Besides, in his comfortably arranged life does he not have his books and his ability to think for himself? And if the everyday dullness "in this small corner" does not respond to intellectual excitement—can it be certain that it responds elsewhere? He doesn't know. No, Pierretis has not

26

straightened this out, no matter how much it has occasionally troubled his mind. And so, always awaiting the next urge, he seeks himself out in the role of the silent worshipper of beauty.

And the land that spreads its quietude here in this end of the island is so beautiful. The small town sits washed in light on its rise and gazes out on the blue sea. And from up there an apron ornamented with gardens and cottages and ruins of ancient splendor spreads down to the shore, to the harbor.

He cultivates his mind, then, to draw excitement from the beauty of the universe and entrenches himself in the task of surveying his inner journey, since nothing happens around him worthy of being surveyed, nothing stirs his boredom, except meaningless events such as the arrival on the day before yesterday of the Dutch freighter.

He came down as usual in the afternoon to take his walk.

The streets in the business sector were full of the foul residue of trampled grapes which clung to the shoes. That morning there had been an unaccustomed commotion among the trucks, which had come down from the vineyards with loads of grapes, and the villagers, who had dumped the grapes in the roads of the market place in protest against the low prices that the wineries, in collusion, had offered for the crop.

The people in the bazaar and some of the passers-by were standing in the shop doorways discussing the incident, taking sides.

And what can come of this hubbub? thought Pierretis. Throwing the grapes in the street and hollering would not increase the demand for our wines overseas, would it?

He quickened his pace to get there before the sun set.

His usual route was down to the harbor, to sit at the seaside restaurant and enjoy the coolness and the sun, which was setting in the arms of the sea in all its purple grandeur.

But he had hardly reached his vantage point when there it was below, the steamer, anchored out in the open sea, writing in smoke on the virgin sky the message it was bearing from the great harbors. Pierretis's heart leaped.

27

In the harbor the lighters, set loose from their inertia, took on sacks of fertilizer from the steamer and one by one followed the motorized felucca which, gasping and puffing, pulled them to the sea-gnawed wharf to unload. The harbor shook off its lethargy and shouted for joy at its temporary activity and its revived hopes.

Night fell and Pierretis was still sitting at the beachside restaurant drinking his third *ouzo,* envious of the steamer with all its lights and its sailors.

He returned late, and when he got back to the height of the overlook, he turned and took another look from up there at the magical lights on the steamer in the night. And then, instead of dropping by the Club as he usually did, he went straight home.

He kept his room very tidy. Shelves loaded with books, papers, and notes, all set in order on his desk. Opposite the desk, hanging on the wall, was a lithograph, Bellini's "The Doge Leonardo Lorentan," which he had once cut out of an illustrated magazine and framed because he was impressed by it.

He sat looking at it. He was fascinated by that austere face with the deep-set eyes, the hard clenched underjaw, the thin lips, which revealed a steel will, diligence, cleverness, and awareness of the power and greatness symbolized in his rich uniform.

Later he sought the inspiration that he wanted to have brought with him. But he found only a ball of inscrutable expectations.

And he lay down to sleep unsatisfied.

PANTELITSA

I WAS LIVING in a ramshackle place, where lack of comfort was compensated by picturesqueness and cheap rent. It was an old two-story mansion crowded all around by the latest neighborhood of the poor. The front part of the building was rented out for storage, the shutters of its spacious rooms boarded shut. In the back a run-down wing formed an angle with the main structure and consisted of a ground floor with two rooms and a second-story room with a wooden outside staircase. The tenant, Melodias, and his family lived on the first floor. And he sublet the little second-floor room to me "with laundry and breakfast."

The inside of the corner, shut off on the other two sides with high walls, was a courtyard. But what a puny one, choked off by the highrises that rose behind its surrounding wall. A bitter orange tree rose with a single branch attempting in vain to reach above its strangling collar. Tins of basil, zinnias, and carnations, breathing with difficulty in this well, were like a pale presence of life in the shade of the ruins of the beautiful mansion and the ugly highrises.

But towards noon-time, when the rays of the sun were falling straight down, reaching to the bottom, to the little courtyard, a wonder took place: all the poor shards of beauty, the little greenery, the flowers, the goldfinch in its cage, the many-colored curtains at the window, the cheerful lines of the mansion with the ancient lattices, shone in a subdued idyllic harmony which entranced me.

That was also the time when I would wake up.

At that time I was studying music, and I made my living playing piano in a nightclub orchestra. I would go to my room to sleep when an imperceptible blue in the sky, a shudder in the air, heralded the impending break of dawn.

29

My steps would echo strangely in the sleepy narrow streets. I opened the fence gate carefully. It squeaked. I usually tarried in the courtyard to smoke a cigarette as I listened to the crystalline bell of the fountain which dripped into the stone basin.

I would tip-toe up the stairs and as soon as I entered my room I took off my shoes to move soundlessly on the decaying boards which separated me from the others asleep down below.

Often before I fell asleep, I would hear Melodias and Titika, his wife, get up and start work, being careful, as I was, not to make noise. They made the *tyropites*, which Melodias would arrange still hot on a three-wheeled cart and would set out selling them on his route at daybreak. He had prepared the ingredients the evening before.

I would sleep well. I was young. I dreamed while awake and was undisturbed by dreams as I slept.

So I would wake up during the brief brightness of the courtyard and go down to wash in the fountain, sit on the parapet, drink my coffee, and eat a *tyropita*—the "breakfast" we had agreed upon. Titika would bring it to me on a tray, which she would place on a chair. Melodias's *tyropites* were famous.

Titika's mother, Pantelou, a muddle-headed old wreck, also awaited as for a eulogy the visit of the sun to the courtyard. She spent her endless days and nights either stretched out in bed or seated on a bench whining and agonizing, troubling herself or troubling Titika, who always had worries of her own, to feed her or take her like a child from bed to bench or from bench to bed, to clean her up, when she had befouled herself, to listen to her endless whimpering. I felt sorry for her—not the old woman, but Titika, whom I watched submit to her, keeping control of her temper, perhaps because she did not want to lose her composure in the presence of a stranger.

As soon as she felt the presence of the sun, Pantelou acted like an impatient child, and she did not calm down till Titika came to support her and take her out step by step to the threshold of the damp ground floor, bring the stool, and set her down leaning against the wall. And when she felt the caress of the sun on her, the old woman calmed down. She sat there in a daze, without the presence of mind to gather her rags about her, which slipped now and then to leave her wretched flesh uncovered. Then I felt embarrassed and looked away.

But my dawn greeter was Pantelitsa, the daughter of the Melodias couple, a charming youngster of about five years, who chattered in the courtyard, splashed in the water, rolled around on the ground, and waited to see me when I came down from the second floor and ran over to me to give me the special good morning which we had both established.

"Life is beautiful!"

Her pale little face was laughing, her brown eyes were laughing and flashing, too, as she looked at me boldly and confidently.

"Life is beautiful, sweetheart."

And I handed her the candy that I took care always to have in my pocket for just this purpose.

It was I who had taught her this original way of telling me good morning.

After spending my first night on the second floor, I came down to the courtyard in a good mood and saw her there in front of me happy and smiling up at me. I said, "Life is beautiful, my child." And I gave her a chocolate that I happened to have in my pocket.

The next morning, I had just washed and toweled down, when there was Pantelitsa in front of me.

"Life is beautiful," she said.

I was troubled not to have foreseen it, and from then on I never forgot to have something for her in my pocket. So it was that my optimistic morning greeting was established with Pantelitsa, for the greater joy of both of us.

On that day as always Pantelitsa came to offer me her unabated optimism, to receive the offering of my gratitude.

Life is beautiful! Your words are a song in my heart, my little sparrow.

The old woman, huddled up on her stool, gasped.

31

I had never seen Pantelitsa go up to her grandmother. Perhaps some instinctive aversion kept the child away from ugliness.

Suddenly the old woman screeched in anger to chase off the rooster which had made bold to peck and scratch around near her feet.

Pantelitsa looked at her, then turned to me and said, "We'll be relieved when she, too, dies."

I was startled.

Nothing had altered in the child's expression. How well did she understand those bitter words that she must have heard fall from wearied lips? In the dimples of her laugh, in her intelligent eyes, which sparkled clearly, I saw all the asperity of her immaculate life.

I got up to go to the local coffee house, where I would perhaps find Pipios, who would have a cup and entertain us with his tasteless jokes.

I wasn't in the mood for serious study.

THE END OF MR. TRIKKOS

EVEN THE MOST PROSAIC BEINGS in the world have their poetic moments. Even the small crab in the sand, who spends his little life hidden in his hole keeping watch in fear, knows lyrical moments when he stands on his threshold, enthralled by the presence of the great sea, and breathes in the rhythm of its pulse.

Mr. Trikkos spent his little life holed up like the crab in his store awaiting profits and fearing drafts, all drafts: those that cause colds, but much more the currents that tend to upset the order of society and the peace of every householder. There were, of course, his nephews and nieces, but he wasn't afraid of them. Why should he be? He only disliked them because they were the cause of his thinking of death and cudgeling his brains for a way to set up his will in such a way that they wouldn't inherit anything.

You grow old unmarried, you suffer want and toil hard till you're well enough off, and then here come the others and find the table already set, just because they happen to have been born your nieces and nephews. Why? Mr. Trikkos was determined to turn it all over to a philanthropic trust, which would carry his name—Ioannis P. Trikkos—forever.

Aside from this nuisance, his days rolled along like a series of tidy nothings, wherein there was room only for his small comforts and his gross personal satisfaction.

Nevertheless, even Mr. Trikkos had his moments, during which a little window opened and aired out the closed-up place of his soul. This was the morning, when he opened his shop. While the apprentice was sweeping, he would take two chairs out to the sidewalk and sit there drinking his coffee, greeting the neighbors, and enjoying the morn-

33

ing coolness and the routine but always new preparations for business on a new day.

The pavement had just been wet down. The gratings of the shops were rolling up one by one with a clatter. The apprentices were sweeping the sidewalks. Working folks were tumbling out of the narrow streets, people bent by years and cares, young men who had not yet unlearned the art of walking tall, girls dauntlessly adorned. They were all moving along in haste, singly or in groups, going to their workplaces.

Enjoying the coolness and his coffee, he knew moments of innocent good humor. Something like a nebula of exaltation lifted him gently and rocked him in the glow of some indefinable magic. If he were in a position to figure out what happens to him during those moments, he would say, Well, you see, we, too, men of the shop, the most prosaic class, as they call us, have a fleeting poetic moment. But he was in no position to do that, nor did he try to figure out anything. He was only enjoying the moment, and the sky, emerging behind the rooftops, gently opened its arms.

He lived in a small apartment over the shop. (The property was his own.) He slept well, awaking very early by old habit, and came downstairs in a good mood, reeking of cologne. And this too, you see, was one of his "principles," to be always well-groomed and well-dressed, because a fine appearance, together with sober manners, elicits trust from the customer and discourages anyone who would like to bargain with you as he might with some novelty salesman. One wastes one's time with this kind of clientele. Mr. Trikkos was interested in attracting only the upper class, and he was very skillful in giving his shop a mannerly and aristocratic air, which served his interests. Where did this man, who had started off unshod and ragged, learn to distinguish whom to greet with condescension and turn over to a clerk, whom to take care of personally, and which lofty lady to accompany bowing and scraping to the door. It is certain that with these talents, and with the invincible power of a limited mind fixed obstinately on a single objective and on rules of life engraved once for all, he arrived at his objective and secured his rules with the indisputable authority of his success. He became Mr. Trikkos, and it was inconceivable to call him just Trikkos.

He slurped a mouthful of coffee and searched his pocket for cigarettes. He radiated well-being. Damn it all! He hadn't had a cigarette since yesterday, determined to break the habit after the stern warning of the doctor. His legs had been wobbly lately under the weight of his body and he often felt dizzy. High blood pressure and who knows what else, said the doctor, and he mercilessly demanded that the terrified Mr. Trikkos deprive himself of smoking and eating so much, which he loved to do.

He got exasperated and barked at Vassilis, his apprentice, a little chap with powerful hands and obedient as a good dog. He had spent his boyhood years and his youth in Mr. Trikkos's employ, doing the heavy work and running errands in the shop, cleaning the house, washing—Vassilis this, Vassilis that!—and with bowed head, in silence, eyes askance under his brows, listening to the mutters and curses of his boss.

Because Mr. Trikkos knew exactly to what point his practiced politeness ceased to be useful and when an employer could become as demanding and ruthless as he pleased.

But his outbreak did him no good. He became dizzy again.

"I don't know what to do with this brute," he said, wiping his sweaty face with his handkerchief.

His hand, heavy and numb, would not respond. He forgot about his cigarette and stood thinking.

He spent the morning sitting moodily in his office without giving a single order to the staff.

About noon he suddenly got a bad headache. Large drops of sweat beaded on his forehead, and he hadn't the strength to lift his hand to wipe them away. He felt nauseated. He braced himself on the desk and made a hopeless attempt to get up. As in a dream, he seemed to get up and walk toward the door at the same time that he had fallen flat, a heavy, flabby mass, onto his desk.

The two clerks and Vassilis came running, and while the clerks were trying to help him somehow, jumping about in confusion, not knowing what to do, Vassilis stood aside and watched, as one magnetized, this deplorable object which only moments before had been to him a merciless force. Something strange was happening within him.

Finally someone thought to telephone the doctor.

People gathered on the sidewalk and commented.

The first thing the doctor did when he arrived was to run everyone out who had crowded into the store. Then he saw to the sick man and telephoned for an ambulance.

"Let's get him to the hospital," he said. "Who's going to take care of him at home!"

Sprawled on a chair which they carried out of the house, the patient looked stupidly around him. His mouth went crooked and his face was repulsively deformed. He sucked in his right cheek with every breath and then breathed out his closed lips . . . pf . . . pf . . . like one smoking a pipe.

When he saw the white uniforms come into the store with the stretcher, there was panic in his eyes. He stretched out his left hand as if he were warding off an undesirable vision. But the effort exhausted him and he sunk back onto the chair.

They asked Vassilis to help them put the patient on the stretcher. And as he hefted the heavy, flaccid mass, he felt again a harshness that waved mercy aside. So many years he had trembled before this carcass! He was holding him under the arms in such a way that, if he should suddenly let go of him, the bald head would hit the tiles and break like a watermelon. I would relish that, he thought.

When they had laid him on the stretcher, Mr. Trikkos began to thrash about hopelessly, as if he wanted to get up. He moved his head from side to side, and, with his eyes and an inarticulate "pa . . . pa . . . pa . . ." out of his crooked mouth, he protested as if saying Where are you taking me? . . . I don't want to, no, I don't want to . . . how am I to leave behind my possessions, everything I love? . . .

Just when they had hefted the stretcher, he found strength to reach out with his left hand and hook on to one of the metal posts of the counter. He gripped it tightly, with all the will remaining to him, stuttering as he pleaded, "pa . . . pa . . . pa . . ."

They turned and looked at the doctor, who nodded: open his hand. Then Vassilis eagerly grabbed the hateful hand and forced it open, mercilessly crushing his hopeless resistance.

36

The patient's gaze, up till then imploring, now fixed venomously on Vassilis for a moment. Then it went out. Exhausted, his head turned to one side.

The doctor, who knew Trikkos and his aristocratic ways, placed him in a single room, first class, and had Vassilis stay and look after him.

In the afternoon a young man and a young woman arrived—his niece and nephew. They appeared awkward in the good clothes they wore for the occasion, and in their attempt to act worried. The girl held a bouquet and did not knew what to do with it. Finally, she found a nurse and had her bring a vase and take the flowers off her hands. They tried to say the proper words to their uncle, but he did not seem pleased by them. He just looked coldly at the flowers and at his niece, who was about to put out her hand and caress, perhaps his forehead, but lost courage and drew her hand back as soon as she met his glance.

Vassilis was sitting out of the way in the hall watching and rose in deference every time a doctor or nurse came by.

When night fell the hospital emptied of visitors. The doctors made their final rounds. The nurses got the patients ready for the night, and a stillness fraught with expectation spread into the half-shadows, in the rooms and corridors.

Vassilis was sitting on a couch which they had arranged for him in the sickroom and watched him puff out his cheek when he exhaled, pf . . . pf . . . pf . . . , insistently, rhythmically, endlessly.

The more the time passed, the more irritated he became. He tried lying down, but shortly found himself sitting up again with his eyes riveted on that hateful being who so insistently disturbed the quiet—as if in this way he was trying even now to exert his importance—and gloom dripped into Vassilis's mind.

The patient opened his eyes, smacked his lips, tongue lolling, turned his head and stammered, "pa . . . pa . . . pa . . . ," looking longingly at the glass of water.

Vassilis went over to him, lifted him, and brought the glass to his lips. The other tried to drink, but found it diffi-

37

cult; Vassilis was clumsy, too. And the water spilled, drenching his front.

"Pa . . . pa . . . pa . . . ," he said in his exasperation, and something blazed in his eyes that reminded Vassilis of the old tormentor and infuriated him.

He put the glass on the cabinet and began madly punching the patient on his sides.

"Pa . . . pa . . . pa . . . ," he screeched and had deep spasms, like a cow being butchered, moving his head left to right and casting wild, hateful looks at Vassilis. Then he became still and looked at the ceiling. The fierceness disappeared from his eyes and an ineffable contrition suffused his face. Two large tears rolled down his cheeks.

Vassilis came back to his senses.

He sprawled out on the couch and soon fell asleep.

Mr. Trikkos died the following morning.

He did not get to make his will.

THE BLUE SLIPPERS

IF YOU HAD TOLD HIM that he had systematically organized his job, Piriklis Sisamos might not even have understood what you meant. He was a peddler in second-hand goods. He traveled the roads all day with a huge sack, sometimes empty, sometimes full, suspended from his shoulder, hanging down to his hips, forcing him to keep his crooked body stooped. Nevertheless, he had elevated this humble enterprise to a well-organized routine, following the suggestions of experience and his natural love for order.

He had divided the neighborhoods into two categories—those where folks sold their cast-offs and those where folks bought the cast-offs of others. There was also another—how would one call it, a neighborhood or a bivouac area?—high up in the Mantides, where folks roosted in various sorts of hovels made of gasoline cans and dismantled wooden crates and mud and had neither a thing to sell nor to buy. Unprofitable area for Piriklis's business, nevertheless that's where he had his own bed.

That neighborhood was picturesque, climbing the bare hillside above the city, with steep lanes and improvised human nests tilting and leaning on each other so as not to fall over, ever finding a multitude of ways to spread out at random and unfold on a few meters of uneven land, here a little terrace with morning-glories on a little stone structure, there a balcony hanging charmingly and daringly out over thin air, elsewhere stairs biting into the rock, courtyards fenced in somehow, with pigs, chickens, dogs, and kids caged in, a swarm of kids, crawling in the mud, eaten up by flies.

"Everything else comes and goes. But these snot-nose kids, why do you unfeeling folk make them and then trample them into the shit pile?" asked Piriklis in exasperation, and continued grumbling incomprehensibly between his teeth.

". . . As if the race will disappear."

He was sitting in the company of three others around a table in the little coffee shop.

The others cackled with laughter.

"As if we had any other amusement," said Mouttas sarcastically. He was the joker of the group. The winking of his good eye and the grimace he made gave his toothless face an expression at once shattering and ridiculous because of his other eye, the bad one, which bulged from its socket swollen and ashy red like an abscess.

He raised his hand with palm stretched out and let it fall significantly on his crotch.

"That's all we've got left." And he laughed aloud.

But suddenly Peyorkis blew his nose. He drank his *raki* in one gulp and banged the glass on the table.

"Why don't you leave us alone in our misery. Did we make you our judge?" he said, glaring provokingly at Piriklis.

"You think I'm really concerned about your misery!" the other said mockingly. "I'm just talking about the children. How are they to blame, you rag-bag, when every bum sows his oats at random?"

Peyorkis's face darkened, but before he could come up with a strong rejoinder, Mastro-Themistos joined in.

"Cut it out, fellas," he said with his bellowing voice and spread his hand out on the table.

Mouttas jerked on his chair, and rubbed his hands together apparently waiting for something important to happen. He was disappointed.

Peyorkis put his anger aside. Ah, the devil with it, he said to himself.

They sat there in silence for some time, looking at their glasses. Finally Piriklis got up.

"Well, goodnight," he said.

". . . night," muttered the others without looking up.

§

He was irritated with himself again. He had told himself a thousand times not to meddle in their business—not that he cared how they would take it; no, he didn't give a hoot. It's just that he could find no reason why he, Piriklis, should worry about the rest of them if they liked living like cockroaches. Let the poor wretches go to hell. Every sheep hangs by his own feet. That's life. Should I, a loner, worry about them when I'm struggling not to end up like them? As if anyone ever worried about me! Let 'em go to hell, he said again to himself as he groped in the dark to find the keyhole to open his door with the big key he had taken from his pocket.

He locked the door behind him and found himself alone in thick darkness. He went to the corner shelf and put his hand exactly on the box of matches, picked it up and lit the lamp. In the low-roofed, damp, ground floor everything was located in its proper place. Piriklis looked about him and sighed. They can all just leave me be. It's enough as long as you don't need anybody and you're not concerned with anybody.

He was quite used to his solitude, where he found refuge in which to love all the things that had surrounded him so solidly and faithfully for so many years, things which he endowed with the guileless dispositions that he never met with in mankind. And if moments came when he tired of it and could no longer rely on such self-deceptions, he sought the company of men, became quickly exasperated, and returned again to his solitude.

He sat in his chair and stayed there for a long time, his head bowed.

A cockroach emerged confused from under the linen-chest and proceeded to the opposite wall, crossing the tile floor diagonally. It set out in a straight line as if with some purpose, stopped for a moment at mid-point, moved its antennae uneasily and set out again hastily till it reached the base of the other wall and crammed itself into a crack. Piriklis followed it with his eye. He hated cockroaches and had tried every method to exterminate them. But his efforts were wasted, for the hated beasties popped up again during the night, millions of them, coming from the courtyards and from the other hovels around. So he finally hung a lamp from the ceiling beam that would at least protect the food.

A pair of blue girl's slippers, tossed on the table, mocked their humble surroundings with their beauty and charming lightness.

When he first saw them, Piriklis remembered Anthoula and almost smiled, but he caught himself. He picked up the slippers and scrutinized them, turning them this way and that with thick fingers that touched them clumsily, as if in fear of wounding these dainty little things. They were practically new. This is how some of the rich girls do, he thought. They choose whatever is the most expensive, they dress up in it two or three times and then toss it to the chambermaid to sell to the rag-man. It's just like new. You could say they were unused. Do they ever touch the ground? These girls, my dear, live like faeries, reclining on pillows, nourished on cream and sugar candies, walking lightly on rugs and parquets. . . . But how the desire flashed in Anthoula's eyes when she saw the slippers! She took them in her hands and marveled at them; she pressed them to her breast, then gave them back to me and looked at me as though pleading. Mystery. What would she do with them with her paralyzed legs? Just for a decoration? . . . But what does it matter to me, he said to himself and tossed the slippers on the table. Did anybody ever give me anything? This is no time to start playing the compassionate and give gifts to anyone's bastards. Next, the world will be stripping us to the hide.

§

At times Hariklou worked at other people's homes, but mostly she struggled to make her living with her needle. She also had this crippled girl, and she had her lazy Peyorkis to provide with pocket money when he took it into his head to look her up from time to time, but she never got smart enough to send him packing and get rid of him. But that was her business. What did it matter to Piriklis? As long as her work for him was satisfactory. He would give her whatever of his purchases needed fixing: this for darning, that for a button, the other for cleaning; and he paid her by the piece.

42

Nor on the matter of the girl would she listen to reason, foolish as she was. Instead, she had her, the apple of her eye, sit around scrubbed and combed, with bows in her hair, looking at the clouds. She was crippled and needed compassion, I know, but nothing comes of compassion and gentle words.

"Send her off to learn dressmaking, you foolish woman," said Piriklis to her one day. "She has strong hands. What will happen to her in the future when you're gone?"

Hariklou turned and gave him a dark look. She was about to retort, but got control of herself, turning to Anthoula, who was sitting next to her looking at her wide-eyed.

"It's time, sweetheart, to water your plants," she said, caressing her hair.

The child understood. She got on her crutches and pushed off adroitly, standing upright, and went off outside—tock, tock, like a grasshopper. Her left foot went on tip-toe, barely supporting her slender body until she jumped and found support on the crutches again, one more step. Her right foot hung like a rag.

The woman lashed out.

"Listen here . . . why do you say such things in front of her? Have you no pity?"

Piriklis had already regretted it, but he didn't want to admit it.

"I say it for her own good, Hariklou. It's true, isn't it?"

She bowed her head.

"What do you want me to do? Sending her out to learn dressmaking is easy to say, but how am I supposed to send her so far away from me into the hubbub of the streets. They'll make fun of her and hurt her. You know how sensitive she is."

"She'll live through that whether you like it or not, Hariklou," answered Piriklis quietly. "Better for her to get through it now while she's still young and has you with her to lean on until she toughens up than to leave her inexperienced and helpless later on. They'll trample her good then."

He fell silent and waited, but the woman remained bowed and quiet.

"I'm just making conversation, Hariklou; just forget it if you want to," said Piriklis finally. "You're the mother. Do as God guides you."

He threw the slippers in his empty sack and left.

He left a few items for mending on the table. These he would stop by for in the morning.

Anthoula was sitting in a corner on the low parapet where the flower pots were lined up. She was watching the sun set. She did not notice Piriklis go by. Perhaps she even pretended not to notice him.

She was a girl of about twelve, fragile and pale. Her face, round and slightly flat-nosed with deep blue eyes, had an open, strangely charming look. Her hair, the color of ripe wheat, divided into two pigtails bound in blue ties. Most of the time she sat by herself as if concentrating on something that only she could see. And if you happened to speak to her, she would come out of her trance, turn around, and look at you as if she were saying, "Oh, if you only knew!"

§

Piriklis usually slept well, wrapped in a sense of security from others' worries, a sense that he obstinately cultivated, considering it as a compensation for all the poisons that life fed him.

Tonight, however, he was not able to calm down. He tossed and turned the entire night, sometimes half-asleep, other times wide awake. He saw and thought about many strange things, as if he walked all alone on the city streets, loaded down by his sack, which, though empty, weighed on his shoulder like lead. The streets were deserted and soundless. At some point they filled with his shout, though he did not realize that it was his own voice.

"*Paliaaaaa!*"

"A! . . . a! . . . a! . . . a! . . ." came the echo from all directions.

His legs were paralyzed, but he was determined to keep walking. Then he found himself before a marvelous vision: a nereid who shone luminously and walked on thin air wearing blue slippers. For some unknown reason he was sure that it was Anthoula, even though she did not look a bit like Anthoula. We are judged by the clothes we wear, he

44

thought. These form the opinion that others have of you and the opinion that you have of yourself. But that was not the issue here. The issue was what you can and cannot do . . . He struggled to grasp something that would give him an answer he could be sure of, but it slipped out of his hands and left him only with the sensation of hurling into an abyss.

He got up. A dim light came in through the crack under the door, which looked eastward, the only opening in his hovel. Shapes and masses were tentatively cast into the half-shadow.

He opened the door and lighted the fire to make coffee. And when shortly thereafter he was calmly sipping his morning coffee, his irritation had subsided. As always, he regained his composure when he sat in the early morning on the threshold, bathed in the light of the new dawn, looking down over the city as it awakened early and ventured slowly forth under a light mist.

But Anthoula's eyes insisted on gazing at him, questioning him, so calmly, so sweetly that he could not resist them. The entire matter would be foolish except for that gaze. Mysterious business, he said to himself as he began to give in.

He put things in order, picked up his sack and went to the door, but turned back, picked up the slippers and threw them in the sack. He went out, locked the door, and went to Hariklou's.

The clothes were ready, folded in a stack on the table, and at the corner of the table sat mother and daughter drinking their tea.

Piriklis greeted them and sat down on a chair opposite.

"Join us!" said Hariklou and got up to bring him a cup.

"No, thanks. I just had my coffee."

"You're out and about early today."

He didn't answer, only lit a cigarette. He kept looking at Anthoula and she smiled shyly.

They passed some time in silence. Finally, Piriklis rose, picked up his clothes and put them in the sack, after removing the slippers, and holding the sack in one hand and the slippers in the other.

45

"Goodbye, then," he said.

Hariklou kept a tab for the clothes and he paid her every Saturday without haggling, because he was sure she never overcharged him. She would not stoop to that level.

He looked at the child and suddenly gave her the slippers.

"They're yours," he said.

Anthoula took the slippers and clutched them to her as if they were a treasure. She was about to say something, but Piriklis did not give her a chance to. He hastily went out the door.

He threw the sack on his shoulder and started down the hill.

"What nonsense," he muttered as he wiped the corners of his misty eyes with the back of his hand.

NICOLETTA

LIKE EVERYONE ELSE, I set out full of fine sentiments and lofty ideas for conquering I know not what. For a time I fought for these *a priori* notions, defending them step by step until there was nothing left for me but the necessity to earn my daily bread some way and to preserve what was left of my pride and enough humanity to keep me from "running with the wolves" or creeping along licking spittle.

Nevertheless, I've no complaints about life. And those small things, pride and humanity, are enough to save one's earthly soul—even if they are thought meaningless by the various rationalists who, because they never tried to go anywhere, had it made comfortably in a corner, and now rubbed their full bellies in satisfaction.

For my bread and butter, however, I had to abandon the great dreams and return with downcast ears to my little town, to the island, where a number of good friends of long standing interceded and managed to soften the heart of the eminent Isaiah. So it was, thanks to his connections, that I secured a minor post as secretary in the customs office.

This was the one and only time my pretentious maternal uncle deigned to support his good-for-nothing nephew, myself.

Everyone, you see, explains life in his own way. And my uncle Isaiah started off by getting his hands on just about all the family property and continued his grasping career until in time he became rich and famous, reserving all his respect for his *self-made* self and all like him. He had, in fact, a special reverence for the term *self-made*, which he waved around on every occasion as an expression of the highest virtue.

You can understand then what sort of opinion such an important uncle would have of a nephew who not only showed from early on no gift for being "self-made," but also decided one fine morning to mortgage the house he had inherited from his mother, so he could go bumming around Europe. Uncle Isaiah simply pointed out that I was worthless, and, as before, he continued to take no interest in my person.

But I wasn't worrying about that once I had decided to take wing. Nor was this what I wanted to talk about. I only wanted to tell about those few things that remain constant and provide support when a person has quit running after the intangible.

One is the ineradicable determination to stand firm in one's faith in oneself. Another is the thirst of the heart, which bonds you with other people as your brothers, whether for the time it takes to round out an entire lifetime with joined hands, or for the moment it takes to touch wine glasses during a chance meeting. These bonds accumulate with the years to form a basis for existence. They are not lost. They are never lost. Neither do they fade with time or distance. Whether you find them right now in the little *taverna* on the beach with whatever folks you come upon who have just got off work, or you have lived through them for years past, they are indispensable, clinging about your heart as the abiding good in your life, a treasury of friendly faces, first one, then another, coming up to smile at you and raise your spirits. And among these for me was the beloved face of Nicoletta, a child I did not know, but whose appearance, as my imagination created it from the circumstances hereafter narrated, is as real as those of others I knew.

§

I spent some three months in Rome tracking down the splendid fountains with the purling waters, wandering around museums, art galleries, churches, palaces, ruins, but most of all the streets and the neighborhoods.

I have not known hours finer than those spent traveling. Each time one comes to places seen for the first time, or that long absence turns again into places seen for the first time. When they are rescued from the mists that familiarity casts over them, all the colors of life and all the faces of man shine before your eyes, which take on youth again and discover beauty even in the most familiar objects: a tree, a beach, a distant mountaintop, a window in a flower shop, a child playing in the park, a worker passing by laden with toil and thoughts.

Bewitched, you watch the great world unfold rich and populated with a million faces. And things you had ceased to notice in your little place appear regenerated before you: the fields and the mountains and the seas and that ant, man, who builds, tears down, and rebuilds endlessly. And everything is so different, yet so much the same. The traveler's greatest joy is to capture every moment a new, yet known, view of life, to feel the world infinite and one.

So, I spent around three months in Rome. I arranged my sojourn there in the way experience had taught me: the first few days in an inexpensive hotel. While I was there I was able to find my way around and get a room by the month in an old neighborhood. It is cheaper that way, but more importantly it is the only way one can get to know the real life of a city: the people who set its pace from day to day. If you do not live openly among them so that they open to you, too, and receive you at the table in the coffee shop, at the counter of the *taverna*, in their simple homes; if you do not sit and break bread with them, how will you see their real face, the real face of the country? In the luxury hotels and various spots where visitors herd together to see some picturesque scene? That's like looking at some image of life through a shop window.

Of course, some prefer it that way, to provide the various Hiltons with living merchandise. That's their business. That's not my purpose at all.

And don't forget that picturesqueness has its value too. You will see it differently when you find out what lies behind it. For example, the little street where I lived was very picturesque, and I enjoyed it. But I knew that on that narrow street my landlady, signora Annuzza, led a difficult life. She was a hefty, big-framed woman with a disproportionately small face. She left her sluggish body and her very quick tongue no moment of peace. From dawn to dusk

49

she worked, struggled, and talked with her neighbors, with passers-by, with her children, with her cat, with her flowers, even with me whenever there was opportunity, though I understood little of what she said to me.

I also knew that from this picturesque and humble little street my landlady's daughter set out one morning for the Mayday parade. Her brother tried to keep her from going and stood in the doorway. But the girl told him to get out of the way with such a tone, and their mother drenched him in such a flood of abuse, that the young bully stepped aside and then began angrily kicking whatever came in his way.

And yet he said that he was a worker and wore a *trayaska*, while his sister, who worked as a salesclerk somewhere, dressed very carefully and tastefully. She was a pale, delicate girl with golden hair. The smile that never left her face, together with a serious, almost sad expression in her blue eyes, revealed a strong character.

But that was Maria, not Nicoletta, though I borrowed Maria's features to fill out the image of my Nicoletta.

§

From the very first day, I heard her name momentarily drown out all the other sounds of the neighborhood.

"Nicoleettaaa!"

It was a woman's singing voice from the narrow street behind signora Annuzza's house.

Of course there is nothing strange or remarkable in hearing someone called by name, even if you like the name and the way it is called. Nevertheless, during the passing days, every time I happened to be at home, I would frequently hear one voice or another calling Nicoletta. I began noticing this and ended up waiting for it.

Rarely did I stay at home. How can you stay home when you have so much to see and are in a rush to get it all seen. I usually went out very early and returned in the evening exhausted. But sometimes I would come back early, when I had to go back out at night. And I would also come back at noon to rest up a bit when I was somewhere close by.

Perhaps you might be a born traveler, ready at any moment to pay the price of separation for each fresh departure. You will find again stations along the road where you will rest ever so briefly, but long enough for your other self, the one longing for domestic permanence which you also carry along, to pretend that you had enough.

This brief respite I found in signora Annuzza's house, where I liked to spend my idle time stretched out with book in hand, feeling about me the warm and vociferous breath of the neighborhood and hearing voices now recognizable to me rise frequently above the confusion. And among them those who called for Nicoletta. Sometimes a woman's voice, sometimes a boy's, sometimes a girl's—never a man's—each one with its own inflection, one musical "Nicoleeettaaa," another entreating "Nicoleeetta," the children's more natural, the girls' warbling like birds "Nicolettaaa," the boys' with a somewhat imperative tone "Nicoleetta," and all these voices laden with affection.

Just who in the world could this Nicoletta be?

I tried to create her looks, but my imagination sought for some model, the seed of an image.

"Who is this Nicoletta?" I asked signora Annuzza.

Her face shone with love.

"Nicoletta! . . . *Carina!* . . . ," she answers.

And she started explaining to me in many words, and more gesticulations, so I would understand that she was a girl of twelve years (she showed this with the fingers of both hands then two fingers of the right), beautiful (she drew the fingertips of one hand together and kissed them), no mother, her father a worker, and she, *poveretta,* did all the housework. And she was so good, the poor little thing, so eager to lend a hand in whatever she could. If one of the neighbor women needed someone to look after the baby while she went to the grocery store for a couple of minutes, she would call Nicoletta. If another needed help folding the wash, "Come, Nicoletta." *"Nicoletta qui, Nicoletta la,"* and Nicoletta ran. But it was the children who could not get along without her. They seemed to have taken her on as leader. Even the boys, who sometimes came to the point of letting Nicoletta step in and settle their differences.

I'm not sure whether I've translated accurately in all the details signora Annuzza's words. But that's the sense that emerged when her endless flow of words combined with her gestures and expression—and my own fondness for the girl whom I did not know.

I wanted to meet her. I could have asked Maria to take a walk down there with me, as soon as a suitable opportunity arose.

But by the time the opportunity came, I changed my mind. People have their worries and their pride. What would they think if someone imposed on them uninvited? What excuse did one have for observing their lives?

Finally the day came for me to make my farewells here, too, and to get on my way again.

Everything else withdrew into the background. Only the magic contained in a train whistle or the blast of a ship's horn at these moments remained and surrounded me.

Early in the morning I said goodbye to Maria before she went to work. I went back to my room to pack my bag.

I finished doing that, but sat around waiting as if to say farewell to the walls or as if asking why go out now, it's still too early. I went through the drawers again to be sure I wasn't forgetting anything. Then I started reckoning the time I would arrive in Venice, when I heard the piercing little voice of a girl.

"Nicolettaaa."

It seems that's what I was waiting for.

I smiled and, for reasons unknown to me, I said, *"Ya hara!"*

THE INCORRIGIBLE

A PERSON OF TASTE can with three conventional phrases put his seal even on a bit of a card, thought Thassos as he looked at the attractive invitation. He meant Verenikis, the secretary of the Council of the Hunter's Club. He placed the invitation back into its envelope and got back to work, opening the mail which the office doorman had just brought in.

He would have to think about the invitation, though his first spontaneous thought was, What am I looking for in the social scene? He wasn't at all sure.

"Look out for your interests, Thassos; don't avoid people that way," Verenikis had said to him once. It's possible that Verenikis, too, had his weaknesses—if his capabilities and talent for compromise, which led to success, are weaknesses—but he always behaved like a good friend toward Thassos.

He smiled and decided that the matter was not important in any case. But he suddenly became serious. That's all we need now, to be flattered about the honor paid us by snobbery, he said, to cover over the spark of satisfaction which jumped up within him and fluttered about as if mocking him.

He concentrated again on his work and shortly had forgotten the invitation. He remembered the Korvelis house and hurried to finish up his routine correspondence so he could resume the planning from where he had left off the night before.

Spread out on the drawing board was a first draft of the house plan, and around it, heaped randomly, a pile of sheets full of hasty pencil sketches. In one corner a thick, tattered notebook of plans and notes lay open. This notebook Thassos

53

took with him everywhere in his sack, whether on hunting trips or on one of his all-day solitary walks which he was wont to make in the isolated areas of the island. In this notebook he kept sketches and notes of all the remains of popular architecture that he might come across.

He sought these things out, taking pleasure in their truth, the beauty which he found woven together with their usefulness. He sought them everywhere and collected them affectionately in his notebook. But in time his obsession ceased being so simple. It became a problem and it troubled him. To what degree can this beauty be embodied in our buildings *today*? How much of its life can be drawn from it? Slavish imitations sickened him. Some admirers of the popular style stuck them up like scenery next to all the other ostentation of their villas. He regarded them as counterfeits which had no respect for the original. But where is the solution? You tell me! You do not get very far making plans on paper. You must have the opportunity to *build* what you envision.

That's how he tortured himself until the Korvelis proposal dropped from the sky.

They were lovable people, Rigas Korvelis and his wife, Kyria Lenia. Lovable both in their virtues and in their whims.

Whenever he had an evening free Thassos would visit them at their small apartment on Katramadou Street. Many times their clear and cultivated thoughts would clarify questions he found confusing. But just as often he would smile at their attachment to all the conventions of the afternoon tea, at their gentle manners with one another after thirty years of marriage, or at their credulousness, which sometimes bordered on naïveté.

Both of them were retired school teachers.

Thassos never hesitated to knock on their door for the reason that they showed no indication that his visit altered their normal routine in the slightest. He spent many peaceful hours with them, smoking his pipe while Korvelis paged through a collection of old engravings, Kyria Lenia knitted, while a concert was playing very softly on the radio.

One evening when the program of classical music came to an end, Thassos reached over and turned off the radio. He thought that it was time to go when the Korvelises

54

glanced at one another, smiled guiltily like children who have behaved badly, and began talking both at once. But after the first volley of words the husband fell silent, and Kyria Lenia explained to Thassos that, well, they had decided to put their savings into a small house on that lot he knew of, and if he wanted to, that is, if he had time, they wanted him to draw up the plans. Just a small house, one that they could afford, as long as it fit into the style of the local architecture.

She said nothing else, but Thassos understood. He knew their views on this matter. (He knew other details too, such as that "our savings," which Kyria Lenia mentioned, consisted of her small inheritance, which included the lot.)

He was happy about it, but was seized immediately by something like uneasiness. He realized that in this easy manner, as if it were of no particular importance, his good friends had placed in his hands the toils and dreams of a lifetime, and now they were looking at him again with that guilty smile, as if they had sought the heavens and the stars and now feared that it was not right to make such great demands upon life.

The Korvelis cottage exercised his thoughts a great deal.

He knew the lot from before, but he went out to it again and again to look at it, to become familiar with the landscape. It was in a piney suburb ten minutes by bus from town. The location was very suitable for a country cottage, which Thassos could design with his eyes closed. But his eagerness to live up to the expectations of his friends and the need he felt in this particular case to bring to life the images that he had repeatedly put on paper, gave the matter a content at once attractive and difficult to achieve. For some time he contemplated a cottage that was low-cost and attractive in its simplicity, one that would join the folk heritage with the technique and the requirements of a modern person. And to this he must add yet another dimension: the Korvelises were eager to adorn this cottage with the small collection of paintings which they had gradually acquired through personal sacrifice.

Everything he has is taken into account and under his control, even his tone of voice, thought Thassos, and smiled.

Verenikis's voice came out of the receiver baritone and affected, but brimming with friendliness. Especially for me, smiled Thassos again as he listened.

The other was phoning to ask him whether he had received the invitation to the dance and whether he would be going.

"But I don't dance," Thassos answered.

"Come now, Thassos. Do you think this is one of those dances where people go to dance? Put aside your monasticism for once and put in an appearance. What's more, this is the right time for it."

He promised that he would come.

"Great. We'll expect you," said Verenikis and hung up the telephone.

He would go. Even though Verenikis's words had set him to thinking, that is, that his appearance would be at the right time. Naturally he was thinking of Thassos's book *Mountain and Game* which had recently come out and had had very good reviews.

Perhaps a circle of ladies and gentlemen would form around him, and each would put on airs in his or her own particular way and speak in deeply thoughtful manner to show how each was in a position to appreciate the work of a successful author. They had no idea how distant their salons and intellectual bubbles were from his thoughts when he lay on his back on the dry, redolent pine needles taking in the secret song in its myriad voices coming from the mountain, from the forest, from the running waters, from the rich life humming around him, unseen to the eyes of the profane. He took it all in through all the pores of his being and left it there to ripen in his heart till one day for unexplained reasons he undertook to sit down and describe it. And then it flowed forth unforced and free onto the paper, like the flow of water in the stream. Because he knew as few did the mysteries of the woods and enjoyed following with the dispassionate love of a genuine hunter the intricate forms of life, its offense and its defense, which lay throughout the extent of this apparent calm.

The Hunter's Club was the most aristocratic and exclusive club on the island. Its annual dance at the Grand Hotel was regarded generally as a very significant social affair. Invitations were sent with utmost selectivity by those who *belonged* to the upper class, and sought after with utmost servility by those who aspired to burrow into, or at least be seen with, the upper class.

"And what do all of you have to do with hunting?" Thassos asked one day, supposedly as a joke, but expressing willy nilly the contempt of a true hunter for the dilettantes.

Verenikis didn't believe a word of the nonsense that identified the lower reaches of his class, but he was one of those people who knew that it was not required to believe in something in order to use it for your own benefit.

"Such naïveté!" he answered, laughing. "Hunting, my good man, has always been a class privilege and has remained by tradition a distinguishing mark of the aristocracy. Not, of course, in the narrow sense you give it, but as a pastime of people who spend their time and means acquiring expensive and luxurious guns, keeping purebred dogs, and organizing first-class hunting expeditions."

§

And there was the matter of his tuxedo. He hadn't worn it for two years, and now it was getting tight in the sleeves, making him feel as wooden and clumsy as a bumpkin.

The dance would begin later. For the time being in the large, brightly-lit hall, where chandeliers, crystals, and showy tapestries sparkled, men in black tuxedos and women in daring décolletage mingled with the confidence of a perfectly rehearsed theatrical troupe, forming together a fluid movement which altered the shape of the whole every moment and was accentuated by slight bows, introductions, expressions of surprise at some supposedly happy encounter and poses of all sorts. The serving staff in white jackets glided gracefully through the throng, some holding great trays of drinks, others plates of select goodies. The guests would reach out indifferently to take something, without paying any attention to the conventional smile of the waiter—what meaning can the smile of a hired waiter have?—and vigorously continued their flattery and chatter, heaping one commonplace atop another as if in fear that the talk might stop, and then how would they deal with the silence?

But Thassos was determined not to fall out of his role as philosophical observer. So he stood to one side and, without realizing that he had taken up a pose himself, was listening to a portly, short-legged gentleman with fat cheeks speaking to a small group on the matter of the silos, as Thassos could gather from the few words that reached his ear. He spoke with obvious enjoyment and had a unique manner of forming his words in his mouth and pronouncing them roundly and resoundingly. He addressed himself chiefly to a middle-aged man with impeccably combed gray hair who stood unnaturally upright and who every now and then pulled down the points of his vest with a sudden nervous movement.

Farther on he spotted Prokas standing with his arms folded behind him and his head thrown to one side. An aged lady, with an aristocratic air, but with something like a violet grape leaf comically decorating her white hair, was trying insistently, as it seemed, to convince him of something. Prokas listened as he rocked his small, compact body, resting now on the toes of his shoes, now on the heels, obviously wanting to show in this way that, yes, he listens out of politeness, but is concerned about other matters. How unbearable successful people can be sometimes, thought Thassos.

Farther down a man with a huge belly was holding his sides, swinging his head back, and laughing out loud. His companion was watching him with the obvious satisfaction of one who has succeeded in accomplishing a desired result.

Suddenly a commotion near the entrance disturbed the monotone of the crowd. The president of the Club, a dapper and perfectly bald little man, who was chatting with a group, turned, forsook his companions and dashed for the entrance, where it appeared that at that moment the "honored guest" of the evening had come in. The president's face took on a festive and radiant expression by the time he crossed the hall to meet him.

Every one of them believes that he is *somebody*, thought Thassos, trying to wrap himself in indifference, to

58

protect himself against his other self which stood ready to be astonished and bow down for nothing. An idiotic feeling of inferiority before these vainglorious men bubbled up corrosively from some dark fold of his being, twisting him into an unnatural position of defense. (So they spend their lives, well-dressed, well-off, and brash, hollow-headed, showing off and rattling off nonsense.) But the next moment he felt disposed to leave, to leave, to climb up by himself to the clean air of the mountain, to leave behind him the garbage of the city and the incomprehensible hierarchy of its values. The loud wall tapestries, whose bad taste had previously made him smile, now revolted him, as did the sickly odor exuded by the half-wilted flowers in the vases.

But he felt relief when Verenikis came smiling and impeccable in his well-made tuxedo, and took him by the arm.

"Come, let me introduce you to a lovely admirer of yours," he said. And as he led him through the crowd, he added in a whisper, "Her spouse is a great entrepreneur and political wheel. Great connections."

Thassos's disdainful disposition evaporated.

The learned lady was in fact beautiful. Her snug black outfit brought out the sheen of the rosy whiteness of her arms and neck. Her large dewy eyes and her somewhat short lower jaw gave her a special charm. Later Thassos observed that her hands, large with thick fingers, almost masculine, were totally incongruous. This observation at once shattered the magic, but, as I said, that came later. For the time being he was enchanted.

"I wanted very much to meet you," said the lady after Verenikis had made the introduction. She extended her hand breast high as if proffering it for him to kiss.

Her honesty and the friendly, personal tone of her voice were very appealing. It was as if she were saying, Let's put formalities aside. They have no place between intellectuals.

With the discretion of a man of the world, Verenikis left them alone to chat. And the learned lady, once it was understood that the conventional phraseology of first acquaintanceship would be out of place under the circumstances, came at once to the point.

She spoke to him about his book, how the spirit of the nature-lover had impressed her, as did the poetry that suffused it from beginning to end.

Curiously, the lovely, learned lady was no fool. She did not resort to those phony displays of admiration which so irritated Thassos. She only spoke of the good features of the book in a way that showed both intelligence and a degree of cultivation.

Flattered, Thassos now fell prey to his inclination to put on his superiority. The conversation took on the profound appearance of an exchange of original ideas between two exceptionally profound people, even though Thassos knew all along that he was not gifted with all the blarney it took to play the role he was trying to play.

". . . The hidden cowardice found at the bottom of every type of compassion . . ."

"Play actor," he heard for a moment his genuine self whispering to him. He could see that those and other words like them which he was sitting there saying, though genuine parts of the train of thought in his book where they flowed forth from a pure source, sounded fake, as he cut them to fit the situation just to impress someone.

The next moment, as we said, he noticed his companion's hands.

But the "honored guest" interrupted them. He was circulating the hall, dealing out handshakes, smiles, and condescension, and when he arrived before the learned lady, he was bathed in sweetness.

"I hope that you're happy with the outcome of the Tsardis matter," he said to her.

She smiled, but did not respond to his remark.

"Allow me to introduce Mr. Maridis," she said in the carefree way of a great lady, gesturing to Thassos.

The other reached out and shook hands.

With his great circular forehead and round, clever eyes, he looked like a bird of prey.

"Pleased to meet you," he said in voice different from the one he had spoken in before.

"So, about the Tsardis business, you think I ought to be happy?" The lady was now serious.

Thassos realized that it was his duty to withdraw. He made a bow in the lady's direction. She gave him her hand, looking at him as if seeing him for the first time, and moved on.

Naturally, philosophy was one thing and the Tsardis business was another, he said to himself and felt like bursting into laughter. But he knew that he would spend a sleepless night later, reproaching himself, cursing his weakness. He knew that against his will he would feel diminished when he saw the Korvelises again.

He wanted to be outside wandering the narrow streets of the old city that he loved so well. But he decided that he would not be the first to leave, especially so early. It's a question of good manners after all, he said, just to provide himself with some excuse, and he set once more to scrutinize the scene.

Until Verenikis was again there before him.

"By yourself again. You're incorrigible," he scolded. "Join our party for dinner."

Obviously his friend made it his business this evening to be his guardian angel.

Thassos was overcome by the mood to be finally rid of any semblance of seriousness. And he succeeded. He stayed with the cheerful company which Verenikis had invited to his table. And he left with them at dawn, half-drunk and dejected.

THE STRUGGLE OF KOSTANTIS
OR
THE STORY OF A DAY'S PAY

HE COULD NOT make up his mind to get a bicycle like everyone else did to make traveling back and forth easier. Not even a used one. He just kept walking from his shack to work, now to one field then to another.

Not that he disagreed with the others. The bicycle is a good thing. You can even say that it has solved a problem for the worker. And yet he had no intention at his age to straddle the old iron frame. Once he struggled with Lazaris's bicycle, to find out how to suit his spindly legs to it and how to control it. "Am I to play around like a kid now?" he could not help asking himself, and gave it up. The others kept encouraging him, but he suspected that they might be doing it to amuse themselves.

But that alone would not have stopped him. There was the other consideration: he had no desire any longer to change his way of life, those patterns formed by the links of his own existence with life and everything in it that he loved.

What if he has to get up an hour earlier? What of it? Is he used to lounging in bed? As soon as dawn breaks he's up for sure, he washes, drinks a cup of coffee, which he brews himself on the stove while his old lady is busy cleaning out the chicken coop. Then he sets out, leisurely at that, without rushing as when he was young, when they would start working at sunrise.

He carried a stout stick over his shoulder, a brightly colored cotton bundle hooked onto the end of it, with sandwich-makings wrapped inside. He walked along clumsily with great, easy-going strides, his lean body rocking like a camel's.

Familiar roads took him sometimes to the open country, sometimes through hedges of cypress, reeds, briars, orange trees standing behind them motionless and thoughtful in the redolent silence of the morning: sloping rays of the sun passing through the trees turning the dew to gold; sparrows bouncing here and there like rubber balls and taking dust baths in the roadway; goldfinches chattering in the hedges. And he would walk along singing to himself as if he hadn't a worry in the world.

A person is not the same all the time, you see. Kostantis felt this sacred morning hour floating on the spray, beyond worries as if life had just now been reborn, untouched—as every morning. He loved this time of day and would not be deprived of it only to escape the fatigue of walking.

Although he was realizing recently that he could not ignore fatigue as he once could.

He was tall and wiry, a bit bowlegged, with large, strong hands, a head small for his height, graying hair and mustache, which drooped from lack of care. The short German boots—military surplus—which he wore, and the black knife sheath, which seemed to stick out from his right boot, gave him a belligerent look. (It was an old knife with a broken point which he used to scrape off dirt that stuck to his hoe.)

§

Work on Sardaina's fields was no joke. The clever and diligent widow of Sardis—once an *artiste*, whom that well-known rake had fallen for and married in his old age—knew how to handle the reins to get the most out of her workers. To be sure, the old ways are passing, you cannot squeeze the workers fiercely and make them live in dread of you, the Union of Field Workers has a voice now, speaks out and makes explicit agreements. But Sardaina adjusted wonderfully well. "Bosh!" she answered contemptuously to the nonsense of the other big vegetable growers about bringing the workers back to their senses. She discusses with the Union as an equal and finds that the agreements give the employer some rights, too, and tend to keep things honest.

The Union has divided workers into classes: first, second, and sometimes a third, according to the capabilities of each, with differences in the day's pay for each. Well, Sardaina always looks for workers of the first class because she has realized that it is worth the difference in rate, and then some, to have the output of a good worker. You only need to know what's in your own interests.

There were five hoers who had taken their places at equal intervals so that they covered the entire breadth of the strip. They would be moving forward in line, each hoeing a wide belt of earth. And the five belts would cover the whole surface so that, when they finished, the entire strip would be hoed. The work was clocked: forty-five minutes of hoeing and a fifteen-minute break to give the workers a breather. Otherwise they would not be able to take it; the work is hard, very hard. They are bent double the whole time, leaning down over the thickly planted orange trees, which spread their branches from the earth at waist level.

They took their places and waited, like athletes waiting for the starting gun.

At the far left end stood Pantelas. He was a short-legged, long-waisted, broad-chested man with the neck of a bull, puffy cheeks, and small, bright eyes. The team charged him with keeping time, since he was wearing a watch. To the right of Pantelas was Kostantis, and to the right of Kostantis was Yoryis Trambas, Yorgaros, a big man the height of Kostantis but twice his girth, which gave him the look of clumsy power. Next came Xapolytos, and at the right end Stelios Klamenos.

Sardaina arrived right on time, too.

A woman of about fifty, well-preserved, slender, with muscular legs, she looked as if she must have been exceptionally beautiful in her youth. Walking along she lit one cigarette off the end of another. She stopped next to Pantelas and said good morning in a hoarse voice. Then she set her watch with Pantelas's.

The five men responded to her greeting.

"Are all five of the first class?" she asked.

"Yes," said Pantelas.

"We'll see," she said, continuing on her way to make her morning inspection tour of the property.

65

Yorgaros followed her out of the corner of his eye, watching her from the waist down amid the tree trunks as she walked with her steady stride until she disappeared from sight. Then he spat into his palms and grabbed his hoe as if he were ready to rush right into the job.

Kostantis spat into his palms, too.

"Come on, lads," said Pantelas and came down strongly with his hoe.

The second to dig in his hoe was Xapolytos, with a "hm!" as if he were getting a weight off his chest. He was a dark, small-framed youngster, all sinews with the mobility of a cat. His ears stuck outward as if they were independent of his head.

Within a few moments the work settled into its usual pace. Each of the five men hoed in his own way, with his own rhythm. Nevertheless, their uncoordinated move-ments, the blows repeated time and again, finally took on a rhythm of their own.

Pantelas was without question the best worker in the Union. With his body bent at the hips to form almost a right angle, he hoed with measured, unhurried movements as if he were making no effort: one, two, three, four blows spread out equally, to cover the breadth of his share of the strip exactly. He took a small pace forward with feet widespread, rooted in the newly hoed soil and quietly be-gan again: one, two, three, four. . . . He was capable of con-tinuing in this way for two whole hours without a breather.

Kostantis looked at him from time to time out of the corner of his eye. What an animal! he would say to himself and remember his own youth. But he was in no fear of him. He knew that Pantelas did not deign to play the bully at work. He only set his pace with that of his comrades, avoid-ing any indication that it would be easy for him to pass them by.

The one who worried Kostantis now and then was the young lion Yorgaros with his bravado. Bravado on the job, the ox. He wasn't very smart.

From the first strokes he felt that pain in his left shoul-der, as if a wedge had been driven into the joint, knifing him with every movement. He gritted his teeth and obsti-nately kept on working. He knew that the worst of it would be now, at the beginning, until his joints and waist had warmed up. For the time being he was having difficulty bending at the waist. A large drop of sweat rolled down his forehead and was dangling at the end of his nose. He thrust out his lower lip and blew it away. The hard part would be getting through the first hour, he thought and grasped the hoe handle as hard as he could.

Kostantis had passed his forty-fifth year and was the only worker of that age to keep his place in the first class. (His contemporaries, as many as were still able to work at all, had moved on one by one to the second class or were shifted to lighter, auxiliary jobs.) The other four of the group were all young men, about thirty. As for Xapolytos, he was not quite twenty-five.

But Kostantis did not put on airs, nor did he think that there was any reason for him to be too proud of himself. It was, of course, no small order to compete at his age as an equal with young men, especially a select group. Kostantis was aware of it and took satisfaction in it from time to time. But what he reckoned especially was the wage: two shillings more was something one could do without only with difficulty. He knew that and thought it natural that he would one day join his contemporaries. But that's the way it is.

"Hang on tight, old man," shouted Yorgaros teasingly.

"Hang on, Kostantis," repeated Kostantis to himself, paying no attention to the other's tone of voice. What can you expect from that fart Yorgaros.

The pain in his shoulder began to abate, and the joint began to work more freely.

The five men continued working in silence for a while. With every stroke they turned up the heavy, sandy soil and buried the dampened grasses. The freshly dug earth and the cut grass exuded an evocative fragrance of fertility, filling Kostantis's lungs with balsam.

But Yorgaros stepped up his pace, as if he suddenly got the urge to challenge his fellow workers. The others strained not to fall behind, because they knew that Sardaina had come and was standing at the end watching them. Kostantis got stubborn and, with a great effort, kept exactly in line with Yorgaros, while the others fell back some. Pantelas was last, to show that he did not pay any attention to this undeclared and pointless competition. Kostantis knew it. Well, if Pantelas wanted to he could make Yorgaros eat dirt before you could bat an eye.

This stretch lasted for about ten minutes. Kostantis began to breathe heavily, but he did not yield, until Sardaina withdrew. She had apparently reckoned the time against the work that was done. Kostantis knew that break time was drawing near.

In fact, Sardaina did not get far before Pantelas gave the signal:

"Oooop!"

They stopped, laid down the hoes, and straightened up. Yorgaros stretched out ostentatiously. Pantelas joined his hands behind his back and stretched them powerfully downward, doubling his back muscles as hard as he could. Kostantis mopped his brow with the back of his hand and then blew his nose on the ground, closing off first one nostril with the thumb, and then the other with the index finger. Xapolytos withdrew farther on to piss.

Klamenos stretched, too.

They went one by one to get water from the jug which one of the girls had brought. They found it leaning on the root of an orange tree nearby, a cup hanging on its neck.

Yorgaros downed a cupful in three big gulps, filled the cup again, drank the second the same way and let out an "aaah!" of pleasure.

Kostantis rinsed his mouth out twice and drank the half cup that remained. Then he sat down on the root of an orange tree, leaning on the trunk.

Pantelas came and sat down crosslegged, a bit farther on. The others, too, sat wherever, lighting up cigarettes, except Klamenos, who lay face downwards, his jaw on his hands. He was a well-built man with a long face, cheeks caved in, and gray-green eyes. His pallor was striking because his way of working revealed no weakness.

"Cut out those antics, will you, Yoryis?" said Pantelas in a tired voice.

"What d' you mean?" asked Yorgaros, playing dumb.

"You know perfectly well what I mean. Don't you know that this kind of stuff won't do anymore?"

Yorgaros did not answer. On his face a half-smile revealed indifference and petty stubbornness.

Pantelas knitted his brow.

68

"How's Yorgaros supposed to understand that?" he said to no one in particular.

Xapolytos spat deftly and hit the trunk of a young orange tree two meters in front of him. He spat again but missed.

It was cool and peaceful under the green cover, held aloft by countless rows of columns in straight lines, the trunks of the trees. There the daylight was filtered and otherworldly.

As Kostantis sat leaning against the orange tree, he heard his blood beat angrily against his temples. He was watching a large, white rooster with a blood red stripe digging nervously at the ground, pecking around as if he had turned something up, and he started cackling and calling his hens, who were browsing for food farther off. They were a crowd of big, fat, white hens, the same breed as the rooster, the famous English chickens belonging to Sardaina. Three of them came running at the rooster's summons, necks stretched out, wings flapping, and when they got there they began greedily scratching and pecking the ground. The rooster stepped aside with an aristocratic air. Then he crowded one of them aside skillfully and jumped on her.

But at that moment Pantelas gave the signal.

"Come on, lads."

They got up immediately and took their places.

Starting off was a little less difficult now than the first time. Kostantis did not feel the stiffness in his waist, his joints were flexible, he worked with ease. Perhaps he would have even rediscovered his old humor had it not been for that deafening ringing in his ears which troubled him. Gone was the time when he was not aware of his ears, his joints, or the resistance of this earth, which he now reckoned as a living opponent pulling with all the weight of its own unstable mass at each swing of the hoe.

"Come on, baby," he murmured every now and then as if coaxing someone, he wasn't clear whom. Perhaps it was this red sandy earth. He was in the habit of chatting with it intimately, except that in the past their chats were different. They were friendly back then, of course; he always loved the earth, but back then he didn't implore it, he didn't seek its goodwill as he did now.

Sardaina passed by again, stood for a while watching the five workers.

Tireless, the dragon-lady, Kostantis said to himself. He had respect for her, even though he knew that the question this morning, whether all five were of the first class, was definitely referring to him. The Union director had told him the other day that Sardaina, during a discussion with him about the new requirements, had tossed in among other things a remark about workers of advanced age who continue on in the first class, and mentioned Kostantis as an example. "We know," she said, "we know what happens should a worker of limited strength be in a group." The director reassured her that the Union pays close attention to that particular point, and, so far as Kostantis is concerned, he is a worker of the first class and then some, and she should not worry about it. The director passed these things on to Kostantis, who took no offense, nor even complained. He found it natural for an employer to demand his rights and for a man's strength to diminish with age. One will endure longer, another less, but the time will come for each to drop out. That's the way it is. As for the director's assurances, Sardaina does not need them; she is in a good position to judge for herself.

Kostantis saw her still standing there. He knew that break time was far off and he grew anxious, for he had begun to tire. The ringing in his ears grew louder. His heart filled his chest and was still swelling to the point of overflow. Ragged thoughts without beginning or end passed through his mind, thoughts without the power to conceal his one and only concern—not to fall behind. Not even an inch.

Finally Sardaina left.

But this time it was quite a while before Pantelas gave the signal.

"Ooop!"

This second break would last a half hour so the workers could have a snack.

Kostantis had difficulty straightening up.

He staggered to the drinking fountain, which was running in the next strip. He plunged his hands into the water and felt the coolness all the way to his innards. He then blew his nose and washed. He went over to where he had

70

left his bundle hanging from the limb of an orange tree. He took it down, returned, and sat by the fountain to enjoy the purling of the waters.

His supplies consisted of half a loaf of bread, a handful of green olives, two tomatoes, and some leftovers from yesterday: stewed potatoes in a little glass pot with a screw-on lid; the last was for lunch.

The other workers came around one by one and sat in a circle, some holding napkins like Kostantis's, others baskets.

"Photiniii! Water!" yelled Yorgaros.

Then he gathered some dry sticks, shaped them into a little pile, started a fire and toasted a herring skewered on his fork. The aroma of the frying salted fish filled the place.

Kostantis watched indifferently, and as the other got up, holding his *meze* with satisfaction, Kostantis noticed the marks pressed in along each hole of the leather belt revealing how much fatter his big stomach got from one year to the next. How old is he? Kostantis wondered, and guessed about twenty-eight, the same age his first son, Christofis, would have been if he had not died as a youngster in the meningitis epidemic. He was the same age as Yorgaros.

Photini arrived hefting the jug of freshly drawn water and set it down next to them. She was plump, but tough, as girls often are who work in the fields, darkish, round-faced, with thick brows and a bit of fuzz on her upper lip.

"Come, join us, Photini," said Xapolytos.

The girl threw him a quick, provocative glance and immediately turned her face elsewhere, as if not paying any attention to him.

"How's it going, Uncle Kostantis?" she asked and smiled, showing a line of little white teeth, which somehow made her look like a small, charming pet animal.

"O.K., my child," Kostantis answered.

He cut up his tomatoes with his penknife, sprinkled them with salt, which he had wrapped in a bit of cloth, and began quietly eating his bread, olives, and tomatoes, chewing each mouthful attentively, without hurrying. He was not in the habit of hurrying with anything; not even when he was as young as these fellows. That's why he liked Pantelas, who had put his basket down in front of him and was eating in the same controlled and patient way as he

71

hoed, while the others went after their food as if they were afraid it would get away from them.

Yorgaros took a whole loaf out of his basket, cut it in half, put half back into the basket and began eating greedily huge mouthfuls of bread, biting them right off the loaf, and slices of herring, which he cut at an angle with his jackknife, throwing them into his huge mouth and then spitting out bones as if they were apricot pits.

As Kostantis watched him, he remembered his grandfather. Kostantis was very young when his grandfather died. Only occasionally out of his childhood memories could he but dimly make out any picture of him except one, which remained vividly drawn: the old man sitting on the parapet in breeches and bare feet greedily gulping down something he was gathering up with his fingers from a clay pot, his saliva running down, dripping on his bare chest and bloated belly. In his last years he had ended up like an animal, with no other volition except when to eat, to bolt down whatever they gave him, all the while whining that he was hungry. Such was the memory Kostantis had of his grandfather.

From the other side of the field came the noise of the hoeing machine which Sardaina had brought in just recently and was hoeing the newly planted parts where the small, widely planted trees did not get in the way. It was an object like a low motorized wheelbarrow, and with one man steering, it could do more work than five good hoers. Of course, the work is not the same. This machine barely breaks the surface. But Sardaina says that agriculturalists now advise that deep hoeing is not necessary. For certain the clever lady is now following up on that and reckoning the results and the cost to make the appropriate adjustments. Kostantis heard the machine shatter the quiet and he disliked it.

He was last to finish lunch. He rolled the bread and the pot in the towel, hung it from a branch, sat down again at the foot of a lemon tree standing by itself at the edge of the furrow, and lit a cigarette. Though he could not state the time in minutes, he knew *exactly* how much time remained before they would pick up their hoes again. And he had not yet felt rested, just sitting, leaning heavily against the tree trunk, without the ambition to stir from there.

He reached out and plucked a soft little leaf from the tree, rubbed it between his fingers and smelled it. His mind was refreshed with the fragrance. I'm just tired and it will pass, he thought, as he heard Pantelas give the signal. He put forth the effort and rose to his feet.

They had no more than begun work when there she was: Sardaina sprang up before them and stood watching. That was the system she had—to appear sometimes a minute before break time or a minute after they had started in again, so those keeping track of time will keep an eye out. She stayed for a while, but fortunately Yorgaros was not in the mood for being clever. She left.

Kostantis bucked up, somehow found the strength to keep his place in line, and did not fall behind. But now another sort of pain was tormenting him, a subtle one, which was spreading all along his left side from his shoulder blade to the tips of his fingers. He was unable to determine exactly where it was coming from. Come on, baby, he would say to himself every now and then as if to exorcise the evil, but this was not like the usual pains that grip you in the joints or in the waist and make it difficult for you, and which you overcome and your limberness returns as you work. This here is something different that smolders inside; you have to fight with it, but you don't overcome it. Instead, after a while, it numbs a little.

Yorgaros shouted.

"Photiniiii! Water!"

The girl came running with the jug and made to hand him the cup, but he grabbed the jug and lifted it with both hands, leaned his head back and without touching the rim of the jug with his lips began pouring water into his open mouth. He gulped it down adroitly without shutting his mouth, his adam's apple moving up and down.

The others continued to hoe.

"Yorgaros has gone mad," said Klamenos.

"It's the herring," teased Xapolytos.

When he had drunk a lot of water, Yorgaros brought the jug down and belched loudly. Then he took up his hoe again and put out all his efforts to make up the distance he had fallen behind.

"If it had been . . . just . . . the herring," he boasted with panting breath. "But last night . . . we drank . . . a fifth of cognac apiece . . . me and Antrikkis."

The way that ruffian is going he won't hold out long, thought Kostantis indifferently.

He was most concerned with holding out himself. As long as he can. He has to. In just a little while Pantelas would give the signal to rest. He would stretch out on the ground, to regain his strength. A quarter of an hour to rest; that was something, anyway, to rest, to manage until the next break, another quarter hour, and then comes the lunch break, which lasts a whole hour . . . Come on, baby. Courage, Kostantis. The time is near enough for you to give it up, but every day you last is a day won.

Now the pain had numbed, seemed more like a void, an oppressive void inside him from the shoulder blade down low through his trunk as if his innards had been emptied. His legs tremble. Sweat runs drop by drop from his forehead. But he hangs on with a fierce determination, clinging to Pantelas's pace, step by step, thrust by thrust, not to fall a hand-span behind.

But he did not stretch out on the ground, so as not to reveal how weak he felt. Instead, as usual, he sat with his back leaning against the trunk of an orange tree. Better that way. If he had stretched out he might have had difficulty getting up.

Pantelas came and sat next to him. They spent their quarter hour break together smoking, not exchanging a word.

The other three were sitting farther on. Xapolytos was telling some story and Yorgaros was holding his sides in laughter.

Pantelas looked at his watch and got up.

"Wherever she is, the dragon-lady will show up," he said as if trying to justify himself, and gave the signal by clapping his hands.

Kostantis got up, took his old knife out of his boot and carefully scraped off his hoe, and, with a manner full of determination, as if he knew how to do it, he began work. One . . . two . . . three . . . four . . .

74

Well, no! . . . he said to himself as if responding to a provocation he would not obey. Oh, no! . . . he said again, strongly gripping the hoe handle. But inside he was uneasy.

He focused whatever willpower and stamina he had left, working with control and attention, avoiding any superfluous motion, even speech, so as not to waste his breath. His movements, which were by nature unhurried and purposeful, became more measured, so that every stroke of the hoe, every step was aimed accurately at the target, only with the expertise of an experienced worker, who had learned to conserve his strength so he could get to the end of the day. Not that he would think of it that way; he was only obeying a necessity which he felt in his body, in his innards; and his mind wrapped itself around it like a ball of twine.

Unconscious of the presence of his comrades, he only glanced from time to time at Pantelas to make sure that he was in line. Their conversations he either did not hear or took them as mere sounds. He paid no more attention to them.

In this way he got through almost the entire hour, and only towards the end did he begin to pant. But his alert inner timekeeper was telling him that any time Pantelas was about to give the signal; and with this to look forward to he lasted without bending a bit.

"Ooop!" Pantelas's bass voice sounded at last.

This time Sardaina did not show up.

Fifteen minutes. Enough to breathe a bit without slackening his resolve, which he had to keep till the next break, the noon break. Then he could rest.

He was quite alone, as if he had been cut off from his comrades. Not that he wanted it that way, that he felt sulky or bitter toward them because he saw them pull indifferently ahead of him as he struggled to keep up with them in line. Naturally he was having difficulties, he thought. It was his turn to. And it never crossed his mind that it could be otherwise, that the others could possibly undertake to cover for him—nor could he accept that. It's just that willynilly he forgot they were there; because all his thoughts were taken up by his one single concern.

Nevertheless Pantelas came and sat by him again, and, as if the two of them were of one mind, as if indifferent to it all, they smoked in silence.

Sardaina was not absent this time.

When they had picked up their hoes again and had hoed for a while, there she was. Kostantis realized that she was coming along unhurriedly, looking at the hoed earth— surely she was measuring up the work they had done—until she came up beside them.

"How's it going?" she asked Pantelas.

"Good," he answered without turning to look at her.

She did not say anything else. She just stood there for a few moments, lit a cigarette, and left.

Some employers make it a practice to observe, scowl, never to show satisfaction, in the belief that this was how they'll get more from their workers. Sardaina was not so stupid as to make demands without cause. As long as she judged the work and found it acceptable, she knew that nothing more can come of making crabby remarks. On the contrary.

Kostantis's determination was still holding out, but his strength was slowly beginning to leave him, and only an un-conquered stubbornness kept him going. He felt like an in-sect which is tormented in the earth, always stumbles and falls over and always gets back on its feet to try again. One more step . . . one, two, three, four . . . And another step . . . one, two, three, four . . . He felt nauseous. Fragments of thoughts teemed in his head. But as if he were a stranger to all that, he heeded only his unbending will, which kept him going till he could make it this time, too, to the break. The others were neither aware nor cared to be aware of *how* he made it. Why should they care? Everyone fights by him-self. *How* is his own business.

He did not feel like eating a bite. He just wanted to lie down. To lie flat on the ground as he had planned, to rest his body. But now that the time had come, he thought that he ought to eat something first. You should rest, yes, but again where will you get the strength to continue? Can a man work without eating? Nor did he want to collapse in front of the others, just like that, and reveal that he didn't even have strength enough left in him to eat.

He left his hoe behind and went over to the ditch to cool off, searching his shadowy mind to remember where he had left his bandana hanging.

But when he got there Pantelas had anticipated him, holding Kostantis's bandana along with is own basket.

"Since I was there . . . ," he apologized and set basket and bandana on the ground.

Kostantis said nothing, only hurried to the water to wash off, as if he had nothing to say. Of course, it was natural as long as the man was going there. . . . Moreover, it was his habit to sit quiet when he felt the way he was feeling now; he could not handle kindheartedness.

He spread out his bandana, unscrewed the lid off his jar, and began eating, using his penknife as a fork.

At first he had to force himself to chew, but little by lit - tle the taste of well-masticated bread in his mouth made him feel better. He watched Pantelas across from him grind his food with brio, his strong teeth shining white. He saw Yorgaros farther down greedily swallowing, his eyes wide open. He saw Photini, who had just hefted the jug of fresh water, having a quiet chat with Xapolytos. And he was no longer all alone.

Nevertheless, he should not waste time. He finished off his lunch and without even lighting a cigarette, got up, moved away from the rest, chose a level spot in the shade, and spread himself out on it. Aaaah!

His tendons relaxed and he became one with the rich sandy earth and the orange trees, which spread searchingly and twined their branches in every direction like thick living tentacles charged with energy and solidified movement. And above them the branches shot with dense, deep green leaves rising, drawing sap, and boldly spreading out.

Without thinking anything, Kostantis wandered with his gaze here and there, stopping now and then on details— a healed wound, a shoot sick with chlorosis, a greedy, impetuous twig—which he studied as if they were his personally, as if he were studying the knots on his own hands. The trees about here were so familiar to him—as were so many others all around the area—from the time he remembered them as newly planted seedlings. An entire lifetime working on them. Just as well known to him was this earth with its green-covered surface and its dark innards, where roots struggle to open passages and move searchingly forward to draw in moisture. He felt as if he were sinking into the earth's bosom, and he, too, was drinking in with every fiber of his body the balsam of life from her great breath . . . until he was in a deep sleep . . .

From the depths he heard Pantelas clapping; he jumped up, stretched, and went to his place. He felt rested and peaceful.

But he knew that the struggle would start up again in the same way as it had in the morning: the pains, the stiffness in his waist, until his joints warmed up with the work and the pains numbed. But he was not afraid. He had stored up enough strength to overcome it. What was there left? Two stops . . . Come on, baby . . . He spat in his palms and started in.

Determined but controlled and unhurried, he labored and moved on step by step.

However, things did not follow exactly the same course as in the morning.

In the beginning and almost to the first break he had had good control over his body and ignored the little pains. But as time rolled on his exhaustion became more and more intense, and he did not have time to recover in the brief breaks.

He'd had it now. That feeling of emptiness in his chest finally became unbearable. Neither his rapid heartbeats nor his rushing, insatiable gasping for air could tame it. The ringing in his ears grew louder and made his isolation complete. Every now and then he would waver in a strange fashion, as if the ground were disappearing from under his feet. But at once he would clench his teeth, and with a shake recover control over himself like one who obstinately resists going to sleep.

Until finally there was nothing supporting him except his will, which remained unbending, to endure, to endure till the end of the day. His thought did not move even once beyond this immediate border to think about what would happen tomorrow . . . To stand upright was everything today, to win the current day, and leave tomorrow to God.

78

But his comrades began to wear out, too. They ceased their chatting, the jokes, and you heard only their heavy breathing and the strokes of the hoes that grappled with the earth.

The closer the time came for them to quit for the day, the more this suffocating silence bore the weight of their fatigue and impatience.

The sun was still high, but its rays fell slantwise, slipped among the branches, and imprinted the earth with a phantasmagoria of bright shapes with green overtones. The area under the orange trees took on the appearance of depth.

In his dizziness Kostantis forgot to wait and watch when Sardaina would appear—it was his practice to be in place right up to the time that the workers would quit for the day—nor did he even realize that she was coming, caught sight of her suddenly only after she had come and stood next to Pantelas looking at her watch. Now he knew that any moment now Pantelas would give the signal. And he felt something like the joy of victory.

When finally Pantelas's "Ooop!" came, Kostantis had difficulty straightening his body, his legs trembled, but on his face played a strange smile, that of a child who wants to be brave.

"We'll continue tomorrow," said Sardaina. "But one more group of five should come. Time is running short and we have to hurry."

§

The four got on their bicycles and, before Kostantis could make it to the gate, had disappeared.

He laid his staff on his shoulder and started towards his shack with the same rocking inelegant walk that he used in the morning. But now he was walking with a stoop as if he was not looking around him, as if the countryside had been stripped of the magic that had washed over it this morning. Not that he was absorbed in any worries or complaints. Not at all. He was just tired, but at peace. Besides, as we said, a person isn't always the same.

He reached his shack late in the evening.

He sat on a bench outside, and by the time he smoked a cigarette his wife put supper on the table and lit the lamp.

The place was deep in half-light. A peaceful sorrow wrapped the voices of the neighborhood and the quiet exchanges of Kostantis and his wife as they were having supper under the vine-arbor.

Kostantis had planned to go waste some time at the coffee shop after supper.

But when they finished eating, he felt dead tired. His eyelids were heavy.

He got up with some difficulty, he went reeling into the shack, took off his shoes, and he fell face down on the mattress just as he was with his clothes on.

In a few moments he was sound asleep.

TIMES OF DIFFICULTY

THE ORANGE GROVE

ALONG THIS SHORE OF CYPRUS the land is blessed. Light, sandy soil, good water, and the breath of the sea, which takes the edge off the winter frosts. Whatever is needed to grow orange trees. A garden land. A bright green belt, that spans the gold of the sand on the entire semicircle of the gulf, to fade into the rocky ground of the cape. During March, whenever it blows off shore, the sea breeze is redolent of orange blossoms all the way to the entrance to the gulf, a distance of two miles.

Talking about growing orange trees is easy. But only men like Petris can turn talk into reality, men who for an entire lifetime bound their toil so tightly to soil and tree that these three basic elements of the garden are inseparable. That's how Petris grew his orange orchard on the edge of the green belt on the boundary toward the cape.

When he left his father's land and set about on his own, he was somewhat advanced in years: almost thirty. He was unable to do so before that because he had two sisters to settle, and both married late. But Petris never took it hard. Not that he was kindhearted or even that it bothered him to leave others unprotected. No. Petris was one of those stoics who follow with composure and determination the fate set for them, and whose capability to live life without considering anyone special makes others revere them. A grave, taciturn, and hard-working man, he followed the primordial way of his kind because that was the way he found it. He took care of his sisters, dividing between them the family estate and the responsibility for watching the old folks. And then, without taking a day's rest, he crossed himself, spit on his palms, and set to digging and putting out trees on his own land. He planted, grafted, set up fences, built a little house and got married. What did it matter whether he had started at thirty instead of twenty? The route was all the same, even the inner route, the tight bonds of his soul with this soil, with these trees; not distinguishing between his own toil and the toil of the young tree struggling to take root, or between his own pain and the pain of the tree attacked by blight; hearing in his dreams the pulse of his trees, and feeling delight when they are sated with water.

Nevertheless, his late start caused one departure from the usual route. Petris was over thirty-five when his wife, almost thirty herself, bore their first child. A boy. They had no others. And upon this boy, Artemis, the middle-aged parents placed affections felt by them for the first time, affections which they clung to but could not sort out, but which cast into the mother's soul the seed of boundless love and into Petris's mind some new ideas. Thus Artemis, the only son, took from his mother an affection unusual in the people of his kind, and from Petris he acquired permission to go to the high school in the city, an hour away from the village.

Nor did the new ideas in Petris's mind stop there. He had the further intention of sending Artemis away to study when he had finished high school. But he never talked about it, nor did he acknowledge to himself that the matter was settled: "let him finish and we'll see," he would say to himself, the hand that worked the pruner suspended for a moment. And with a smile playing in his eyes, he would go back to his pruning.

Now Petris's world became strange, in that it was divided between his immovable devotion to his land and his dreams for Artemis. It was as if he were living two lives, which in his primitive thought had no common point of contact, yet no cause for splitting up, either. The dreams merely opened a window from which new light flooded the heart of Petris.

And that's how the years rolled on. The orange trees spread their branches, joined their crowns, and Artemis became an eighteen-year-old graduating student. A dark-skinned young man, terse, saying little, just like his father. As Artemis grew up and found success, the light in Petris's heart spread with quiet assurance, as if the child's success confirmed his own on the land.

However, a new wind had arisen recently, one which stirred the minds of men. Like a quite obvious and shocking message from the depths of time saying that the hour had come and the framework of everyday life was too small for the good islanders. In the coffee shops, in the market place, in the homes, the work places, the schools, a wave of alarm, of expectation, of justification raised souls above the logic of compromise and routine. The youth girded themselves with the panoply of their enthusiasm and sought out opportunities for self-sacrifice. They came, they went, they met in out-of-the-way places, and they talked in whispers, then suddenly they jumped on their bicycles and took off for town. With them went Artemis.

Petris had suspected something from the start. Nevertheless, he held his peace, and, like a wild animal, he sniffed the coming storm in the air. He waited cautiously and observed Artemis. But one day, when his wife was trying to tell him her fears for the boy, who could not be curbed, he scolded her.

"Leave him be. He knows what he is doing. What do you want him to do, stay behind, a great towering fellow, and hide behind your skirts?"

Later a feeling gradually began taming his reservations, the feeling that all this commotion around him was as if surging from the roots of his own existence, deeply, very deeply, from where his consciousness of nationalism drew its own sap.

On a sunbathed day in the fall Petris was sitting on his threshold fixing his sulphur sprayer, making it ready for use when the right weather came along, when the fence gate of his garden opened abruptly. In came two young men panting. They came over and stood facing him twisting their school caps in embarrassment. Petris tensed, but he did not show it. He just kept looking at them and waited for them to speak. Finally, one of the lads, forgetting the words he seemed to have prepared, blurted out the whole story hastily and incoherently: The students had gone down to a demonstration. The "security forces" opened fire. Artemis, who was out front with the flag, fell. "Two others were wounded, too, but Artemis . . . fell," repeated the boy loudly.

Petris understood and was suddenly on his feet. A fiery column of wrath rose within him and burst out. The mother, who was in the room listening, let out a wail and tried to rush out. But Petris reached out and stopped her. He put his arms around her with unusual tenderness, and had her sit down.

Everything that followed, that day and the next, seemed to Petris to take place in a separate area of his life, in an area where nothing ended and nothing began, because the moment, each moment, solitary and dominating, was so intense with inner vibration that filled everything. In his affliction he felt as one elevated by a remarkable if vague identity between his own drama and the pulse of everything around him.

But after Artemis's funeral, night came, and people began discreetly to leave, with a squeeze of the hand and a good word. And finally, when midnight had passed, the aged parents were left alone, without anyone to stand by them in their grief.

Then Petris felt that he had come back to reality. He turned and looked at the mother, who was sitting in silence, the now useless wings of her affection folded. And he felt once again that tenderness in his heart and the itch of a restrained caress in his palms.

Later, exhausted, she lay down as if to sleep, and Petris, who no longer fit there, opened the door and went into the garden.

The living presence of his trees, their familiar breath under the starlight, drew him as always into their own orbit.

It was the pleasantest hour, the one that heralds the dawn. The cricket was sewing the tapestry of its trills onto the veil of silence. A hen stretched her wings out in the coop. A cow was mooing in the distance. Then the horizon started to turn red, and Petris noticed that the weather was dry and calm. "Time for sulphur spraying," he thought. And the worker, awakening in him, automatically joining thought to deed, went to the shed where he kept his tools, picked up the sulphur sprayer, and started working.

The sprayer filled the silence of the dawn with a strange sound resembling the insistent and rhythmical moaning of an animal, as if it were calling to the sun as it grew brighter and the light of dawn spread, giving everything a special meaning.

AUTO-DA-FÉ

EVERY EVENING when the sun was about to set in royal colors, Father Kyriakos would go out through the courtyard door of his house and, leaning on his stout cane, walk to Trifonas's coffee shop to relax from being cooped up all day.

His large frame was too heavy for his old legs, but with the help of his cane he would walk upright and proud. He would arrive at the coffee shop, scale the three steps one by one, and go sit in his usual place near the low surrounding wall.

Trifonas's coffee shop is located on the edge of the main village, a straw-covered hut with a courtyard like a terrace, at the overlook. From his seat, which was like a lookout post, Father Kyriakos muses, looking out at the plain, which spreads in waves; at the few little houses of Alia, slowly cooking dry on its baking dish in the middle of the plain; and beyond, at the whole line of the horizon, the mass of the barren mountain range which raises its peaks like an unapproachable boundary.

This eternal dialogue between consent of the gentle plain and the proud "no" of the mountain fills the old man's soul so full that he cannot separate it from his own being. How many years has he spent loving this place and its people, living the goodness of the plain and the struggles of the people, the dignity of the mountains and the poverty of the people! He stopped counting the years and trying to keep up with people long ago. He has become one with this plain and with those mountains beyond. And just as the wind-swept peaks of Pentadactylos raise their bulk over the envies of the plain, so does Father Kyriakos raise the stature of his long and honorable life over the trivialities of ordinary

life and look about himself with understanding and serenity.

Trifonas brought the tray with coffee, placed it on a chair
in front of the old man, and returned to the task of sprin-
kling the courtyard. At this time the coffee shop is empty
and the kind cafe owner tidies up while waiting for his regular customers, a few workers of the neighborhood who
would come in one by one as they got off work.

Dimitros came in earlier than usual, straight from work, his
clothes covered with lime dust and his basket in hand. He
went to the corner where Father Kyriakos was sitting,
greeted him with "Good evening, teacher," and sat down
next to him.

He was about thirty-five, tall and stooped, with blue
eyes. He spoke in the muffled tones of those with weak
lungs. But he looked strong. His broad hands and dry,
dusty skin revealed his trade—masonry.

He sat with palms on knees and waited in the attentive
silence of one possessed of some overmastering purpose.
The old man looked at him sympathetically, then returned
to his own reflections. They both gazed out at the plain and
had the same thought, each in his own way.

Father Kyriakos spoke first, as if resuming a conversation started once before.

"Yesterday I went to Alia. I talked with the elders of the
church, but they weren't willing to listen to anything. I also
talked with one or two others. . . . You can't get a straight answer from any of them, but they are all in agreement not to
put up with Loizos. . . ."

"Why? Did he annoy them somehow?" asked Dimitros.

"You ask them and they say, 'He's a leftist; he's a com-
munist.' What's more, they even remembered his past,
when he was a bully and they were afraid of him."

Dimitros listened thoughtfully. He made a broad gesture as if moving aside some impediment and said,

"But that's ancient history. Everybody knows that
Loizos has become a different person since he's been in the
union here with us. Why are they now remembering things
from the past?"

The old man moved his head.

"What can I tell you, my boy? Dissension has flared up among us; you'd think that God has forsaken us. I agree with you that Loizos has changed, although I don't know whether it's because he's moved in with you, as you say. More than a few people have found the right path by coming to me, or rather to God, whom I serve. . . . But that's another matter. Today Loizos is a good man, and I love him even more when I think of what he was yesterday. But the fellow bless his soul does have his quirks, too. The brass and stubbornness that he had once, he still has, but in another way. For a poor worker to stand up to the whole village as if he had no need of anyone . . ."

The sun was setting opposite the mountain and bathed it in the last rays, causing the folds of its bare surface to appear in relief, while the plain, which had broiled all day under the heat of the sun, became mild and gentle. A bus was seen coming from far away, raising a cloud of dust on the white ribbon of the road which wound snakelike up and down the folds of the plain. A barefoot boy passed along the front of the coffee shop guiding a team of huge oxen, which moved peacefully, swaying back and forth. Trifonas's regulars began arriving one by one and the cool open-air coffee shop filled with quiet conversations.

"Everyone has his pride, teacher," said Dimitros. "Does Loizos hurt anyone by not renouncing his ideas? No. . . . Did he ask the others to renounce their ideas? Why does it bother them so much that some poor struggler won't con- sent to live with his head hanging?"

"What children you all are!" said Father Kyriakos impa- tiently. "This is the point where passions have flamed, where men have lost their heads. I'm looking for a way we might prevent an incident which could break out any minute, and you sit and tell me your theories. . . . Listen, you know Sotiris, the son of Harillis. I didn't try to get hold of him, but when he found out why I had come to Alia he sought me out on his own to say two words to me neat and simple: 'The robber Loizos is a leftist dog and we don't want the likes of him in the village.' Sotiris was like a wild bull. It seems like yesterday when he was squalling as I dipped him into the baptistery. I kept quiet, when in another situa- tion I would have pulled his ears. . . . No, Dimitros, such

91

fires are not put out with theories. Tell Loizos to let it pass. It's the only way to prevent an incident."

Dimitros remained quiet for a moment. Finally, he sighed:

"Perhaps . . ."

To all appearances life went on unchanged. Except that a fluttering of excitement, uneasiness, and fear was turning into a flood and permeating everything.

The most excitable people opened up to enjoy finally the high winds, while the others, the lukewarm, who wanted their peace, curled into their cocoons and trembled with anxiety.

Heavy weather was rolling in all the while and hid the faces of men in its darkness. And every now and then hatred flashed, portending disaster.

Loizos would grit his teeth and struggle. For his wages. For whatever he believed was his right. He was a lean forty-year-old. The perfect proportions of his build and an easy suppleness of movement gave his medium stature an appearance of power and neutralized every impression of ill fortune which might be conveyed by his poor, patched clothing and his army boots, which he wore without socks. His jet black eyes, his face, which was rather ugly, shone with the expression of one who was inured to hardship and driven by determination.

He arrived on the bus along with the other workers who came from the military base an hour away. But Loizos had another three miles on bicycle to his modest house in Alia. He made this trip every day: going in the morning at daybreak, returning in the evening: a half hour on bicycle, an hour on the bus.

He stopped by the Co-op, put a few items in the basket he carried, and went to the Union, where he had left his bicycle since morning and where he would sit for a while before leaving for Alia.

Here and only here could he find peace. He was riled and closed up all the rest of the day. In the village the unexplainable hatred of the others hounded him every moment. At home he battled with poverty. At work—drudgery, rather—he held his peace, waiting only for this

day, too, to end. In the village, at home, at work, in the tiresome coming and going, everywhere, there was nothing but
this affliction surrounding him, and the smoldering desire
to pursue his search. Only here, in his union building, was
he where he belonged, among friends in the struggle, feeling that somewhere down deep a seed sprouts that will rise
up—it has to be—rise up one day and give forth the fruits of
justice. But above all the amoebic shapes of hope belonging
to a wronged, uncultured man, Loizos found for the first
time right here the pride one feels when he believes that
his life has taken on meaning. This transport of feeling
suddenly elevated his humble and difficult life to a level of
dignity beyond poverty, beyond the false criteria of inequal-
ity, and restored his much-wounded pride. It was like a
conquest which no one had the right to take from him. *No
one*, he would say to himself, his eyes sparking.

When it passes the last houses of the village, the road starts
uphill, gently at first, more steeply as it goes on, until it
reaches the crest, straddles it, and starts down the other
side.

Loizos got halfway up the slope, found it too difficult to
do on the bicycle, jumped off and continued on foot, pushing the bicycle with his right hand. Usually when he would
reach the top he would straddle the bicycle again and coast
down the slope to the ravine. But this time, as soon as he
reached the point where he could see over the crest, he saw
a vehicle parked next to the narrow bridge over the ravine.
It was Sotiris's truck. He recognized it. Next to the parked
vehicle stood four people. They seemed to be talking and
looking his way.

Loizos got suspicious. Why were they waiting just there
just then? . . . He leaned his bicycle against the trunk of a
wild olive, sat down at its roots, and lit a cigarette. He had
to think.

Recently Sotiris and his gang had taken to threatening
Loizos wherever they came across him, sometimes with
vague remarks, sometimes blatantly. Loizos would attempt
to play ignorant, but rage would flame up. How long could
he hold it back? . . . But there had been other incidents, too.
The other day his older son had come home crying, upset

because some of the other kids had been spitting on him and he could not deal with them; there were too many of them. Loizos grabbed the boy by the hand and rushed back towards the school, but they did not have to go that far. The thoughtless young tormentors had followed their victim, and as soon as Loizos had turned the corner, he was confronting them.

"Are these the ones?" he asked his son, who was already pointing at them.

He picked out the oldest, hauled off and slapped him. The youngsters vanished. And Loizos bellowed loudly enough to be heard at the coffee shop a bit farther down the street.

"From now on anyone who bothers me or my kids will regret it!"

But the next moment he had second thoughts about that.

§

They could be waiting for him down there . . . What should he do? . . . Should he turn back to find his friends and tell them I saw this and that and I got suspicious and I'm not going home? . . . And then? Would the matter end if he ran away this time? If they have something in mind, they'll just look for another opportunity. Unless he decides to pick up and leave town. Oh, no! Not that. It won't do for him to put his tail between his legs and run like a hunted dog just because they want him to. And besides, where will he and his children go to find shelter, or is he making enough that he can even pay rent? . . .

He had thought about this several times. And he always ended up knitting his eyebrows and working himself into a rage to meet the threat head-on. Let's get it over with. After all, if they're just coming to pick a fight, he should remind them that he is not just a wet hen. Have they forgotten when they were afraid of his shadow? Enough is enough. Why don't they leave him alone?

He took a last drag, threw away his cigarette, and got up. He had made up his mind. If they were in fact waiting for him, he was not going to run away. He would clear up the matter man to man. He got on his bicycle and headed down the slope.

94

And it turned out as he had suspected. When he drew up to the bridge, they barred his way.

"Stop! We've been looking for you!" shouted Sotiris.

He got off his bicycle and let it fall to the ground so he would have both hands free. He walked up to them, waiting to see what they would say.

But from that point on matters proceeded differently than he had imagined. Without a word all four of them attacked.

"Tie the *traitor's* hands behind his back," he heard Sotiris say.

At first he was confused.

He had been ready for anything: to hear their hatred and threats, to talk plainly to them, clarifying what each party wanted from the other, what there was to be afraid of, even to come to blows, though they might cripple him since they were so many. But this treachery, throwing him on his face, such a dirty trick with no explanations; no, that had never crossed his mind. Exasperation choked him. He turned into a wild beast and began striking out madly with hands, feet, head, with such rage that his adversaries fell into confusion. He struck out and screamed like one possessed.

"Why? . . . Why? . . . Traitor! . . . Why! . . ."

And he found nothing else to say, but his madness intensified in each word he screamed.

The others were wearing down, but Sotiris stepped in.

"Lean on him, fellas."

They jumped on Loizos again and after a nasty fight they were able to break his resistance. They held him tightly. He was panting, but silent. His mouth was swollen. He spat. Blood.

They tied his hands behind his back with a cord and hoisted him onto the truck. Then they got in and set out for the main village.

The bicycle was left lying where it was.

Loizos was silent. He knew that whatever he might say would be pointless. These men had already made up their minds.

They stopped the truck at the square, in front of the church. They took Loizos off and bound him to the trunk of the old eucalyptus tree, which stood like a sentry before the courtyard gate of the church. And immediately they began

95

hitting him on the chest, in the face, in the stomach, at random.

"Traitor . . . Rat . . . There! . . ."

One of them went and started ringing the church bell.

"Come on folks. Come and spit on the traitor."

Within a few moments a number of young men were in the square. Without asking anything they began hooting at Loizos and cursing him for his treachery and his disgrace, which was obvious.

Some went the rounds of the streets and proclaimed a mass gathering.

Pandemonium ensued. The relentless ringing of the bell, the shouts, the running about roused the village from end to end.

"Hurry . . . Hurry . . . They're punishing a traitor in the church square."

Everyone was astir. They came pouring out of the coffee shops, out of the houses, out of the stores—which hurriedly closed up—and made for the square: old men who had trouble keeping up; young men on the run; women who were weighted down and slow-moving, carrying children in their arms and dragging others at their skirts; girls who didn't dare go alone, calling to one another, gathering quickly in every narrow street, in every neighborhood, forming colorful clusters and coiling down the slope; children—a gang of children—barefoot and disheveled, abandoning their games and rushing to get in on this other game, one that was unknown and compelling.

Startled and uneasy, the crowd poured out from all sides. Some were completely exasperated in their gullible hearts at the disgraceful deed of the traitor. Some, calculating, lest they be left behind, were counted as indifferent. Others came trembling, torn between their faintheartedness and their merciless curiosity. Some were excited without even knowing why. There were even jokers shouting "Hoorah!" And fear, the maddening fear that paralyzes man and turns him into a wild beast, wandered like a black fog over all these varied, amassed, and unformed emotions.

The ancient land was shaken, and from the depths again emerged dark, hard times. On these stressed faces, the gaping, shouting mouths, the maddened eyes, the ancestors, who were on watch, buried in the depths of time, turned to vampires. And like vampires they were going to stone the excommunicate.

At first Loizos tried to resist, but no longer could. When he found himself tied to the tree trunk, he began to rave.

"Why traitor? . . . Lies! . . . Lies!"

But how could he be heard above the din of the crowd? There was also the pain from their blows and his own helpless, choking rage. Exhausted, he would rest awhile, then begin his shouts afresh, until someone crammed a rag in his mouth and tied a big colorful bandana over it. Now all he had left was his eyes to continue his hopeless protest. But when he saw some of them come out of the crowd and come up and spit at him, he lowered his head to his chest. Not a single sympathetic glance to be found in this entire hell! . . .

Only Trifonas, who had also come out to see what was going on and was standing among the crowd with frozen heart, could not bear it.

Suddenly, he shouted, "Enough, brothers, enough. You'll finish him off."

He approached the suffering man and only then did he recognize Loizos's face behind the gag. He leaned over and attempted to loosen his bonds. Those nearby stood back. The crowd roared. Loizos lifted his head and looked at Trifonas. In his tearing eyes there flashed a warm thank you.

But from the roar of the crowd an angry voice stood out.

"He's an accomplice . . ."

Trifonas turned and, in the first row of circles closing in on him he saw one, two, three hard faces marking him down.

"Stay out of this if you know what's good for you," someone said quickly and quietly.

He saw the danger and shuddered. He was alone against a blind, maddened mob. Their insanity has to calm down first, he thought. I had better go tell Dimitros and the others . . . or the police . . . but why aren't the police here? . . . I'll tell them . . . maybe they can get here in time . . .

He was confused. He turned his face elsewhere so as not to see Loizos's eyes, moved away, and hid in the crush

and was gradually able to get out of the square. He hurried
to get to them in time . . .

When Loizos saw Trifonas leave him, he closed his eyes
and put his head down. If he would only die! He could
take no more . . .

Someone cast the first stone but missed and hit the eucalyptus trunk. Then others threw who found the mark . . .

And suddenly their eyes, blinded by the panic fomented
by the rioting voices among them, saw what they did not see
a moment before—that they were beating and booing a rag,
hanging motionless and heavy from its bonds. A cold breath
of terror touched their hearts and their ferocity began to
abate. The women cried out in horror, then from many a
breast arose a low-toned "Oooo." And the square began to
empty.

The sun had set long ago, and the dusk, gradually thick-
ening, dripped fear into souls. Pensive and speechless, the
people moved away. Some asked who the bound traitor
might be, but no one was found to answer.

They did not want, no, they never meant it to end this
way.

The deserted square sunk slowly into shadow, and above
the shadow rose the crown of the eucalyptus, solitary, motionless, pensive.

Father Kyriakos watched Sotiris leave the courtyard and
slam the outer door angrily behind him. Then he sank
deeply into thought.

He had spent all last night in the courtyard, now sitting,
now pacing, as if trying to find something. Finally, towards
dawn, he went to bed.

He arose late the next morning, and as soon as he had
gone into the courtyard and washed, Sotiris came rushing
in.

"I have a couple of things to tell you, teacher," he said
abruptly, without greeting.

The old man gently interrupted him.

"Good morning, Sotiris. Sit down and have some coffee."

Sotiris realized that Father Kyriakos would not allow
him to go too far. He said good morning and sat down.

"Fix two cups of coffee, *papadia*," the old man called to his wife, who was in the kitchen fixing his breakfast.

Sotiris had to make an effort to restore the threatening look which he had practiced.

Finally, he said, looking sternly at the priest, "They're going to have his funeral in Alia and they say you've agreed to officiate."

"Why shouldn't I agree. That's my duty."

"Father Stephanos refused."

"Everyone has his own opinion, my child."

A deep silence followed.

The priest's wife brought out the coffee on a tray, which she placed on a chair. She looked uneasily at the two men and went back into the house.

"I'll say only this, Father, and take good note of it," said Sotiris angrily. "We don't want a display of that traitor's corpse under our noses in our own church. Let them bury him somewhere else, wherever the devil they want."

He was quiet for a short time. He watched the priest significantly. Then he added,

"Withdraw from this business if you want your peace."

The old man's face clouded, his eyes flashed, but he made the effort to control himself.

"I only know this, Sotiris," he said calmly. "I was asked to do the funeral service for the dead man, and I have a duty to do it. If I refuse, for the sake of my peace, as you say, then I shall have to take off this robe, which I have worn for forty years without shame. Everything else is in the hands of God."

Sotiris got up in a fury and left, slamming the courtyard door behind him.

And the old man fell into bitter thoughts.

All his long life he has stood upright in his quest for the goodness that each person has hidden within, seeking it out and always finding it with the patience granted by his faith. All else were details incapable of unsettling him. But now hard times have come and enmity and fear have throttled everything. For the first time he was inquiring within himself and not getting an answer.

Three days passed before Father Kyriakos rediscovered his old habits: to go out when the sun was about to set, to go to Trifonas's coffee shop, to take up his conversation again with the plain and with Mt. Pentadactylos.

Trifonas was glad. He had been eager to see the old man. Nevertheless, he did not approach him right away. He just brought him his coffee and then wandered about pre-tending to straighten up tables and chairs. Finally, he came over, sat down, and began talking in haste and agitation.

"I think about him all day, teacher . . . he comes at night in my sleep . . . I get no peace . . ."

Father Kyriakos listened to him in silence. He had learned of Trifonas's affliction. What could he tell him?

Trifonas raised his shoulders and spread his two hands in a posture of wretched helplessness. Then he struck his palms against his thighs.

"I keep seeing his eyes in front of me, just as he was looking at me when I went up to him . . . How his eyes flashed, as if they were embracing me! . . . But I lost heart . . . How embittered he must have been to watch me leave . . . Now those eyes hunt me down, full of hurt . . ."

He spoke non-stop, saying the same things over and over, and the hungry glow of his eyes sought help.

In spite of himself Father Kyriakos felt impatience with this weak soul, which had broken at a critical moment and now goes begging.

If he had stood his ground or if they had knocked him down or killed him, it would have been better than ending up like this. What does he expect from other people? . . . What can they give him? . . .

Father Kyriakos drifted away, looking into the distance.

The beloved favorite spot no longer spoke to him of the boundless power of the good. Nevertheless, the aroma of hearths, the purple sunset drawing its splendor over the mountain brought peace to his heart.

Trifonas rambled on and on, but Father Kyriakos was not listening to him.

THE TRAITOR

HE COULD NOT even find the focus of his anguish. His mind was floundering in a nightmare, and he sought tortuously to trace some coherence. Where did all this start? How long has he been wandering about in the fog of this unbelievable town?

Occasionally he seemed to calm down somewhat. The streets, the buildings, the parks of London would acquire substance. He would look about bewildered. Everything was so big—shapes, masses, and dimensions—that it seemed to him now that he and not the town was nonexistent.

He was walking about muttering to himself. And suddenly he found himself awash in a river of humanity that continually broadened and condensed and drew him along swiftly and ever more swiftly as it flowed across the broad pavement toward some unseen goal. From the shops, the exits of highrises, and the side streets, new crowds gushed forth, joining with the great river.

Mihailos fell into confusion. He tried to escape, but could not; he abandoned himself to the current and felt something like consolation, as if he had finally discovered what he had been seeking: to escape from the sense of self, dissolution into the masses.

From where he stood in his isolation, he saw the others living collectively and mechanically, and he formed in his mind a sense of the blessedness of the herd, wherein each individual moves in security, unmindful of the hows and whys. Oh, how he would like to join such an ideal herd! To put out this furnace, this inner raving that breaks out of him in his exile and tyrannizes his brains!

The swelling wave of humanity swept him away, and he, too, joined in the oblivion and relief. Sometimes one of the thousand faces would draw his attention. It would cease being identical to the others and become this blond, rosy-cheeked girl with the green scarf around her neck; or this slender gent with the gray mustache and black hat, just coming out of an exit with a clutch of newspapers under his arm and a closed umbrella in his hand . . . or that big kid with the tousled hair, a head taller than anyone else and the clumsy grace of a young animal in his every movement . . . or that fat lady, decisively pounding the pavement with her heels, tock, tock, tock, her cheek quivering with every step . . . or him over there with the recessed chin, walking along casting quick glances about him like a scared rabbit . . . or that funny little number who glitters and moves like a wind-up toy . . . or that one there . . . or the other beyond . . . each one with his own features, his own manner. But the next moment they all became one again, a gigantic, thousand-faced entity rolling along, emitting a vast hum composed of a thousand whispers, and whisking Mihailos tightly enwrapped toward a longed-for forgetfulness.

The human flood would bunch up and move on, bunch up and move on, till it came to a bridge. There it jammed onto the narrow walkway on the bridge until it issued forth on the other end, thinning out again fan-like and moving on a short distance to confront a flat, low building that was all gates gaping open. The mass would then step up its pace as though drawn by a magnet, would reach the gates and be swallowed up by them. Behind the building were the waiting trains and the tracks that shot gleaming to the horizon straight as an arrow.

Finally Mihailos stopped, drew back, and leaned against the damp wall of a house. He turned and looked back. The crowd was overflowing like ants from every direction, and rolled on towards the station and did not end, no, it would never end. Nevertheless, it was not long before the place was suddenly empty. A few late-comers hurried to escape the void pursuing them.

He felt like crying, out of envy, as the cranky boy he once was would do. In the excitement of his imagination he saw each one of these thousands of people comfortable in his own everydayness and sharing with others like him a common fate. Each of them will go now and find at the end of the daily trek the warmth of a loved one. How many moments of happiness, my God, find their nest in the single-minded crowd!

Nevertheless, he set out to go back.

When he reached the middle of the bridge, he stopped, leaned on the railing, and fastened his attention on the broad waters of the Thames. The subdued power of this liquid embrace magnetized him. He shuddered and drew back quickly. And continued on his way.

He remembered Mouzouris again, his countryman. From the day he arrived he planned on going to find him, but couldn't make up his mind. Something made him afraid of meeting his old friend, an expatriate.

Suddenly a reason hit him. If that block-headed captain had not been there to receive him with smiles and handshakes when he entered the barbed-wire enclosure, the rest would not have happened. Ah, the scoundrel! What devil impelled him to give it all away with his ceremonies right in front of the whole town? . . . He remembered the scene again now and cried out.

The villagers were entering one by one into the barbed-wire enclosure. The soldiers shoved them along to take their places in line. In charge of the garrison was that same red-headed captain with whom Mihailos had conversed the night before last at the police station. And the moment Mihailos entered, in his turn, the captain smiled at him and extended his hand as though they were at a reception. Mihailos did not think in time and he was caught like a fish. But the next moment he realized what he had done and froze. He saw the villagers look at one another and draw back from him. But the Englishman continued to smile. For surely he had planned it that way, the dog, to close off once and for all any other escape, exposing him to the villagers. From that moment he felt an abyss open all around him.

The more he thinks about it now, the more certain he is that, yes, that treacherous greeting by the Englishman was the ineradicable moment that sealed his fate. Up till then he had not even imagined that it was necessary to think much about where he was headed. Confident in his ability to make the right moves and slip away, he blindly followed his whims just as he followed out the obstinacy that took him over when Petrakis, his cousin, came to warn him.

Petrakis loved Mihailos and supported him by his rank in the sector.

They had grown up together. Their houses were separated by a courtyard, and in spite of the fact—or perhaps because of it—that the older they got the more different they became, they always remained inseparable and loved one another.

Petrakis was a quiet, blond-headed young man, unshakably faithful to himself and others. He loved his cousin and was more lenient with him than he was with himself.

Mihailos was a dark, strongly-built fellow with heavy, square hands and firm muscles in his palms. His only law was to do as he pleased, and this he carried out with irresistible gusto. He admired Petrakis. He worshipped him as we usually worship people who embody that which is inaccessible to us. Moreover, he always had something to gain from his cousin's friendship. Wasn't it Petrakis who suggested him for the post responsible to the village for bringing together and provisioning the ones who went off to the mountain? Although in this case he was not guided only by his fondness for Mihailos. They needed a man who was ingenious, daring, and tireless. Such was Mihailos and, in truth, he offered valuable services.

But in this whole enterprise Mihailos chiefly saw the adventure, which he lived with all his passion. With time, however, his untamable egocentrism began to create problems for him.

One night Petrakis came down to the village and sent for Mihailos to come find him at Perkentis's house, where he was hiding out. It had been a while since they had seen one another, because lately their contacts had got more and more difficult.

The lamp was turned down low and Mihailos had trouble recognizing Petrakis in the person of this pale Christ with the blond beard, who was seated opposite him and speaking tersely in a low voice.

"It's a serious matter, Mihailos. Understand that and leave off the foolery."

Mihailos was smoking quietly. The other continued.

"There are not just rumors. Responsible reports are being made. You're wasting money that may not be all yours. And that business with Maroula has become the village scandal. And she's not the first. Wise up, Mihailos."

Mihailos could hold back no longer. He brought his fist down on the table.

"They're lying about the money. I'm well enough off and I'll spend if I feel like it."

He said nothing about Maroula. He could not. He would not stoop to making excuses. That was his own business. Completely his own. Why should anyone else care?

"It's not the time for doing whatever we want, Mihailos," answered Petrakis. "A man with a wife and kid like you can't chase around the village with every girl who thinks you're a hero. Don't forget you're responsible to the organization."

A whistle was heard from outside, a musical phrase of four notes. Petrakis got up and strapped on his pistol.

"You stay put," he said.

He blew out the lamp. His voice now sounded in the darkness.

"Kosmas went wild when he heard about Maroula. We told him that it couldn't be true, but we could hardly hold him down. Shape up, Mihailos," he said again, and his voice softened. "I want what's best for you."

A squeak of the door was heard, then it was quiet. Then the outer door shut almost noiselessly. As if it had been waiting for precisely this moment, a cricket filled the silence with two melodic trills and fell silent.

Mihailos lit a cigarette and stayed right where he was, smoking. He was totally enraged. But he had to stay in the dark without stirring for some time before he, too, could leave. And nothing was more unbearable than times like this spent in silent solitude. Their quietude drove him crazy, especially when he was already on edge.

In a few minutes, which seemed endless to him, he got up. He couldn't take it anymore. He opened the door, but paused there. The orders were explicit: Do not leave one right after the other after such meetings. Should he stay here inside? No, he would explode.

"Devil with it," he muttered.

He shut the door behind him without a sound and left when he was certain that no one was in the street.

It was late and dark, and everything in the village was closed up.

Again he felt a great desire for Maroula. But they had made no arrangements for tonight, and she would be at home now. She must be asleep. To get her up now supposedly for some mission would be crazy. Her father, who was getting suspicious, would never swallow such a line.

He set out for home.

As always Katina was waiting for him. She was doing her mending. Her finely elliptical face with its gentle features and her carefully groomed brown hair gave off a soft radiance.

"Good evening, Mihailos," she said.

And he grew calm. He always did. It was completely different with his wife than with the other women. A longing to be with her never tyrannized him, nor did that madness to subjugate and annihilate with his passion any female within his grasp. No. With Katina he felt the beast in him tamed, without his ever considering how or why. Perhaps it was her way of being always centered, as one unapproachable yet devoted. Though she never asked him where he was going or what he was doing, Mihailos felt that he was expiated by that motherly glance of hers, which knew everything and fully understood.

Katina rose to set the table, and Mihailos went over to the bed where his son was sleeping. The curly-headed five-year-old had his fists clenched and wore an expression of determined resistance.

Levendi mou, said Mihailos to himself and smiled.

They had supper and went to bed.

And when later he leaned his head over and devotedly kissed her soft breast, Katina was gazing at the darkness with wide open, ecstatic eyes.

Nevertheless, the days began again to roll, and Mihailos began again to live his turbulent and carefree life.

The long nights of August had come when Petrakis summoned him again one evening to come see him out at Saint Marina's fig tree, which stood alone in the field next to the solitary little church.

This time Petrakis was clipped and edgy.

"I warned you, Mihailos, but you paid no attention. Listen to me now at least and come to your senses. . . . The boys are demanding that matters be cleared up. Tomorrow night I and three others are coming expressly to reach an understanding with you. Be at Perkentis's at eleven."

Mihailos did not answer.

"Bear in mind, cousin," continued Petrakis. "You're on the defense. Go along with this. And above all, no bullying tomorrow."

" . . ."

"The boys are exasperated. You know what hardships we're going through."

"So, have I been lazing around?"

"No. You've been helping. But your behavior in the village is a scandal. It's damaging. They're right about that. They've about had it. Even Kosmas is getting stoked up about it . . . and he's right."

"Will he be with you tomorrow?"

"Perhaps."

"Ah . . ." said Mihailos so softly that Petrakis perhaps did not hear.

"They carry guns and stake their lives every minute. Understand that and don't stir them up, since you are in the wrong. Do you want to get killed?"

"What do you mean? . . ."

Petrakis got up.

"I came to tell you these things for your own good and in the interests of the struggle. I've done my job. . . . Think carefully, Mihailos. This isn't the time for games. . . . Now I have to go. See you."

The night swallowed him up.

So that's the way it is, then? The gang has got up a court to pass judgment on us? Mihailos said to himself. That is, sit still like a good little student so we can scold you and you can say, 'I was wrong,' and not do it again. Otherwise, we're carrying guns and we'll clean up on you.

He got up and left.

What do you say, kid? . . . Why didn't you dare come up to me one by one—you especially, Kosmas—to settle this like men? . . . Sure, you bring up the organization, and whatever the organization does is well done. You're just a gang of hoods, that's what you are. But I am Mihailos. Mihailos! he shouted into the night.

He paused, startled by his own voice. He looked around the way a hunted animal looks. The deep summer sky smiled broadly with its countless shining spots. The breeze came laden with the aromas of summer. The plain was spreading out in every direction, undulant and blessed. But the balsam of the azure night could not touch Mihailos's soul tonight. His wounded pride was dripping blood, burning-hot blood, which dyed everything around it the scarlet hue of rage.

He attempted to collect the scattered shards of his common sense, to think, but the fires raged again and blinded him.

Now he was walking with great strides, stumbling now and then in the darkness, talking to himself; and the more he listened to himself, the more he took fire.

Can you believe that? . . . Me! . . . Me, Mihailos, who no one till now has dared to question . . . Me, who did not count the costs, who defied danger . . . What would have happened to you, in your hiding-places, if I weren't down here looking out for you and protecting you? . . . Don't you think the English understood that? They've tried hard to win me over. They'd have loaded me down with gold if I'd wanted it . . .

The small enchanting voice—which at other times, too, had whispered in his ear the song of the siren, but he had rejected it—now returned more insistently. Mihailos was shaken. He chased it away. But it kept coming back as if it were sure of him.

Now he was walking, stoop-shouldered, teeth clenched. Out of the fire exploding within him a black, shining serpent was born. It stood upright on its tail and swayed back and forth alluringly, hypnotizing Mihailos with the green glow of its eyes.

His heart shuddered, making a final desperate resistance. The rending within him became so horrible that Mihailos began to tremble from head to foot. He stood as if nailed to the ground, every sinew of his body stretched to the breaking point. From his chest emerged a moan that did not resemble a human voice.

But to give in and have Kosmas come around later and jeer that Mihailos had turned into a little lamb! . . . No! Never! . . .

Within the next moment he had come to a decision.

He looked around him, stepped off the path, and began a stealthy passage across the plain, so as not to run across anyone. (During this season the villagers happened to be working on the plain.) A glow on the horizon revealed where the next town was, to which he directed his steps.

In two hours he was there. Walking along the wall through the darkest side streets, he went to the police station, looked about and around, and slipped in.

The stars had begun to fade, and only the Dawn Star was shining when the courtyard door of the police station shut with a click and he was on his way. Then [a car] came to within a short distance of the village. It stopped and its lights went out. A soldier got out, looked around with weapon raised, and got back in. Then Mihailos came down, curled up in the ditch along the road, waited until the car left, and set out across the plain for the village.

The first roosters were crowing. Mihailos took precautions on his way but felt nothing but a dullness in his brain and exhaustion. He just wanted to get home undetected, go to bed, and sleep. Nothing else.

As soon as he entered the house, Katina, who had been asleep, got up and set about fixing him something to eat. She asked no questions. Was this the first time he had come home at dawn since he had taken on his responsibilities? She never asked questions nor bothered him with her worries and advice. Only her eyes, when she looked at him, betrayed how anxious she was.

This time you will never guess where I've been, my lady, Mihailos joked to himself.

She fried eggs for him, he ate, drank two glasses of *raki*, went to bed and straight to sleep.

It was past noon when he awoke. And until dusk he spent his time at the coffee shop joking and quarreling, trying to cover with racket some annoying questions that he felt surfacing from deep down. Later he went to the Club, where he was sure he could find Maroula. But when he saw her he did not talk to her much, nor did he miss her at all; he only thought with satisfaction how eager she would be to follow him. He would shortly have all the means he needed to take her and go abroad—if he took a notion to. But that thought did not stir him. And in the end he decided that, no, that was stupid. Women should not be mixed up with this matter.

He was at Perkentis's before the others.

Perkentis, who had been notified, left the ground floor open. He and his wife, supposedly because of the heat, retired to the roof to keep watch.

Petrakis soon arrived; he said hello and sat down.

Some moments passed before Ornitharis, and Kosmas right afterwards, emerged from the shadows into the circle dimly lit by the lowered lamp. Mihailos saw a smile on Kosmas's face, a repulsive one, he thought. Petrakis and Kosmas were wearing revolvers. Ornitharis had a sten gun propped against the wall behind him.

But they had scarcely sat down when hasty steps were heard on the road. Someone came into the courtyard and went up the wooden stairs to the upper floor.

Petrakis blew out the lamp. They waited. Ornitharis reached back for his gun. They soon heard the footsteps descending the stairs again. The visitor was gone. A gentle knock came at the door, silence, two more in succession; the door squeaked and Perkentis's voice was heard in the darkness.

"They're blockading the village."

"Isn't Stivaros here yet?" asked Petrakis.

"Just got here," answered a voice at the door.

"Did you hear what Perkentis said?"

"Yes."

110

"We'll divide into pairs. Kosmas and Stivaros go down towards Saint Marina's. Ornitharis and I toward Lagoudera. We've got to escape from the ring. You, Mihailos, stay here for a bit."

Petrakis led the way, opened the door, and went out into the courtyard. He was battling a suspicion that had wrapped around him like a cold snake. The other three followed him.

Perkentis was standing in the half-open courtyard door keeping watch. Petrakis drew him aside and hastily whispered something to him.

All four left in single file, moving from wall to wall, till they left the last houses in the village behind. Now and then they could hear someone running in the dark, or shutting a window, or barring a door. . . . From the field they could hear dogs barking.

"Listen," said Petrakis to his companions. "As we said, we'll try to escape. But if we see that that's impossible, retreat to the oil press. Maybe just two of us can get away. At any rate, those who get to the oil press first should wait for the others as long as possible before entering the hide-out. I told Perkentis to wait at the oil press to seal the entrance behind us. Now let's split up."

Mihailos returned home uneasy. He listened for rifle fire. Will they get through? he wondered.

It was almost dawn and nothing could be heard but dogs barking.

All at once the harsh screech of a megaphone split the silence.

"Attention. Attention . . . All residents are to remain indoors until further orders."

In a little while.

"Attention. Attention . . ." the screech was heard again from the next street.

The child was asleep. Katina was making coffee. Mihailos was looking through the shutters at the street and saw a company of English soldiers in two ranks, one on each side of the road, moving cautiously, weapons at the ready, and fingers on the triggers. He gritted his teeth. Did they get away? he wondered. And he did not know whether he wanted them to have gotten away or not.

Dawn broke; the sun rose high in the sky, and the search continued from house to house.

In the nightmarish immobility of the closed houses and empty streets one could hear now and then the tramp of the patrols and the plaintive bleat of sheep left in a state of confusion locked in their folds. The dogs were still, huddled in corners watching in disbelief this inexplicable situation. But the moment the search party came into Mihailos's courtyard, Arapis could be heard barking madly; a gunshot followed and the howl of the stricken dog.

"Arapis!" shouted Mihailos and rushed to open the door.

But he was pinned to the threshold by a gunbarrel pointed at him and a human bark. Someone gave him a shove and the soldiers came in. He was about to grab a chair but Katina's scream checked him. He leaned against the wall. There was a cloud before his eyes and within the cloud scenes unfolded that drove him mad.

The sergeant in charge stood at the door, a cocked automatic in his hand, and the soldiers set to searching everywhere. One of them went to the armoir, pushed Katina, who was standing in front of it, aside with the butt of his gun, opened it, and scattered on the floor whatever came to hand. Katina braced herself on the bedpost and watched with pinched lips, eyes wide open, pale as a ghost. She clutched tightly with both arms the terrified child wrapped in her apron. And Mihailos saw the boy's gaze riveted upon him as if to ask "how can you let them do this, father! . . ." He was ashamed and lowered his head. And at that very moment by a grotesque coincidence, he remembered a song he liked to sing when the mood struck him:

I took the earth to turn it on its head.

He was sure back then that, if he just grasped the earth with the gigantic hands his enthusiasm provided him with, he would indeed turn it upside down. And now look: Mihailos was just a snot-nose kid . . .

112

When they finally left and their steps were heard fading away, Mihailos turned to the wall and began battering it furiously with his fists till his hands were bloody.

Katina drew water and washed her face, as if she wanted to clean off the filth left on her by their gaze. She did not speak, only bound up her hair and began tidying up. And in a short time her spirit put the haze to flight and the place became good again. Mihailos cooled down somewhat.

The child withdrew angrily to a corner, tore a strip of wood from somewhere, took a knife, and set to carving a sword. He chopped away at it, now and then hefting the sword handle and stabbing pitilessly at the enemy.

Suddenly they heard the metallic voice screeching again.

"Attention! Attention! . . ."

And giving an order:

". . . All male residents twelve and above, assemble at the area fenced off next to the school."

The courtyard doors began one by one to inch open, and men and boys began to emerge and move wondering towards the school. There they saw their playground fenced off with barbed wire and two large tents set up inside. And everywhere were soldiers with sten guns.

Mihailos was one of the last to arrive. He saw the others enter that sinister pen one by one, the English prodding them through with their rifle butts until they put them in line with the others, young and old, faces turned to the wire, looking into the sun, which burned their eyes, their hands held high, and armed men at their backs watching their every move and barking at whoever would venture to lower his upstretched hands.

Then something happened that ruined his calculations. He would have made it. Surely he would have made it. But this he had not foreseen: that that rat would give everything away with his officious greetings . . . He had his reason, that was as clear as day. Now? What will Mihailos do? . . . He went in by himself and stood in line with his hands up. But soon one of the soldiers came and fetched him away for interrogation.

And here he was again, old pimply-face, here in the tent sitting behind a table looking at Mihailos with his dull fish eyes. A strange smile shone pallidly on his face, perhaps one of cunning, perhaps of irony, perhaps even an invitation to licentiousness. So it looked to Mihailos, both here and at the police station the other night. For a moment he had a wild notion to show this fellow up for what he was, and then wring his neck, just to get it out of his system.

But the other brought him back to reality. Coldly, without haste, he unraveled persuasive arguments. He was speaking Greek.

"This is to your advantage . . ."

Mihailos was silent. I see, he thought. I see, you cursed scoundrel, that it's to my advantage . . .

Exhausted, he told about the hiding place at the oil press. If they couldn't escape, they were to hole up there. Where else?

And now it was all getting bitterly tiresome. The Englishman saw that.

"Sit down," he said.

Later they took him to the other tent, where there were two others being held for further interrogation. So they're holding others, too, he thought. Why should the village be suspicious of just me . . . But this thought did not seem to him to carry much weight . . . He lay down on the ground. Oh, brother! Let happen what will.

Towards noon they put the three of them into a closed vehicle and took them into town.

They did not exchange many words, and those few came forth like vapor out of a cesspool of suspicion. Mihailos took out his pack and offered cigarettes. The others accepted, but one of them, in bored tones, said:

"Didn't they take your cigarettes away from you?"

Mihailos was upset by that. You've cast aspersions, he thought, but you took your cigarette . . . Later he got angry with himself for not answering.

They put them off at the police station and separated them, putting Mihailos into a cell by himself. Better this way, he said to himself.

So he was not at home that night to see Katina wakeful next to the sleeping child, her face an expression of frenzy. Nor was he there the following morning, when the battle at

114

the oil press took place, to hear the volleys of shots and to see Katina, shut in at home pacing incessantly back and forth from one wall to the other, wringing her hands hopelessly, blocking her ears whenever she heard bursts of gun fire. Sometimes she would lean her head against the wall and break into silent sobs . . . The news had already circulated to the closed-up houses courtyard to courtyard about the reception given Mihailos by the Englishman. It had reached Katina, too.

The battle started in the morning.

Within the hideout were four young men determined to fire even their last shot with no thought about what would happen later. Later? Light and vindication will follow. But right here at this supreme moment there are just four proud souls who defy death. And all around, a ring of death's implements and of death's agents encircles them, a heavy ring, which tightens methodically and cautiously, and now and then screams a threat—Surrender! . . .—an idiotic threat which the wind carries away.

And beyond the circle of death, all about, as silent witnesses, are the village houses. And behind shut windows stand the villagers, respectfully containing their emotions and listening and holding their peace.

And beyond the village, the plain that nourished the four young men spreads quietly and sympathetically.

The ring kept closing in, machine guns stitching the low walls of the oil press, which had become a fortress.

The besieged respond with sporadic rifle fire, carefully, on target. Although the besiegers saw that their prey would definitely not escape them, they began finally to fret at the heavy price they would pay. For four hours now the land they held in slavery was drinking their blood! Such had not been their prediction. How many were they? How many were still alive behind that hole-ridden jug to hold out against their barrage of fire? Two? Three? One? . . . The situation had become unbearable. Let's put an end to it. Surely in the ledgers of our experience we have very effective techniques for dealing with wrong-headed people who think that the human spirit can prevail against armed force . . . They sat down, riffled through their experiences, found

115

their solution, and rubbed their hands together in satisfaction. Very simple. The human spirit? Nonsense.

Soon the oil press, washed down with gasoline, was burning like a torch.

A blond young man with a weapon came bounding through the flames. For a moment, a very brief moment indeed, he took stock, looking for a place to take refuge. But the automatics lying in wait did not give him time. Struck from every direction, the blond young man, Petrakis, fell on his face.

All at once there was silence.

Only the crackling fire could be heard.

Locked up at the police station "for his own protection," Mihailos fought to keep himself from panic, which pursued him with cackling laughter. He found no other refuge than to sit and reckon how he would arrange his life abroad, where they had agreed to send him. He would have the means, and life would pass pleasantly. Especially if Katina came with him . . . And why should she not come? She would have all the comforts, and what else can a woman look for besides comforts and her husband? . . . So he sat and worked over every minute detail, setting up a sensible edifice. But he could not quite get it set up before a wind would arise and send it scattering. And he would begin walking again back and forth within the four walls like a beast in a cage, walking back and forth in search of he knew not what.

He had sent word to Katina to come where he wanted to meet her. He was waiting. How he was waiting! He thought that her presence would bring order into the chaos. He just needed to hear her speak in that calm way of hers that simplified everything. He had not even given thought to the other woman all these days. He had no need of her. Katina would surely save him. . . . But he would have to approach the matter convincingly, design a story that would hold up from beginning to end. He thought about it, took it this way, then turned it around differently, but he was not satisfied.

He was sitting and pondering these matters when they came to tell him that Katina was there waiting for him.

116

He found her sitting in the office, affable and patient.

His heart was racing. He grew angry with himself. That's all you need, Mihailos, to fall into confusion now like a little girl, he said to himself, and he tried to speak like someone confident, seeking explanations.

"Why didn't you bring the boy with you?"

"I decided I shouldn't . . . around here . . . Anyway, we have to talk about matters that . . ."

So it's your voice that's wavering now, thought Mihailos with satisfaction.

But Katina kept looking at him and waiting.

And here he was with no decision about how to present these things to her.

". . . They've tortured me, Katina."

He saw a pained expression on her face.

Should he keep silent . . . think first . . . but how could he stand this silence between them? . . .

"Come with me, Katina . . . Let's take the child and go abroad . . . It's beautiful; life is easy there. You'll have everything you want . . ."

Katina grew pale. For a moment he thought her eyes flashed anger. But her quiet grievance reasserted itself and silenced him. Finally, with some effort, Katina rose. Her lips were trembling.

"No, Mihailos . . . No!"

She hid her face in her hands and ran toward the door.

Mihailos saw her back shudder with her sobs and he lost control.

He went out of his mind. He rushed after her to call her, to plead with her, but instead of that he slammed the door with all his might, grabbed the chair in front of him, and hurled it at the iron-barred window. The glass shattered with a loud crash.

A demon howled within him.

At the London dock a well-dressed gentleman received him, put him in a taxi, and took him to a small, quiet hotel. He gave him a telephone number to call should he have need of anything, and left him there to rest up, as he said. To rest up! . . . What a strange notion!

At first he was distracted by the unbelievable atmosphere of the hotel, where everything was relaxed and very dignified.

Not having anything else to do, he threw himself at the chamber maid, a fresh lass who seemed made of cream. She received his caresses with a smiling passivity that bored him.

Where the devil has life hidden around here? he would ask himself. It must have gone to sleep somewhere and they've all decided to go about whispering for fear of waking it up. How do they keep from cracking up! Mihailos would certainly crack up if he stayed any longer immobilized in this box, turning over in his mind memories of the sun, his countrymen, and Katina. Only she would be able to gather up the scattered remains of himself and give them some kind of shape again. But Katina was no longer anything but a heart-rending memory.

The next evening the same well-dressed gentleman came by to ask whether he felt like going out. They did. Mihailos started drinking and found some relief in non-stop chatter, even if it was with this impeccable man who only listened and refilled his glass, nodded encouragingly and made an occasional mark in a little notebook.

When he returned to his room, he fell into bed without undressing. Morning found him now sunk in a torpor, now with wide-open eyes, feeling like an empty shell.

Nevertheless, when the Englishman returned the next evening, Mihailos went out with him again. How else would he spend these endless hours?

As last night, he looked about in confusion, incapable of putting order to the floods of movement, luxury, lights that tumbled down from everywhere and repelled the sky till there remained up there only a thick, completely hostile shadow. The only clear impression that Mihailos retained was the striking contrast between the motionless, dimly-lighted street where his hotel was located—and where old-fashioned houses and a few ghostly trees stood dignified and sleepy behind the fences—and the whirlwind surrounding one as soon as he stepped out onto this four-laned main street.

On the sidewalk a great crowd was gathered waiting for who knows what. His escort stood near them, as did Mihailos, who marveled at the cars and the red double-decker buses that passed by endlessly in many rows, some going up one way and others coming down the other end, until someone apparently gave a signal, and the cars stopped all at once and left a passage for the mass of waiting humanity, which rushed hastily across. The Englishman and Mihailos followed the herd. They walked a bit farther along the opposite sidewalk next to the bright store windows, until they turned off onto the side street and entered the same, long, narrow, low-ceilinged bar that they had been in last night. It resembled a railroad car the way it was divided into two parallel rows of small booths. They went and sat at the back in the same place they were last night . . .

§

No. He could no longer stand their isolation. So he decided to go find Mouzouris, to talk to one of his own people.

He had not seen Mouzouris since the latter had taken a trip back to the village to show off his money, his gold chain, and his goodheartedness. When young, they had been schoolmates in the village. Later Mouzouris went abroad and settled in London, where he had his own successful business, a restaurant in Camden Town. In the summer of '53 he had come to the village, where he stayed for two months, having a good time with his old friends. (There was also a rumor that he would get married in the village, but it seems he could not in the end make up his mind to it.) Mihailos had had his address since then.

As soon as he crossed the bridge he flagged down a taxi and handed the address to the driver.

Mouzouris's little restaurant did not resemble that luxury railcar where you felt like a prisoner in the walnut dividers and coffee-colored wall-hangings. There were a few tables with white oil-cloths. Mihailos was reminded of his homeland, though he couldn't have told you exactly why. At that hour it was empty of customers. Mihailos saw Mouzouris chatting with two others around a table in the back. He would rather have found him alone.

119

Nevertheless, he approached the group confidently, tried to appear nonchalant, and said hello.

Mouzouris looked up, measuring him from head to foot.

"Hello," he answered without haste. He did not invite him to sit down.

Mihailos noticed that one of the other two was also from his village, but he gave no sign of recognition. Could it be that this other man didn't recognize him? Then why did he jump up, say, "Let's go, Kostis," to the third man, and leave?

Kostis followed him out.

Mihailos smoldered with anger, but set his jaw and controlled himself. He sat down without being invited.

"Don't you recognize me, Mouzouris?"

"Of course . . . but I can't say I'm proud to have known you," said Mouzouris.

Then he lit a cigarette and took a long deep draw.

Oh, this was too much. Mihailos could not stand it, nor could he make up his mind to get up and leave. He slammed his hand on the table.

"Is that the way you greet your old friends? Or did you think that I came here to ask you for help?"

"I think you've gone beyond that," Mouzouris answered abruptly. "Old friend! . . . Petrakis too was an old friend. Don't you think we hear what goes on back home?"

"What did you hear?"

Mouzouris did not answer. He simply raised his hand and stirred up the air. He lit another cigarette and said:

"Tell me, who brought you to London at such a time."

" . . ."

"I've just one word for you, Mihailos. Don't come back to my restaurant. Many of our people gather here and I don't know what might happen. And I don't want any trouble in my place. You saw them just now . . ."

He got up and continued.

"It's getting close to busy time and I've got to go to the kitchen. God go with you."

Mihailos saw the walls spin around him. What was he to do? Grab whatever was at hand and smash the place apart? He stood there hesitating, lost in strange surroundings. He steadied himself on the table and got up. Heading for the exit, he turned back and shouted:

"You'll pay for this, Mouzouris. All of you will pay for this."

He was shaking from head to foot.

Once in the street he walked, not knowing where he was going. He walked quickly, teeth clenched, as if he had to get somewhere immediately. In this state he wandered for hours with no sense of time, seeing around him nothing but a grotesquely huge, chaotic, and hostile inferno.

Finally he was exhausted; his fit of anger cooled until it broke down completely. His knees grew weak. He stopped, looked around him, and felt totally alone and wretched. Where was he? . . . He hailed a taxi and gave the driver the address of his hotel.

At the hotel he found two letters waiting for him, and when he saw the stamps, his heart leapt. They were from the island. The first that he had gotten from there. Have his parents and Katina finally answered the letters he had sent them?

He locked himself in his room and opened them. The first was from his mother. Without reading it he opened the second with trembling fingers. No. It wasn't from Katina. He was disappointed but also surprised when he saw the signature: "Your friend, Perkentis . . ." What does this mean?

He read the letters hastily, first Perkentis's then his mother's. Then he read them again more carefully.

His mother informed him that everybody was well and that "Katina and the child are staying with us and Katina sends you lots of greetings and will write you herself and you have greetings from your father. And Perkentis asked me for your address so he could write to you."

Poor old woman, he thought. She's trying to console me with fairy tales. Greetings from Katina, greetings from the old man, but she went and got someone else to write the letter for her, for this is not Katina's hand nor the old man's.

Perkentis wrote him amiably, making some vague re-marks and finally inviting him to the village. ". . . We're human and we make mistakes. We want you with us again; just come and don't be afraid . . . ," and other such things.

121

To him it seemed that a miracle had taken place. This letter was so unexpected and liberating. He kept looking at it and felt like crying out for joy.

But when his initial amazement had passed and he began to collect his thoughts, he fell into reflection. Something is hidden here. It can't be. Something must be hidden behind this unbelievably favorable solution . . . The cunning animal in him sniffed uneasily and struggled to see clearly, to set aside the exultation that his heated soul absorbed. He was distressed. His breathing was ragged. Suspicion would not allow him to believe in the marvel.

There was a knock at the door. It was the chambermaid, to tell him that "that gentleman" had come and was waiting in the salon.

"Tell him I'm sick."

"Thank you," said the girl, and shut the door.

To hell with that "thank you," he thought, they keep pounding it in all the time. It's as if they are telling you they don't give a damn whether you exist or not. He felt like slapping one of them to see whether he would say "thank you" again.

And again his hopes and fears started whirling through his mind in confusion.

For two days and two nights he wrestled with the imponderable difficulty. It was unprecedented and torturous that this man of spontaneous reactions should sit motionless, nerves strained to the breaking point, pondering and not discovering an explicit impulse to follow up on. How has this happened? It's as if he had been split into two incompatible parts, one side believing that Perkentis's letter was lighting his way back to his lost joys, and the other finding that, no, it's a trap and beware, Mihailos, lest you play the chump. They're uneasy because you're over here alive and you know so much . . . He shouldn't make anything of Perkentis's remarks. What he must do is stay put . . . Stay put? Impossible. He will go mad. He will go howling down the streets. He should realize that, because of a single suspicion (which could, after all, be mistaken), he is sitting here by himself longing for the light. How long will he last? And, after all, why should he last? Is this hell a life, to be in a world where there are no people you can call your own?

A whirlwind spun in his brain. He hadn't slept, had hardly eaten for two days and nights. Sometimes he would walk the noisy streets in a daze; sometimes he would stay in his room stretched out on the bed staring at the ceiling.

One time the chambermaid discreetly knocked on the door. She opened it part way and stuck her little doll's head in to tell him . . . To tell him what? . . . To hell with her. He grabbed a shoe from the floor and hurled it at her. She barely got the door shut in time.

Finally he had had enough. He would leave. Go back home. Walk the beloved soil again . . . Not that he had reached a conclusion and believed Perkentis. He just wanted—Oh, how much he wanted—for it to be true. He would come alive again. Otherwise? . . . What will happen will happen.

He was overrun with haste, in a fever to set out as quickly as possible.

He was waiting impatiently for his Englishman. When he came Mihailos showed him the letter, saying that it was an opportunity to go . . . and to find out . . . (let me fool him this time and we'll see, he thought). The Englishman took the letter, put it in his briefcase, and said he would bring him an answer tomorrow.

The next day he returned and said, "I presume that you have considered all eventualities. But since you've made up your mind to go, it's your business."

He lifted his hands and shrugged his shoulders to indicate that he had no say in the matter.

He continued, "If everything goes well and you're reunited with your friends, you know, of course, that every piece of information has its value . . . Hm . . . Hm . . . As for the money you are entitled to, it is always at your disposal . . . here." And he pointed to the ground.

And if things do not go well, you've gotten rid of me cheaply, Mihailos reckoned. He felt again like an insect caught in a spider's web. But he was not concerned about that now. He just wanted to leave. To go to his homeland. Then he would see.

The Mihailos that set out on his journey home was a strange creature, born from the red-hot mass left over from the old Mihailos. He carried his old self within, restrained and speechless, but this new self was looking about as if seeing for the first time the world outside it. And he was searching for his homeland, as a deliverance, and the fulfillment of his contrition.

For as long as the journey lasted, days and nights, he would shift from agony to calm, from plans of action to indifference, but down deep he longed for but one thing—forgiveness.

From the train window he saw spreading before him the rich fields of a foreign land, its lakes, its snow-clad mountains. He looked at them in wonder, as if he had not seen them when passing through these same places before. He took them in with a quiet passiveness, but they were not, certainly not, the simple and bright plains of his homeland.

For a moment he thought, it was better that they kept the money in London. When the time comes it will be mine again. But if I don't live through this, it's better that the money not turn up. It's not proper to bequeath such money to his child. The thought took shape in his mind peacefully, as if it were intended for someone other than himself.

But for the most part he was not thinking at all, but simply coming to terms with life and mankind through an emotional revelation.

It was night-time in Venice. He wandered for hours on the shores of the canals and in the narrow inner streets, watching the movement of the crowd, looking at the gorgeous palaces, the tile-colored dollhouses, and the couples who walked along hugging and kissing. And he found that perhaps life could be good.

Later his sea journey began. This sea, however, was profound and heavy, not like the aery light sea of his homeland, which sparkled good-naturedly in the sunlight. Mihailos was bored.

At Peiraeus he did not get off the ship. Leaning on the gunwale he watched the movement of the harbor, but his mind was elsewhere. He would lift up his eyes and insatiably take in the gentle landscape, the light, the bluest of waters, and it was all the same, all exactly the same as those he was so impatient to see again.

Far out at sea, he thought no more of anything. Just waited.

And one early morning the island appeared dimly on the horizon. His eyes became misty. And from that moment until the end Mihailos was a man handed over to fate. He was receiving with affirmation some vague message of forgiveness, like one volunteering to die.

He got on the tender along with his few fellow passengers, went with them through all the waiting and customs, patient and indifferent, as if all this was meaningless detail, unrelated to the sense of a deeper, inaccessible reality that shook him without feeling at all the need to explain it.

He got on the mainline bus that would take him as far as the village crossroads. And during the entire trip he had his gaze fixed beyond, turning into a sensitive antenna to discover new vibrations in familiar places.

The bus stopped briefly in the middle of the road in front of the station. But Mihailos did not get off for food and drink as he used to, once. He merely gazed at the oranges and longed to taste them.

And the bus set out again. From where he was sitting his glance fell upon the small round mirror outside the driver's window. In this crystal screen he saw the reflection of a sweet, shawl-wrapped face of the young woman seated in the last row. The shape and long-suffering expression of her face reminded him one moment of Katina, and another of the compassionate Virgin Mary. He stared as if magnetized at this comforting vision, which took on a magical texture surrounded as it was by the constantly changing view of the landscape.

It was noon when they reached the crossroads. Right on time. Strouthos's vehicle, which made the connection between the crossroads and the village, was there waiting. But as soon as Strouthos saw Mihailos get off the bus, he set off hastily with his two passengers without giving him a chance to fetch his suitcase.

Mihailos understood. It was as if he stumbled against something hard and woke up. He sat down at the edge of the road and reflected. Now what? . . .

But his indecision did not last long. He had to expect things like that. He decided to walk to the village. He would be there in an hour. His suitcase was not heavy; he hefted it onto his shoulder and set out, but much saddened.

A little before he arrived at the entrance to the village, he saw three men heading in his direction. They came up to him and stopped. One of them was Perkentis; the other two strangers. Uneasy, Mihailos set his suitcase down.

"Hello," he said.

"Hi," answered Perkentis. "Give me your suitcase to take home while you go with these two. They need to talk with you." He pointed at the two strangers.

Mihailos wanted to say that he needed to see Katina first, and the child. What do they have to tell me right now before I go to my house? . . . But he realized that that was pointless—that whatever was going to happen would happen in any case. A numbness had paralyzed his once quick reflexes. He handed his suitcase over to Perkentis and followed the others, who took the path up to Saint Marina's.

They walked along in silence, the two strangers with Mihailos between them. Suddenly his old self awakened and he began looking for a way to escape them. They've trapped me, clear as day, he thought; they've planned it all out in advance. How can I slip away from them now? . . . Too difficult to fight them—there are two of them . . . Cut out running across the open field? Dangerous. They might be armed . . . There must be some way of tricking them, but how? . . . For some time his mind searched feverishly, until all at once again the chord of his old will stretched tight and broke. Again a longing for the end spread out and covered him.

He forgot his companions and everything else. With his gaze he measured the kind plain, the village down below behind a fold in the earth, the small, charming dome of Saint Marina's. He breathed in their presence to the depths of his soul. And within this strange prayer a small voice of complaint called on Katina and the child, just to look at them, to see that the fear and harshness in her eye the last

126

time he saw her were not there, to see that her gaze fell upon him softly, like a pardon.

And there it was. The fig tree spread its deep shadows affectionately with open arms. With his glance Mihailos caressed its rough foliage. He breathed in like a dew of love its sharp aroma. But the next moment he remembered his companions . . . The one, there he was, standing opposite a few steps away, a revolver in his hand, looking at him strangely. The other was not there, but he appeared shortly from the direction of Saint Marina's, carrying a sten gun. He came up and stood next to his partner.

"We have orders to execute you," he said.

Mihailos paled, but did not answer. He knew it could not be otherwise. With his eyes he worshipped the beautiful little church there below, and its little cypress tree, which waved slowly, pointing at the sky.

The next moments were so intense that they passed beyond the boundaries of time and the boundaries of the intelligible world. He who was about to die became a bow stretched ever more by teeming emotions between two opposite passions—fear and the longing for the end.

And all at once a fountain of forgiving fire blazed forth and struck him in the chest. He fell face downward exactly as Petrakis had fallen. His spread palms grabbed at Mother Earth, and his fingers in a final spasm dug into her soil.

TIMES OF DIFFICULTY

AND SO, in undefined fashion, with no consideration on his part of the appropriateness or the timeliness of it, his strict injunction to live in solitude, binding on him for four years now, gradually began to lose its edge. His former self, the peaceful, good-hearted fellow, was emerging in the imperceptible but sure way that the young moon emerges in its season, and it embued his life with its former colors. Without his consent or his resistance the freshness of his soul was struggling alone for regeneration from the ashes, now that the conflagration surrounding him was abating.

Makis had spent about four years tightly bound by the determination that forcefully put aside his every need to return to the sources of his joy.

Later came the "Long live!" . . . "Long live" victory!— What victory?—"Long live" this . . . "Long live" that . . . "Long live" everything . . . A celebration that left him pensive and out of sorts.

Nevertheless he leaned once again on Loukas's confidence.

Loukas was one of those people who are never rattled, because they are above all sure of themselves, people who, proceeding from this innate and basic given, believe that the truth exists definitely—and exclusively—there where their own activity lies.

This confidence of Loukas, his driving egotism, fascinated Makis, who had realized how much his own thoughtful disposition, the tormenting disinterestedness of his thinking, corroded and paralyzed his will.

Loukas shined his boots and the buttons on his military tunic and marched in the parade triumphantly, head held high.

Makis, who was behind him in line, smiled. Loukas believes in victory, he thought, because victory gives him greater dimensions in his own eyes. But he was immediately ashamed of that notion and forced himself to rediscover his old devotion to his friend, who had been his guide through all his difficult moments. He is able to defend himself, to strike out, to make decisions. These are the things that we need nowadays. Everything else is smoke and fantasy, he thought, now steadily digging his heels, too, into the pavement.

Nevertheless, the confusion in his mind did not let up. It was as if a swell in midsea found him, tossed him about, tormented him, with no consequences except exhaustion, an insuperable penchant to lie down on the ground and sleep. Nothing more.

After the celebrations in the City, they returned to the village, where each in his own way, according to his own understanding, set about living out in practice what all were agreed to call the continuation of the struggle by peaceful means.

Loukas found himself in charge again, channeling energies, proposing resolutions, fanning the flames, certain about everything and ready to head off any contrary opinions by presenting categorical views and statements taken from the few texts that made up his limited but stable ideological equipment. And Makis was following him without hesitation, sure of the superiority of his friend in the sphere of action and immediate necessity. But he felt his own sense of inadequacy, which sprang from his realization that he would, of course, find those same texts correct, but not a part of his heart and soul. They could not stir him to enthusiasm, because every point of view in his brain dragged a tangle of questions behind it. Is it because I've read so much other material? he would ask himself and become pensive.

Nevertheless, in spite of these irritations, his former self surfaced insistently and quietly, extending itself with a subtle movement punctuated by moments of intense feeling triggered by the most insignificant events.

One morning he stopped by to greet master Kyriazis at his carpenter shop.

The good little old fellow carried on like a child, so pleased he was. He laid aside his plane, shaking the shavings off his *vraka*, and ordered coffee. After they had sat chatting about one thing and another, Makis broached the subject of the outcome of the struggle and of the new objectives now before them.

He was speaking with an enthusiasm which he drew from the will to do his duty in the task of enlightenment assigned to him. His effort to convince the other man ended in strengthening his own conviction. The smiling agreement mirrored on the calm face, in the old blue eyes of his listener, gave sanctity to Makis's words and put to flight the questions that constantly tortured him.

But, then, Master Kyriazis had no need of arguments. It was simply his own heart that confirmed the rightness of Makis and the other young men whom he loved because they set out so bravely and fearlessly in the struggle. Why ask so many questions? Do you suppose he ever asked a lot of questions in order to get, with that same smiling consent, a whole life, with all its worries and poisons? No-o-o. Master Kyriazis never sat and asked himself why we are tortured in this life; he only knew that the entire universe was there so he could lay out his furrow till the end like a man. Even the sow has her joys. One had a craft, to do good and solid work with the loving care of one's own two hands: a cedar chest, a loom, an icon stand. And in some unexplainable way he identified with these finely wrought works, which would abide for a long time among people who would bless him for their usefulness and their beauty.

But Makis, who liked refreshing his soul in the serenity of his old friend, did not yet know the secret of that serenity.

As he was talking, the aroma of sawdust would flood over him suddenly laden with all the sense of return that spread root-like within him. He fell silent. He opened up and breathed it all in, could not get enough of it, and it was like a joyful message that he was eagerly awaiting and look! there it was.

Without knowing why, he returned home happy.

131

That noon he decided to go for a walk. He took the up-hill slope that led to Pentalona.

It was a pleasant day in mid-May with a perfectly clear sky and golden grain moving in waves across the field, ready for harvest. The green had withered and withdrawn into the ravines. And of the colors of the brief spring, which was already past, there remained only a few scattered clumps, red, pink, and white, upon the oleanders.

Makis, with his shirt open, climbed the slope in the sunlight, taking in with deep breaths all this beauty, but without really seeing it. He was occupied with the fantasy wherein memories of the past and events of the present merge and become one. Bright fragments of memory with the magical power to submerge you stripped of all weight into golden realms of pure fantasy, to rest on impassable ground, in the bitter salt sea, on the roof tiles of houses, amid the concerns that torment you—upon all reality that surrounds you and all reality that you carry within—and to make everything unreal, changing all into an aery play of light and color and lucid sensation. It is not memories as much as a happy mood, by which some unexplainable connection crystallizes into the images that well up from the memory:

The painted little wooden horses went round in a circle propelled by a faint, incoherent music played on wooden pipes and small bells, like the laughter of children . . . The festival at Saint Yalos and the dancers in *vrakes* with flying feet and hands stretched open like wings, gazing at the sea as though seeking to embrace it . . . When they brought him near the body, the father, totally blind from cataracts, reached out and gropingly caressed the face of the dead companion of his life. And Makis, who never remembered the old man ever showing tenderness, looked in confusion at that trembling hand as one looks at a hidden treasure revealed where it was unexpected . . . Dark-eyed Christinoula, who was their leader in the games, made a sign with colored pencils on a sheet of paper: "Intrance [*sic*] to Karagiozis." She nailed the sheet to the wall and pointed out in no uncertain terms that that was indeed the entrance and not anywhere else. And the other children obeyed, including her brother Apostolis and her cousin Makis. What else could they do? Christinoula was determined to have her own way. On the other hand, without her the games always went awry. That's why the children were devoted to her; they all loved her for her willful personality and her inexhaustible high spirits . . .

Her big dark eyes still kept their beauty—even her twenty-six years had not taken that away—but they were but a dim reflection of those laughing eyes of his little cousin, whom Makis kept ever locked in his heart. Now Christina was looking at him, eyes laden with humiliation and annoyance, as she gave him Apostolis's letter to read for himself to see how unfairly her brother was treating her, he who did not consider that he had an unprotected sister, and that we sold everything so he could go abroad, and he forgot us and now is marrying a foreign woman. . . . Makis was holding the letter waiting for her to leave off finally so he could read it. He was sorry for her, but again, like it or not, he felt something like exasperation before this frantic soul, who was not willing to know any darkness but her own. But, then, wasn't just about everyone around him like that? Embittered folk, for whom life had failed to keep its promises, their souls charred stumps, cripples, tormented by suspicions and hatred. He saw each and every one of them in the grips of fear lest they be wronged, and at the same time ready to wrong someone else. Fine for the others, but Christina, too? . . . But, on the other hand, why not Christina, too? Hasn't she been living amid the same slavery, in the same misery that we've all lived in. Why shouldn't she knuckle under, too? . . .

But these things have come to an end, he said to himself, the slavery, the misery. Now we'll build up a new life. And he fell to thinking for a long time, until the field, spreading now under his feet, caught his attention again. He had reached the rise and was seated on the parapet of the bridge, turned towards the cliff.

The field was bathed in sunlight, stretched out all the way to the horizon, where the sea dimly appeared as a blue line. And Makis abandoned himself to this golden embrace, with the trust that a child abandons itself to its mother's arms. There he found again the mystical bond that caused him to feel in his blood, like a perceptible presence, the invincible power, the indestructible permanence that the earth of his homeland kept hidden beneath its calm exte-

133

rior. In the light of this great truth everyday events are confined to their actual dimensions, the face of mankind is chastened, and his journey takes on another meaning. Makis breathed deeply again and remained there plunged into fathomless thoughts.

But all at once his eye caught sight of someone coming towards him up the slope, at a quick pace, almost running. He was watching him until he disappeared where the road dipped, but he reappeared shortly at the turn. Although it was too far for him to make out the face, Makis knew who it was from the long strides and wide swing of the long arms, as of one swimming. It was Phoebus, who shortly perceived him and waved a signal: It's you I'm looking for.

What could this be about? thought Makis.

He got up and went to meet his friend.

As soon as they met, Phoebus said, "I've been looking for you. I went by your house and they said that you came this way."

Makis smiled at him, this young giant with a child's heart who was so lovable. Phoebus continued, panting.

"Mavroyannos is in town . . . Several men have him blockaded in his house."

"But how did he get to the village?"

"They say a military car brought him, dropped him off, and left."

With no more discussion they set off for the village.

Mavroyannos himself was a police informant who had sold out. A person of no consequence. The villagers had never trusted him enough for him to be able to learn much of anything. Nevertheless, he had done quite a bit of damage up till the time he was discovered. Then he fled to the English looking for protection. They kept him in town, at the castle where they had installed their headquarters and prisons. And since he felt secure there, the worm began playing the bully and sending his boasts and threats to the village. Finally, word came out that they would be sending him off to England.

"It seems they must have brought him back to get ready and to say goodbye to his wife," said Makis.

"To hell with him," muttered Phoebus, and spat.

"Does Loukas know this?" asked Makis.

"Yes. We were together at the coffee shop, and he went off to see what was happening."

To get to Mavroyannos's by coming down from Pentaloma, it was necessary to cross the village from one end to the other.

The narrow streets were deserted, more deserted than usual, as were the village courtyards and the vacant lots, where, amid heaps of dung, ruins, and rubbish, dust-covered prickly pears fought the aridity, presenting a picture of abandonment and unfulfilled promises.

A fat woman, bent over, legs widely spread, wiped off her baby who had just done its duty on the dung heap. She indifferently allowed her thighs to show.

A lean yellow dog with dry mud clinging like scales to its fur was moving very busily along the wall sticking its muzzle here and there as if searching for something and not finding it. As soon as it heard the steps of the two companions coming from behind, it crouched down in fear, thrust its tail between its legs, and hid behind the tumbledown wall of an animal fold. It could soon be heard barking as if it didn't care any longer.

A donkey snorted and stuck its head out from behind the fence. He stretched his ears towards the two unfamiliar and hastily-moving passers-by and watched them in wonderment with his kindly eyes.

The house was among the last in the village, somewhat isolated. It was a stone cottage with dirt roofing, white - washed only on the front side. Out in back was a small courtyard surrounded by the remains of a neglected fence of stakes.

A crowd of men and women had formed a close circle around the house. They stood in their groups chatting, shouting, and gesticulating in exasperation. A mob of children, too, had gathered. Some were passing from one group to another, listening to the grown-ups' conversations and drawing their own conclusions. But most of them sat in a line on the high embankment, following this unexpected event.

The two friends saw Loukas in the middle of the biggest group, and they, too, joined it. Loukas was talking and the rest were hanging upon his words, occasionally turning to

135

flash angry glances towards the house. Mavroyannos is in for it, thought Makis, and without knowing why he felt choked up about it, even though he agreed with Loukas that Mavroyannos was a scumbag.

Only a few of the women were mixed in with the groups of men. Most of them were gathered at the side watching. Among them Makis saw Christina, who was talking, and he could see from the way she gestured now and then in the direction of the house that she was upset.

Soon the door opened and Mavroyannos's wife came out onto the threshold. She stood with hands on hips.

"What do you want with my husband?" she asked defiantly.

"Some man! hiding behind his wife's skirts!" someone shouted offensively.

"Just like he's hiding behind the English," another was heard to say.

Some began to hoot. Others shouted, "Send him out here."

"He won't get away. Where would he go?"

There was a loud outcry, the crowd getting angrier and angrier and jostling in closer from all sides. The wife got confused.

"Leave him alone, neighbors," she cried. "Leave him alone. He'll go away. Have some pity for me, too, the wretched one."

But her voice could not be heard any more. She withdrew, shut the door behind her and began tearing her hair.

"Oooh! What a mess we're in."

The shouts, curses, and hoots went on and on. But everyone felt that something had to happen. Then a young fellow went to the fence, crouched down for a moment, then rose and stepped away. Shortly the stakes were aflame.

"Fire! . . ." Many voices rose. "Fire! . . ."

"That's the way . . . set a fire to drive the fox out," someone shouted.

"Bring some kerosene," another shouted.

Then Makis saw Christina leave hurriedly in the direction of her house, after she had first called and took with her the oldest of the children who were seated on the embankment.

All at once the door opened again and Mavroyannos came flying out brandishing a pitchfork. With his back to the wall he stood holding the pitchfork at the ready and casting looks of panic and rage about him like a trapped animal. With his dark face, his front teeth jutting from his mouth, which opened in a threatening grimace, the hairs of his thin mustache standing on end, he in fact resembled a dog who was harried and dazed.

The crowd hooted and started moving in closer. But when some of them came in too close, he lunged at them with the determination born of despair and almost speared one of them. They lurched back. He stood with his back again to the wall, then moved side-stepping to the corner of the house. With a quick, measuring glance, he took a deep breath and made a dash for it, intending to escape to the field and the nearby woods.

Everyone on that side gave chase. Some threw stones. Someone chanced upon a heavy stick and threw it at him. It caught him between the legs and tripped him up. He fell on his face, his pitchfork flying from his hands. Bracing himself on his palms, he tried to get up, but the other, who had in the meantime retrieved the stick, began beating him repeatedly as hard as he could. There he stayed, face down, arms splayed, panting, till he finally clutched his hands in back of his head to protect it.

They mobbed around him; some began beating him with sticks, some threw stones, some kicked, some spat. It was a savage outburst of rage, merciless hatred, madness, against the shifty and despised enemy.

People were moving now from every direction to the place where Mavroyannos had fallen. Some were running, some were walking swiftly, some were hanging back and came in their own good time. And when they arrived, some of them crowded into the circle around the fallen man. Others were standing aside and watching.

Loukas and his company set out with the first ones, but Makis did not follow them. He was left by himself.

He saw Christina return with the boy she had left with and another, who were clutching opposite handles of a bucket. He saw them arrive at the embankment to find none of the other children there, and then approach three women who were standing farther on. The women pointed at the house, then to the place where the people had gathered. And then the children with the bucket set off in that direction as quickly as their burden would allow. Christina followed without hurrying, and when she got to a certain distance from the crowd, she stopped. Makis went, too, and stopped a bit farther back.

When the two youngsters could go no farther in the flow of the crowd, they set the bucket on the ground and said something to the people standing in front of them. The others turned, looked at the children, looked at the bucket, and began talking among themselves. It turned into a commotion till one of them shoved his way through decisively and grabbed the bucket. The rest made way as he came up and poured the contents of the bucket on the fallen man. He threw away the bucket, put his hand in his pocket, and bent over . . . Flames soon leaped up with thick black smoke. The people broke and ran.

The flaming body jumped up and tried to brace itself on all fours, but could not and fell back in the same place. It moved its hands and legs sporadically as if battling to escape the flames by swimming. Finally it was paralyzed.

Makis turned his eyes to where Christina was and saw her cover her mouth tightly with both hands, her body tense, bent forward. She was aghast, watching the horrific scene.

He went over to her and took her by the arm. She was trembling from head to foot.

"Come, Christina. Let's go," he said.

She turned and looked at him with the gaze of a person awakening in terror from a nightmare and does not yet recognize those around her. She let her hands drop.

He drew her along gently and they moved without exchanging a word.

As they passed by the accursed house, Makis glanced over at the wide-open door. The rays of the setting sun lighted up a table covered with a colorfully printed tablecloth with a fringe. And on the table was a glass fruit bowl filled with faded artificial fruit: oranges and apples.

They continued down the road without stopping.

But Makis was now engrossed in listening to the story that those poor abandoned decorations were telling him with their wretched unsightliness.

TIMES OF AFFLUENCE

NOTHING BEFORE THE END . . .

They did not know how to love anyone but the dead.
Pushkin

LATER, the local bigwigs began to put in an appearance, as is usual on these occasions.

Each one in turn approached the casket, unfolded his papers, prattled to the "great man lying in state" an encomium made up of ringing platitudes, placed next to the others the wilting wreath he was holding, and returned to his seat so the next could take his turn.

It was a monotonous flow of words that made both the crowd and the heat even more unbearable for me. And in my confusion I felt his presence again. He seemed alive, standing in his usual place at the candle stall attending the service. With his great, heavy-boned face, square chin, and that stern look of his lying in ambush behind his thick eyebrows. I had the impression that the local bigwigs, too, felt his presence, because they seemed to me hesitant to put on their airs. Who among them ever dared to strut in front of him when he was alive . . .

Such a funeral was a rare occurrence in our town, the boys and girls from the high school marching out in front, the priests following them with the cross, the bier heaped with wreaths, and a huge crowd, anyone who was considered of any importance. You see, the funeral of the great Isaiah was a significant event. It would occupy people's thoughts for a long time, and everyone took care not to miss it.

Metropolis Street—with its dusty pines, scattered houses with their little gardens, and vacant lots, usually deserted during these afternoon hours—stirred as if startled out of its torpor.

Women and children come out to the fence gates and stare, some of them make the sign of the cross; a hefty girl

141

comes out of the lane wiping her hands on her apron; an old man leans on his cane with his right hand and takes his straw hat off with his left, holding it to shade his eyes; a little old woman with a censer stops the bier and perfumes it with incense; shops let down their shutters; the flag at the high school flies at half-mast; customers in the coffee shop rise reverently . . . And the procession moves along in the burning heat, disturbing the stillness with its passing.

I was following the bier along with the crowd of heirs, who moved with slow steps under a burden of hopes and suspicions. And as I walked, the sensation of his presence came and covered my wandering thoughts, and it seemed to me that he was satisfied with these public observances. Indeed, he had been fond of honors . . .

But at a turn in the road my attention was captured by the horse that was hitched to the bier. I recognized him as belonging to Menikos, the carter. An old horse, swaybacked, with swollen knees and bony hindquarters. I used to see him often at the customs house and would feel a great affection for him as I watched him strain his neck and put everything he had into his effort to unstick the heavily laden cart, and later, bathed in sweat, to pull it along panting towards the town.

But now he was setting his own pace, rigged up formally with a black blanket thrown across his back hanging down to his belly.

I looked up expecting to see Menikos in the driver's seat, but it was not he. They must have rented just the horse. Where could they have gotten one more presentable? There are no wagons in our town any more, only this ancient bier.

Still, I kept seeing Isaiah in my mind's eye. And I continue to contemplate even to this day the thoughts of that hard-edged man, who, since the time I came to know the world, has occupied my thoughts and feelings in spite of my determination not to know him.

Without intending to I often found myself examining Isaiah's discourse. But how can you, if you are not narrow-minded or fanatic—or both—measure up a living person, classifying his personality and ideas? And what moment of his life do you select to draw your conclusion from? The next moment life may give him another form made from the stuff already within him.

Only death, putting an end to the different shapes a person can take, will once and for all encase his face in a composition made up of memories.

The Isaiah whom I was then seeing in my mind's eye was a composition made up of memories.

I made mention on another occasion of Isaiah, when I told you the story of Nicoletta.

He was one of those persons who know what they want. Without hesitation he would decide on his own what he was entitled to and take it. As for what others were entitled to . . . what would that be? Isaiah did not consider whether anyone else even existed. (Perhaps this was the reason he had never married.)

Gifted with this advantage and with tireless industry, he amassed great wealth and made his presence felt not only in our town but on the entire island. Because he got involved in politics, too—that is, the rivalry for primacy and influence for the purpose of exploitation which was called politics in our land—and acquired one of the top positions in the shadow of the foreign government, which had singled him out for an important decoration.

He became, then, for the rest of us, "the great Isaiah." That was what we called him among ourselves as a joke, though I'm not sure that it was just a joke. Do we not become sarcastic about the person who corrects things beyond our power to correct?

My judgment has always been ambivalent about this steely man, whom I admired and disliked, whom I would have liked to cast out of my thoughts with the same ease that he cast me from his. But I could not, because for good or ill I saw him towering over our fellow-citizens, over their distorted proprieties, their cheap virtues, and their sentimentality.

Not that he was exceptional and perfect, as if he had sprouted from some novel. People are not created from thin air; they are made out of whatever they sink their roots into. So Isaiah, too, shared the faith of everyone else in the values that kept our town inert: a fanaticism about ownership,

143

the right of each person to despise anyone with a smaller in-
come, and all the other bigotries that float like foam on
marsh water. But in contrast to the trembling pettiness of
the others, Isaiah had a dynamic personality. That fascinated me, because I never did anything in my whole life
except follow my desires and fill my hands with dreams,
only to end up a clerk in the customs office.

Uncle Isaiah occupied my thoughts ever since I was a child.
I remember elevating him to about the same level as the
bishop, who came two or three times a year to honor our
house with his visit.

For all of us, young and old, those visits by the bishop
were like an Easter celebration. And they strengthened our
position in the community—though I realized that only
much later. What excited me when I was a child was the
holiday atmosphere, the preparations, the wind of expectation that blew across the neighborhood. And finally the car-
riage drawn by two horses would stop at our door, the
bishop in all his dignity alighting and after him Uncle
Isaiah, who would accompany him.

The deacon came along, too. But he would sit on a chair
in the gallery and wait, while Uncle Isaiah would enter the
salon right after the bishop. Father would follow, then
Mother and Aunt Euridice. We children, dressed in our
finest, would stand in the gallery and watch through the
doorway while they took their places in the circle of easy-
chairs. We waited for Mother's signal to come into the salon and kiss the bishop's hand.

Later I went to grade school.
I was in the third or fourth grade when a sudden commotion blew up around us: people coming and going all day
long at the big ancestral house where Uncle Isaiah lived;
many were coming even to our house to talk with Father in
the salon till far into the night. Until one day the disturbance reached its culmination. That noon they sent us children into the kitchen to eat by ourselves. The grown-ups
did not seem to eat at all. During the night it was like a festival. And I heard them say that Uncle Isaiah had become

144

the mayor . . . Mother started to cry, and I was surprised to see Father laughing, but they told me that she was crying for joy. How does that happen? I asked myself.

Two years later we took down the hanging oil lamps and replaced them with light bulbs, which suddenly lit up one night by themselves. It occurred to me then that people with magical power were not just in fairy tales. For what else could this be but magic? And everyone was saying that Uncle Isaiah brought it all about.

Aunt Euridice told very movingly of all the marvels she had seen at the dedication ceremony for the coming of electricity.

"Isaiah did this; Isaiah said that. He also gave a speech that ended only when it began to grow dark. Then he was quiet for a short time, cast a glance around the room, and thundered, 'Let there be light.' And all at once, snap! The lights came on. Everyone clapped and shouted hurrah. But it's one thing to hear about it, another to see it."

I was in eighth grade before I began to realize that Isaiah might not have had magical powers, but that he was nevertheless a person of ability and determination. Then I began to measure him up, to admire him for this and dislike him for that, sometimes admiring and disliking for the same reason. And I began to see his performance, at the celebration for electricity and other such things he devised from time to time, as evidence of his demagogic demon.

He was mayor for about thirty years. And during all that time he worked for our town in the same capable and obstinate way that had ensured his own success in life.

There is something about that which I could not figure out: how a man as egotistical as he was could be equally dedicated to himself and to the progress of his town. How did the two become reconciled in his soul? But can we untangle what happens in the soul of another person? Does his being egotistical mean that he cannot have any sentiment? Perhaps his town was the object of his sentiment. Perhaps,

145

too, by some mystical twist in his soul he identified himself with his town, seeing it as an indestructible extension of himself . . . In this way I was always delving to the very roots of his every act, not seeing the substance, that is, the deed itself and its consequences.

The truth was that Isaiah took over our small, unlovely, neglected town, a great, dirty village, and transformed it within a few years. Streets were paved. Neighborhoods cleared of dung heaps and ruins. The little harbor was dressed up with a quay and a line of electric lights that reflect on the water at night and invite us out for a stroll.

His determination to modernize extended beyond the mayoral jurisdiction, such as schools, for which he succeeded in acquiring new buildings.

It is not my intention to list all his accomplishments here. Whoever is interested will find them in their proper order and with all the details in the local newspaper *Ramparts*, a weekly sheet that circulated back then in our town. It was put out by a self-styled intellectual who lived clinging like a leech to whatever political party would agree to make him some return for *his intellectual services.*

So the man clung to Isaiah and for a long time sang the praises of the *enterprising* mayor in his newspaper, describing the progress being made in our town with words so resounding that one would have said that a historical renaissance was under way on our end of the island.

But if you ignore the hoopla and keep paging through the complete series of the *Ramparts*, found piled in bundles on a shelf at the Club, you will see, starting in one of the issues and continuing thereafter, articles equally bombastic but against the *despotic* mayor. The editor of the newspaper, for whatever reason, went over to the other party.

But that is not very significant. Business as usual. What is worth noting is that neither *Ramparts* nor any of his other rivals ever dared to accuse Isaiah of self-interest. They told much to his discredit, truths and falsehoods, explicit and implicit, about his greed, his megalomania, his unfairness, but about self-interest in connection with all the work he did as mayor, no, not a word. How could they say anything? That matter was so clear that not even his most perfidious rival could blur it. Isaiah was tightfisted and never gave anything to anyone. But to build what he did in our town he often spent money from his own pocket. He even made significant bequests.

That was one of his contradictions, of course, which I would try to solve: although he was indifferent to humanity, to the human creature next to him, he was interested in the town, as an impersonal entity, to the point of spending his own money on it.

When he got an idea into his head, he could only with difficulty acknowledge it as infeasible. Without rushing, but also without forgetting, he would draw circles around his target, trying one way, then another, until he found the right way.

It is neither easy nor uncomplicated to accomplish anything in a small, abandoned town under English colonial rule. At every step you stumble against a wall of indifference, mistrust, requirements, safeguarded privilege, and the deliberate inertia of the government, a wall that you have to tear down, if you can, or turn it upside down.

But the wily Isaiah knew many paths: sometimes with flattery, sometimes through bargaining, sometimes with outrage, and if the work did not get done he finally had recourse to heavy measures which were not in the hands of just anyone, but only in his own. The English took pains to get around men like him, to do favors for, to get on their side. Isaiah finally attained free entrance to the office of the governor himself. So it was not difficult for him to effect, when he needed it, an order of expropriation or an item of exceptional expenditure for the completion of some project or other. What did it cost the English? Would it change the misery of the country?

He became very powerful.

But we youngsters in high school held his power against him. It was based on the goodwill of the English. We knew that he was not a participant in the happenings of '31. Moreover, he himself did not hide his opinions. I heard him many times right in our own household arguing the case that our connection with a rich and powerful empire was to our own advantage.

147

The war came.

Hard put, the governor wore another countenance and smiled at us, telling us that we were all one, colony and homeland, and we were protecting the popular concepts of freedom and democracy. Come, then, and let's battle together against the enemy of democracy.

"Onward for freedom!" we bellowed, along with the governor.

It was irrelevant that the governor thought one way and we another, we who saw freedom as having the color of the sky. And he ceased forbidding us the color of the sky only to make a virtue of necessity.

"There is no oppression," he told us, "in the free world that we are defending. And if anything like that happened, it was a misunderstanding. Hurrah!"

"Hurrah!" we cheered.

And we unfurled our sky-colored flags, which we had kept hidden in chests. Our hopes began to sail high.

After that honeymoon, when the 25th of March came, we celebrated without restraint as our hearts had yearned to do. And Isaiah delivered the panegyric.

He was a good orator. But on that occasion his elation and bombast excelled all previous occasions. He spoke with inspiration about the great works and the destiny of our people and praised the Idea which he saw with the eyes of his soul rise up to a crest and flash lightening.

The audience abandoned itself to the sweetness of emotion. Many were crying. Even I felt that my eyes would at any moment fill with tears, but I resisted. The words of Papadiamantis came to mind about those who practice the profession of patriotism. It annoyed me that Isaiah was getting up now and turning into vapid rhetorical tropes the vivid idea of the fatherland that was inspiring us.

But I knew that I was doing him an injustice by likening him to the professional patriot of Papadiamantis. No. Isaiah was not a fake. His emotion at that moment was genuine. I knew that he believed what he was saying. I had heard him say these things passionately on other occasions when he was not holding forth before an audience. But I could not figure out how he squared these patriotic themes with his view that we were better off as an English colony.

But I did not impute to him any intention to deceive. Don't we all have our peculiarities? The entire course of his life, his place in the community, had shaped his thoughts to compromise between an attachment to an ideal Greece and the perception of a rich and freedom-loving England. His education predisposed him to this. He possessed some knowledge of the classics and took for genuine philhellenes a few of his English acquaintances, high-level functionaries in the colonial service who had acquired at Oxford and Cambridge a culture similar to his own and were admirers of Greek antiquity.

He insisted on maintaining these beliefs even after the war. He refused to admit that the governor and his free world deceived us again.

But I was accustomed to paying attention to his every phrase, and I saw that the more time passed and our hopes vanished, the more stubbornly he persisted in the beliefs he felt tottering within.

He stopped keeping me at a distance and began chatting with me as if I was no longer a good-for-nothing, as he used to refer to me before. I saw that something was irritating him. For the first time he showed signs of not being sure of himself.

It took ten years for even the most naive to understand what exactly the governor meant when he was weaving the romance concerning freedom and democracy.

And this last realization of ours brought us to the conclusion that we were not about to gain our freedom by exchanging sweet talk with its counterfeiter.

We broke free, then, from the stupidity of running around in tight circles that came out nowhere. And we took the open road of revolt.

And if we could not reach the desired goal on the first try, we knew that the road did not end there. For the time being the good islanders unstuck themselves from the limetwig proffered by the promoters of good intentions. They opened their eyes. They saw the English and the various other supporters of colonization wipe off their smiles and expose their inhuman faces. For this reason, when the signal was given for a Protest March against the military bases which the crown maintained in our country, thousands mustered from every corner of the island.

All the time of the uprising and thereafter, Isaiah was baffled and speechless.

Those who did not care to find out where the man stood said he was indifferent. Others looked at him suspiciously. They had not forgotten his friendship with the English and the medal they gave him. But it never mattered to Isaiah what people would say.

I saw him only rarely. But when we met by chance and talked, I was aware, as I said before, that something was troubling him.

One evening I happened upon him at the Club. He was sitting in the drawing room listening to the radio. It was time for the news report. The radio was on a small low table, and he was bent over it with his ear perked up and his elbows resting on his knees. In his right hand he held his worry-beads and from time to time he would let a bead drop, tock, as if he were punctuating the reporter's account.

When the broadcast was finished, he straightened up, turned off the radio, and pointed to a chair next to him.

"Sit down," he said.

There were others in the drawing-room. A discussion arose. The former publisher of the *Ramparts*, who was now applying *his intellectual services* to other objectives, set about advancing the old subject of what is in our interests, with fresh allurements. He fluttered his cunning eyes, caressed his well-groomed mustache, like a man who knows a lot . . . He seemed pitiful to me.

Isaiah listened, still letting a bead drop now and then. All at once he interrupted the speaker.

"They're not kidding anyone any more," he said. He twirled his worry-beads on his finger and added, "They're liars."

The other raised his eyebrows.

"You're saying that?" he said, as if perplexed.

Isaiah did not answer. He only turned and looked at him. Then he shifted back to me and paid no further attention to him.

The proclamation that called the people to the March was a remarkable document. It revealed the role of the military bases and ended with a call for their removal from our land. It circulated from hand to hand in a typed version and whoever agreed signed it. The purpose was to collect signatures of people with clout and publish the proclamation together with their names.

I had taken part in this enterprise and intended to present the document to Uncle Isaiah. If he signed it, it would have a significant effect. But would he sign it? My friends shook their heads doubtfully. Isaiah?

I wasn't sure, either. I had some reasons for hoping, but on the other hand I knew that Isaiah was not one to sign anything casually, on the spur of the moment, or just to do someone a favor. He had to ponder his decision. But it was worth a try. Just think, Isaiah's name on the proclamation . . .

I handed him the typed sheet and waited. Knowing his character, I did not attempt to persuade him. He would decide for himself.

He put on his glasses, read the text carefully, placed the sheet on the table, and took off his glasses without saying a word.

"Shall we have some coffee?" he asked. He clapped his hands for the waiter.

Good sign, I said to myself.

While we drank our coffee, we talked about other matters. He asked about one thing and another, whether I was still swimming in the sea, whether there were difficulties with the loading procedures down at the docks. . . . He was curious about everything, wanted to learn it all.

He put out his cigarette and put his glasses back on. He took out his fountain pen, straightened the sheet, and without hurrying, wrote his signature.

"They should leave," he muttered.

151

He raised his head and looked me in the eye. I felt as if he were looking straight into me. He was struggling with his emotions, but was soon in control. His face turned stern again.

"They should leave," he said again determinedly, and handed me the sheet.

I, however, didn't have the strength to fight down my emotions. I searched my head for an appropriate word to say to him, but I couldn't find one. I only pressed his hand and left.

It was his last signature.

He died in six months. Suddenly. There where he was sitting. Heart-failure. He was seventy-eight years old.

TIMES OF AFFLUENCE

PRELUDE

THERE ARE ALL KINDS OF PEOPLE living during times of affluence, just as at other times. And they are divided into two general types: those who, satisfied with whatever surrounds them, are sure of themselves; and those who by chasing in vain whatever surfaces in their dreams end up doubting themselves.

(This does not mean that people are all cut from the same pattern. Each one is created after his own fashion in the circumstances of his life. It only means that the springs welling up from within drift him toward one or the other of the two types.)

The difference between this and the other times is that during times of affluence, circumstances on the island permit the rich to multiply, to know that they are in charge, to show off their wealth to the extent that folks of the other type shy from revealing who they really are and follow as best they can the ways of the rich, abandoning to decay whatever might set them apart.

The observer wondered why those granted the grace of living beyond their own limitations made the shabby decision to be likened to the rich.

But he did not attempt to reach a sensible conclusion that might resolve his perplexity, because as a person experienced in life he knows that answers of that kind only serve deceptively to quiet our feverish minds. And he who follows the ways of art will not accept them and yet fall asleep midstream; he investigates life such as it is: fickle and many-faced. He will need to labor judiciously, embracing with his thought each of its facets in order to grasp and express some wrinkle of truth.

153

For the time being, then, let us stay with the observer's first impressions of those within whom a sun happens to shine. They live, as it were, a double life: on the surface they imitate the rich so they can get along. And for as long as each of them can hold out, they keep to themselves their private worship of the mystical substance of their hope and the dreams that they make with it.

And let us speak of the sovereign group of the rich, who give to the times their particular character.

That which characterizes the rich is that each of them is certain of his own value as an individual.

Like comfortable frogs, they prosper in their bogs and, casting disdainful glances at the starry sky, they croak:

"We have it good right here. What, after all, are the sky and its stars? Can they be eaten? Or are they expensive items of luxury that one can acquire and show off? Or do they present opportunities for lucrative investments? No. They are none of these things. Then what meaning can they have for sensible people?"

For the rich, the sensible person is a worthy role model. By that they mean the person who is gifted with that sort of narrowmindedness needed to succeed in the pursuit of advantages.

Having concentrated all their small intelligence and their small heart exclusively on their pursuit, sensible people reach their goals and acquire power and glory in times dominated by the rage for acquisition. And as is natural, even when they happen not to be blockheads, they end up admiring themselves for the same reasons that blockheads admire them. And they smell danger in whatever there is beyond the limits of their success, in whatever promotes thought, which hides in the little corner of the mind to wake them up and disturb them, shaking up all that is comfortable without thought.

It is not only thought that they avoid. They even avoid the sight of the beauty of their country, the mountains and plains and sea, the people and the thirst of their hearts, even the recollection of themselves when they were children.

This last they flee more quickly than anything else, because they sense that they could not be so sure of their sensible selves if any of their childhood was still alive. For those who believe in wealth it is a sign of naïveté to see life with eyes and heart wide open as you saw it when you were a child—to behave like a child, according to their perception, that is, not to have placed blinders on your eyes and your heart in order to get ahead.

You understand now why the few others we spoke of end up doubting themselves and avoid revealing who they really are. It is not easy to believe that you are on the right road when so many of your high-living countrymen pass you haughtily by, leaving you in the exhaust of their limousines, telling you that you're not progressive—you who go on foot because you want to preserve your initial sense of reverence.

What is left for you to do, then, under such circumstances?

The time comes when exhaustion weighs you down and you want to run away! . . . But the next moment you realize that it's only an inner lament, because one cannot escape from one's own life.

At other times you are swept away by the thought, why can't you be like the majority who may live in today's reality while you, with your ideas, feelings, and difficult life, are left in the void . . . But the next moment you know that this is just another kind of lament, that people do not change just because they suddenly make up their minds to.

And there are also thoughtful moments that find you once again on your feet standing firmly on your beloved island, knowing in mind and soul that this whole situation which wounds you is only dirt on the foam that the times have brought forth. Underneath, the deeper waters are still unsullied. They toil and wait.

During these good times you cease to doubt yourself. It is no longer a question of whether you have a place in your country, you being such as you are. The country is yours. It does not belong to the rich, who hide their real faces behind a smokescreen of farts.

DREAMS AND REALITY

*Money, like drink, makes a
person strange.*
                              Anton Chekhov

ONE POLE OF HIS LIFE in Africa was his concern for
putting aside money. The other was his dreams, where his
soul found refuge. Between these two inclinations he
shaped a lifestyle based on two interrelated expectations:
economic security upon his return to the island and re-
sumption of his youthful plans at the point where he had
left them.

That is how he endured thirty years as a clerk. They
seemed endless but could not shake him from the beloved
and steadfast image of his island, once he had stowed it
away .

But when the time came for him to return . . . How
quickly the years passed! it seemed to him. And he felt as if
he were going abroad a second time.

His perception of time altered yet again when he arrived
at the island and found himself confronted by a reality different from the image he had preserved in his dreams. The
time he had left as an emigrant now seems very distant indeed.

Yet moments come when the unbridgeable distance is
reduced to nothing, and, as in a waking dream, he sees with
the eyes of memory worlds other than those confronting
him in actuality . . . Here it is, Alkamenous Street . . . As
Loukis walks up the slope, sunk in his thoughts, the present
street with its pretentious modern houses vanishes, and he
sees instead the green expanses of another time, with towering pines and widely-spaced stone houses in gardens surrounded by fences.

Alkamenous Street back then was out in the country, far
from the center of the small town. It did not lead anywhere, but only came to an end at the overview on the ridge

157

atop the sandy slope that stretched from there all the way down to the sea.

(When by chance you wandered up there and the sun-drenched expanse opened suddenly before you with the sea glistening down below, you experienced something like purification and you went in delight down the winding path that led to the shore.)

But when he reached the overview, the spell vanished all at once. He found himself at a crossing of paved streets. Before him stretched a mosaic of lots and newly-built houses, and the view of the sea was shattered by tall apartment buildings erected on the seashore.

He turned to the street he had just crossed and examined its motley confusion of new houses standing haughtily next to the few old ones that were left. He looked over the latter, the familiar houses, and it was like rediscovering lost friends. Among them was Thalia's house. It looked bare until he realized that the two pine trees which once hid it were gone. He smiled. Thalia and Anestis's house . . .

He and Anestis had been classmates during high school. They were united by the ideal friendship which binds youngsters of the same age when they have interests and dreams in common. Together with a few others of that age they comprised a company of intellectuals-to-be, a company of the sort that forms at the heart of each new generation, absorbed by a vague feeling of uniqueness and responsibility. This mystical passion leaps indestructible from generation to generation. And if it appears to change, it is only because it mirrors the hues of the current era. Sometimes it finds the times suitable and it becomes fruitful; other times it finds them contrary and withers before it can form a fruit.

Loukis, Anestis, and their company found the times immovable. They were shut into the narrow confines of the provincial life of the then-subject island. They had no exit from their dreams, which in time settled like crystal on the bottom of their bogged-down existence, to remind them with their brilliance of lost dawns.

But Loukis, who left the country as soon as he had finished high school, thought to take his dreams with him while they were still fresh. And since they had bonds with neither place nor employment in the foreign land, he kept his dreams immaculate in a corner of his mind. There he adapted them to the changes and progress he was learning about in his now-liberated island, and he created his own image of the new era, which he expected to find upon his return. Surely the good that had no way of thriving in the previous era would be blossoming now.

Thalia, too, had been a member of the company. Not that she would routinely run around with the boys—that would have been scandalous in those days—but she was among the first girls who dared to play roles in the theatrical productions at the Amateurs' Club. For that boldness and for her serene beauty the boys secretly loved her. And in their jealousy they found occasions for annoying Anestis, who was her fiancé.

Loukis was not surprised, then, to receive a wedding invitation and a friendly letter with the encoded signature: A + Th = 1.

He opened the fence gate of the garden.

The old house seemed smaller to him than he remembered it.

A middle-aged couple was sitting in the shade of the grape arbor. They looked at him expectantly. Who could they be? he asked himself. But when he approached and got a good look at the woman's eyes, he knew. Naturally. So many years had passed . . . He smiled at them, but they continued to look him over circumspectly.

"Thalia! . . . Anestis! . . ."

"Hey, hey, hey!" cried Anestis as he got up. He appeared to be happy to see him, but something in his manner checked Loukis's inclination to embrace him. They shook hands.

The woman got up and began exclaiming: "Tassia! . . . Tassia! . . ."

"Yes," answered a girl who appeared on the threshold.

"Bring a chair!" Thalia called and immediately calmed down.

"Welcome, Loukis," she said and gave him her hand.

When they had exhausted the questions that people ask one another on such occasions, they fell silent.

Loukis studied this fat fifty-year-old with the flabby face and swollen eyelids and this languid, pale wife, and found nothing to say to them. Finally Anestis asked:

"Did you make any money?"

"I've got enough," answered Loukis.

The other seemed to come alive.

"If you want my advice, I tell you as a friend to put your money into lots. There's no security in interest any more, what with the continuous devaluation of the pound. Whereas the value of land keeps rising steadily and you have a definite increase in wealth."

He was quiet for a while, then continued.

"Think about it. And if you decide to do it, I'll get you a lot in the most promising area. You'll thank me some day."

So much for Anestis! Loukis said to himself, as his good humor slipped away. Nevertheless, he was not surprised. From the day he set foot on the island the subject of lots, how much for that one, how much the other went up, a thousand details and examples, came up again and again monotonously in the conversations he heard all around him, as if it was the only concern people had. Moreover, he even understood what Anestis meant when he talked about lots in promising areas. He had heard mention of the high value of some meadowland near the seashore which Thalia had inherited from her mother.

"Should we go in?" said Thalia as she got up. "The sun is getting to us here."

She seemed angry. As if something had upset her.

The large living room on the ground floor reminded Loukis of the rehearsals they used to hold there when they were getting ready to put on *Popolaros*. The same ancient furniture, the easy chairs with tassels on the armrests, the piano with candlesticks on it . . . He became distracted as he breathed in the aromas rising from the past.

"Do you still play the piano, Thalia?" he asked.

"Piano?" she replied, surprised. "Who plays the piano any more, Loukis? . . . The television is enough for us," she added in a tone so tired that Loukis was confused. What could it be? . . . Bitterness? . . . Sarcasm? . . . or was it . . .

160

"Have you seen my beret, mama?" asked a voice in a fit of temper, and at the same moment a girl appeared in the doorway. She stood looking at Loukis.

"What beret?" answered Thalia.

"The green one, what else!" the girl turned and said.

"No-o-o, . . . I don't think so . . ."

"You haven't seen it; Tassia hasn't seen it . . ."

"Why don't you ask yourself, Marcia, where you put it . . . But come and meet Mr. Papachristou," and to Loukis, "Our daughter Marcia."

The girl approached boldly and extended her hand to Loukis, who rose.

"Glad to meet you," she said and, without paying him any further attention, turned back to her mother.

"Come on, mama. Help me find where the heck it's got to. I'm in a hurry."

She was about eighteen, with the great, blue eyes of Thalia when she was that age, the blond hair, the broad forehead, and yet you could not say she looked like her. She was wearing a light, colorful shirt and a black leather skirt, very short. She has fine legs and she knows it, said Loukis to himself. Marcia! . . . Where did they find that name!

Thalia got up and followed her without saying a word.

Anestis took his worry-beads out of his pocket and began counting off beads.

Soon Tassia came in wearing a white starched apron and carrying sweets and two cups of coffee on a silver tray.

Loukis looked in confusion at Anestis but waited for the server to leave.

"Don't pay any attention to Thalia," he said.

He took an engraved box off the table and offered Loukis a cigarette.

"Do you smoke? . . . I gave it up."

Loukis took a cigarette and lit it.

"My remarks about the lots have set her off," Anestis continued. "Thalia gets upset whenever I talk about selling a spot of land. This subject always sets us to wrangling. Ever since we started selling a lot once in a while, prices have been rising and alerting us that we could have gotten more if we'd waited . . . I can't argue with her; it is a loss, she's right about that. Can't I see that someone else profits

161

from the rise in price that I lost by selling yesterday instead of today? But on the other hand she ought not take it to such extremes. It's become an obsession with her. She sits and totes up figures, what we sold, for how much, how much they're selling for today, each time she gets a bigger sum of our losses and hollers that we're being ruined . . . What do you want us to do? I say to her. Live in poverty? How will we maintain our place in society? Thank God we have land enough to live comfortably and provide our daughter with a generous dowry. Why are you so distressed? . . . Her, nothing . . ."

Loukis was tired of this.

"It's time for me to go," he said, rising.

Anestis got up, too.

". . . Don't think anything about it," he continued, shaking Loukis's hand. "It's just nerves. It'll go away . . . Think about what I told you."

They went out into the garden. Thalia didn't appear.

Just then a big, shiny yellow car with Marcia at the wheel came out from behind the house, moving down the driveway.

"Marcia!" shouted Anestis.

The car stopped.

"Take Mr. Papachristou with you."

She reached over and opened the door, showing Loukis the seat next to her. He said goodbye to his friend and got into the car, though he would rather have walked.

The girl started out and as soon as they reached the highway she suddenly accelerated. She drove boldly and skillfully, without paying any attention to the passenger seated next to her.

MARRIAGE

*The woman has no authority over
her own body; the man does.*
                    Paul, Corinthians I

MRS. JULIA PELOPIDI'S day begins as a rule with her
tending to the flower garden.

Then will follow in their order all the other cares and
obligations that mark her hours and trick her into feeling
that, as long as she arranges her life in a fashion befitting
her social station, all is well and she lacks for nothing.

The same view is shared by many of the elderly ladies in
her circle who have known her since she was a child. They
would say, with tenderness in their voices, that she was the
same as her departed mother. She, too, they say, was in her
time a beautiful woman who knew how to maintain her position as a genuine lady.

Except that the elderly ladies do not seem to have noticed that her mother did not have in her eyes that look of
fatigue bordering on hopelessness such as Julia's had when
she attended to what was and what was not proper.

Finally she cut a few carnations for the vases and undid the
kerchief that bound her hair.

As she was climbing the marble stairway of the veranda,
she saw that someone was opening the garden gate. That
will be the artist, she thought. She was annoyed at being
caught so untidy and tried to slip inside. But at the same
moment she thought that the visitor might already have
seen her, and it would be unseemly to appear to be avoiding
him. In the meantime the stranger was walking up to her.

The artist taught at the high school. Newly appointed.
Kyria Julia was seeing him for the first time. She knew,
however, that he had been assigned the task of decorating
the hall where the national celebration would be held and

163

that he would have come to see her husband about that very matter.

He was a tall, sunburnt young man with almond-shaped eyes and thick, black hair. He had a long roll of paper clamped under his arm and climbed the veranda steps with the light-footed nimbleness of a cat. He greeted her somewhat clumsily, introduced himself as Nikos Avgoustos, and stood there looking at her. A sparkle of pleasant surprise twinkled in his eyes as he wondered whether this sweet-browed young woman could be Pelopides' wife.

She again thought of her wrinkled blouse and disheveled hair.

"Excuse my appearance," she said. "Mr. Pelopides is in his office. He's waiting for you."

She opened one of the French doors of the veranda and, without letting go of the knob, said, "Mr. Avgoustos is here."

In a few moments Pelopides appeared on the threshold to receive him with a polite, condescending smile. He was a middle-aged, bald man with a clumsy frame, heavy brows, and distrustful eyes.

He could be her father, thought Avgoustos, though their difference in age was not at first the only reason he was disconcerted.

Kyria Julia entered the house by the other French door. She was again feeling choked by the undefinable sensation of emptiness, which frightened her and impelled her to seize upon the superficialities of life, as one would seize a life-preserver, in order to combat the loneliness of this spacious and well-appointed house, which has remained empty for the ten years since her wedding.

But Pelopides sees the situation differently, inasmuch as he is able to fill the entire space with his own presence and with his prominent position as lawyer and political leader in the little town and in the entire district.

He invited Avgoustos to sit down, showing him an armchair, and sat down opposite him. He broached the subject only after sitting with his eyes closed a few moments in order to show that he considered what he was about to say of special importance.

164

"You will agree, I believe, that the national celebration demands close supervision in every respect."

Avgoustos indicated with an approving nod that he certainly agreed. But he was also thinking that Pelopides was particularly concerned because he was to deliver the keynote address.

"As an artist, you recognize that the decor, the artistic side, so to speak, contributes to the creation of an appropriate atmosphere . . ."

Not finding words to respond suitably, Avgoustos again confined himself to a nod of the head. He then spread out his papers on the coffee table and began explaining his plan, taking as much care as he could to appear to consider the matter significant. Among the other posts that Pelopides had succeeded in acquiring—and which gave him all kinds of authority over other people's fortunes—was that of member of the School Board.

Before long Kyria Julia appeared with coffee and *koulourakia* on a silver tray. She was wearing a cinnamon dress which left her beautiful arms exposed. Seeing the table covered with the plans, she paused indecisively for a moment. Pelopides then rose, bent over with difficulty to gather up the papers, and spread them out on the desk. He was about to take the tray from her.

"Let me help you, dear."

But before he could do so she set the tray on the table and said, "A cup of coffee, Mr. Avgoustos?"

It was difficult for her to cast off the wave of displeasure that welled up whenever Pelopides showed affection for her in front of company. She took everything else as her due because of the prominent position in polite society that Pelopides' importance ensured her. But these gestures of affection upset her.

"See what we've come to, sir. On Sunday the lady of the house does the servant's duty because the staff has off," objected Pelopides, emphasizing the "off." He fell heavily back into his chair, where he sat looking angrily at a small gypsum bust of Alexander the Great on the bookshelf.

"Come on, you poor thing . . . ," his wife said calmly as she sat down on the sofa.

165

"I'm putting you folks to a lot of trouble . . . ," began Avgoustos.

"On the contrary," she assured him. "Don't listen to Andreas. He is bothered by the difficulties we have with the help. But what can we do? . . . We must come to terms with the fact that times have changed."

She sat leaning forward, her hands folded, and spoke in a wearied manner as though she was unconcerned with what she was saying.

Is this a pose? Avgoustos asked himself. But a faint smile in response to his gaze lit up her face and convinced him that, no, it was not a pose. Then he felt the spark of affection, which had flashed when they first met, spread, become a wave, and engulf him.

All at once she rose, took the plate of *koulourakia*, offered it first to Avgoustos, then to her husband, and sat down again at the other end of the sofa.

Avgoustos returned to the subject of decorating the hall, trying to remember where he had left off.

Kyria Julia quickly refocused her attention on the forms of good behavior.

"I'll leave you to do your work," she said, and left.

As soon as she was in the hallway, she hurried her step as though seeking somewhere to escape to as quickly as possible. She was hounded by the strange feeling that not she but someone else within her was living moments of dangerous enchantment.

Mr. Pelopides showed his satisfaction with the plans by seeing the artist to the head of the veranda stairs, where he proffered his hand for a handshake. Avgoustos, whose mind was elsewhere, took the extended hand, but stopped short of gripping it as he normally would, because it felt lifeless and soft, like dough.

He left taking the cold touch with him on his fingertips.

PARASITES

I hate them because I cannot make them good
and because I cannot become evil.
                    Panayiotis Panas (1832-1896)

MR. KELARIDES lost the match.   Exasperated, he
abruptly closed up the *tavli* game.   The playing pieces rattled.   The cat, sitting the while on the sill of the open window with its eyes half-closed as if trying to remember something, was startled, got up, cast them a look of disapproval,
and jumped outside.

Strongos regretted being carried away by the game and
winning. He was a master of *tavli*. But with Mr. Kelarides
he applied his mastery to making the game challenging and
uncertain, but he saw to it that his opponent won.

To be sure, gone are the days when his relationship with
Mr. Kelarides was all flattery. Now there is a bond between
them of common interests in supplies and operations, in
which Kelarides contributes high position, connections, and
great resources, and Strongos the know-how and the big
businessmen that he has behind him.

Nevertheless, he does not forget that Kelarides is wont
to think of himself as an important person, that he is suscep-
tible to flattery, and that he does not like to lose at cards or
tavli.

"It's all in the dice, Kyr Grigori," he said. "But now it's
time for our whisky, don't you think? . . . Would you rather
go into the garden?"

As it began to cool off, many had gone out into the Club
garden and were sitting around in groups.   The voices of a
few loudmouths reached them.

"No, it's better right here," said Kelarides. "It's qui-
eter."

They went to a corner and sat down in easy chairs to wait
for the drinks that Strongos had ordered. They were alone
in the salon. Kelarides was as always nonchalant and dis-

dainful. He glanced distrustfully at whoever chanced to walk by.

Something is not going well, thought Strongos. But the other did not say a word until the waiter had brought their drinks and left.

"Do you know Karneris?" he asked.

"Stathis? . . . Of course! . . . We were classmates in high school, but I haven't seen him in quite a while. He went into public service right out of high school and has been climbing up the rungs ever since. I think he's a department head now . . ."

"Yes," answered Kelarides. He took a swallow, lit a cigarette, and continued.

"The file on the crane matter has to go through channels, including Karneris. It's already in his hands. And he's a real stickler in whatever he regards as his business! . . . He could ruin the whole deal if he thinks the purchase isn't indispensable . . ."

Strongos hurriedly assessed the situation: the negotiation is at risk . . . But what is Karneris looking for? . . . I'll have to talk with him . . . Perhaps that's what Kelarides means for me to do . . . Surely . . . That's what he means.

They said no more about the matter. They just drank their drinks a sip at a time, chatting disinterestedly like the perfect men of the world that they were. Finally Kelarides looked at his watch.

"Time for me to go," he said. "I've got to go to the reception."

§

Karneris had stopped lounging in bed Sunday mornings long ago. Ever since the atmosphere of intimacy and the lawful pleasures afforded by their bedroom had ceased to buoy him up with its sensual comforts and had begun to weigh on his soul and impel him out into the fresh air.

Seeking refuge in the few little trees that need tending in the courtyard, he gets up to look after them on Sundays and holidays at the same time that he gets up every other day to go to work. And he leaves Kyria Aglaitsa to lounge by herself.

Aglaitsa nurses a grievance for this against Stathis, who used to be so affectionate. Look how self-centered he is now! And she feels ill-treated and worthy of admiration since she lacks the imagination required to understand that Stathis has had enough of her plump beauty, her housewifeliness, and her dignity, and he feels more alone now than he did before he married her.

But today Stathis does not have it in him to get out of bed. It is not the fatigue of last night's wakefulness that keeps him lying there in exhaustion. It is a heaviness of spirit, a bitter feeling of disappointment—without a distinction between whether it springs from other people's dirty business or his own attempt to keep his hands clean.

So he pretends to sleep in order to avoid Aglaitsa's questions. Aglaitsa is certain to be impatient to learn everything.

When he had explained Strongos's unexpected invitation, he expected to see her pull a sour expression and fall silent. She does not like his friends nor the interests they share with him.

"Everyone else is concerned about accomplishing something, about how to lead a happy life, but these people sit around worrying over ideas and what's happening at the other end of the earth. Pf!"

But no, this time her face lit up. Aglaitsa knows well who is who. And she does not lump Strongos in with Stathis's boring friends.

"Go ahead, Stathis," she urged him.

Behind her heavy eyelids Stathis saw her oft-repeated complaint: "Let's us get out into the world a bit, too . . ."

But this time it was not a complaint, but a hope.

Strongos had telephoned Stathis at his office, as if recollecting their old friendship.

"We've lost touch, my friend. What do you say we get together tomorrow evening at the Papagalos? . . . No, not at the Club. It's better at the Papagalos for going on a bit of a spree . . . I'm a married man, too. No matter about that. Once in a while we need a bachelor's outing . . . Don't tell me you can't."

Stathis said yes and hung up the phone smiling.   He liked Strongos for his audaciousness and his good nature.

Shortly afterwards, when he was immersed in his paperwork, he smiled again.   He remembered how skillfully Strongos used to be able to walk on his hands.   The rest of us would scarcely stay upside down for a minute or do more than a step or two, swaying back and forth.   But he would walk along straight up on his hands for perhaps twenty steps.

To be sure Stathis was somewhat perplexed by the unexpected call.   But since he was among those who take what others tell them at face value, he suspected nothing.

That night at the Papagalos he continued to see Strongos's hospitality, his good humor, his insistence on refilling glasses again and again as spontaneous proofs of goodheartedness.   Consequently, he was in high spirits and enjoyed reliving their friendship and shared memories until the moment that Strongos, half-joking, half-serious, brought up the matter of the crane and ended up by saying:

"Just listen to what I'm telling you . . . You'll not come out the worse for it . . ."

Immediately Stathis's festive mood darkened.   But he kept control of himself.   He pretended not to understand . . . Among all the things that Strongos had said was a sort of hint whose meaning Stathis now understood:

"You're a good official, Stathis, I know, but . . . I don't see that you have backers to protect you if by chance some bigwig should trip you up, let's say, with a transfer . . ."

So it wasn't just idle chatter over drinks, reckoned Stathis suspiciously.   He's pretending to talk at random as if he were tipsy in order to have room to retreat until he figures what your own intentions are.

For a moment Kelarides came to mind.   Is he the one Strongos has in mind? . . . He's powerful, to be sure.   But . . . Kelarides! . . .

They stayed on for a while at the night spot.   Stathis kept up his efforts to appear happy, that he was enjoying the soft, romantic music, which was in fact choking him in a fog of sadness . . . for himself? . . . for the others? . . . he could not tell.

But Strongos continued in the same voluble, effusive good humor. And when they finally said good night, he leaned his hand on Stathis's shoulder as if he were drunk and said:

"Don't you see, Stathis, that times have changed? . . ."

Aglaitsa had risen long ago. He heard her busying herself about the kitchen. What would he say to her? . . . Reveal to her what he really felt? Out of the question. In her little head all these prosperous wheeler-dealers were right, since they prospered and multiplied . . .

Suddenly he gave himself a good shake and threw off the covers and stood up. He stretched as far as he could and went into the bathroom and splashed himself good with cold water.

"Parasites," he said to himself. And he felt better.

ARRANGED MARRIAGE

*They call him crazy at first, then an observer, eccentric,
odd, until they understand the betrayal of those who are
sensible, practical, and sober.*

Th. I. Kolokotronis
"A gift of Skiadistis, a box of matches" (1869)

THE ROAR that rocked him in his lethargy for so many
hours all at once stopped.

Makis opened his eyes, straightened himself in his seat,
and saw the dull light of the window next to him. It's
dawn, he realized . . .

Another image rushed lightning fast into his memory,
one quite similar to the present, when about three years ago
he was returning to the island on a plane of the same air-
line. Back then he was returning from Europe as a doctor,
having completed his studies and two years of internship.
It was dawn then, too, as the plane started downward.

This coincidence created in him the singular circum-
stance wherein memory and the present became one.

He concentrated expectantly on the dull window-pane.
Though he could see clearly in his memory the view that
would be unfolding before him, he could not wait to see the
reality again, to touch it, to rediscover every detail, all the
beauty that he cherished in his island.

Very slowly, as in a crystal ball, the fog began to thin,
until it cleared off . . . Behind the perfectly clear surface
now appeared the infinite background shining in the golden
light of dawn . . . Then the light grew brighter and the infinite became dazzling, joyful, spherical, embracing the
azure surface of the sea . . .

Makis concentrated his gaze insistently . . . and all at
once, as if in answer to his summons, a dull stripe appeared
where sky and sea met. He shuddered. And from that moment he was lost in the images that succeeded one another.
He lived a past and present that were raveled together: the
hopeful enthusiasm of his first return and the down-to-
earth feelings of the present one.

Slowly and steadily the dull stripe drew nearer . . . until the shore appeared, washed in sunlight, playing and laughing in the spray.

(Somewhere a crackling sound was heard and behind him a metallic woman's voice announced: the aircraft will land shortly at the Nicosia airport.)

The other views of the island followed successively, with ever-hastening rhythm, sparkling with undefined promises: the first barren mountains, like castles confronting the sea . . . the peaceful, the so ineffably peaceful, plain, its grasses rippling at the touch of the wind . . . the other mountains, with their forests sunk deep in reflection . . . the villages, fastened midplain or on the slopes . . . the town, with buildings twirling, chasing one another as the airplane came down in a rush towards the runway . . . the heavy thud of the touchdown and the final roar of the propellers . . .

The silence that followed pulled him out of his reverie. His mind, as if come in for its own landing, turned to Aunt Merope, who was waiting . . . I have to make up my mind, he thought.

This, after all, was the reason for his trip: to give himself time to think coolly, far from the intrigues of Aunt Merope, uninfluenced by her love and his own feelings for her.

He knew that her interest in getting him settled sprang from her affection, the same affection that had impelled her to underwrite the expenses of his education, which his father, a teacher for thirty years, had been in no position to do. And for that very reason he wanted to get far away, not so much because of her well-intentioned maneuvers and admonitions, but because of her arguments, the knowing way she had of seeing reality and of showing him that his ideas—his illusions, as she would call them—did not go over in our country.

For a while he felt as if he was trapped, vacillating between the invincible logic of Aunt Merope and the values which formed the basis of his life. At times he would admit that, yes, Aunt Merope was right. And at times he would pity himself for sitting around listening to the arguments of the virtuous self-promoters. Have the dreams been lost, then? . . . Our first love during our mission in our freed land, so generously dedicated? . . .

Compelled perhaps by a longing for spiritual renewal, he chose to revisit the places where as a student he had lived with his friends. The beautiful beginning, the promises and the hopes that succeeded the struggling years in high school. And it was good, this journey to meet with his former self.

But there he was, bringing back the same load of uncertainties that he had taken with him when he set out . . . Living the realities of the island for three years had darkened the clarity of his vision.

§

In spite of her humble origins, Merope had for years been well-received at the Mentrinoses, and at other houses, too, which were also considered the distinguished families of the island. (Families which, because of their great fortunes, passed off as profoundly significant the worthless genealogical documents which appropriated and imitated the airs of an authentic aristocracy that never existed in our land.)

Within this circle, Spanides belonged to the best family.

His marriage to Merope, who was a teacher at the time, was regarded as unsuitable, and the "young Mrs. Spanidou" was received in the salons with conspicuous condescension.

But the mere teacher was not disconcerted. Blessed as she was with a sensible head and steady nerves, she charted her course and followed it through without haste and without deviation, assuming from the first moment a position of equality with the aristocratic ladies.

As a consequence of this policy, they were the ones who were disconcerted. They raised their noses high and attempted in every way to put her in her place . . . until they realized that in this subtle war of nerves she was stronger than they, that their vexation was in vain. And so, little by little, their opposition faded; they grew tired of poking fun at the origins of the "young Mrs. Spanidou" and confined themselves to gossiping about "Merope" in the same way they gossiped about everyone else in their circle. This meant that she was regarded thereafter as one of their own.

Now everyone knew how strong-willed Makis's good aunt was and how dexterously she had set her scheme to work to marry her nephew to Tereza, the elder of the   two Mentrinos daughters.

She expected no difficulties from the parents.   She knew that they would count on Makis to be her heir, since she had no children of her own and regarded him as her child.   Spanides, who died relatively young, left her a sizable estate.

In fact, it turned out as she had foreseen.   When in a conversation with Tereza's mother she dropped a word in about her nephew, a serious young man and a brilliant doctor, and about Tereza, who was adorable, Kyria Haricleia did not say anything, but her expression revealed that she understood and took it as a good idea.   And when a few days later she was invited back to the Mentrinos house "for an intimate dinner," she was assured by the couple's particularly friendly gestures and by some half-spoken words that she could approach the two young people.

Where it was necessary to proceed circumspectly was with Tereza, who, as a young woman of the times, would surely bridle at any open indication of an arranged marriage.

And this was true of Makis, too, who seemed not yet to have cast aside the foolishness of youth.   But he did not give her any opportunity to beat about the bush.   He caught on from her first hint.

"Are you set on getting me married off, Aunt Merope?" he said, his eyes flashing with irony.

And they both broke into a wholehearted guffaw.

She liked his unpretentious personality, the candor of his words.   He reminded her of herself before she became accustomed to concealing her thoughts.   These two, who seemed so different, were deep down very similar.   Even in their features they had a definite if indefinable resemblance—the large elderly woman with the look of a peasant in her square, innocent but clever face; and the tall man with broad shoulders and thoughtful expression.

But Aunt Merope's laughter did not last long.

"It's time you thought of your future, Makis," she said seriously.   She waited a spell, but saw that he was not about to reply. He was only looking at her thoughtfully.   She continued.

"Your opinions are praiseworthy, my child.   But how far do you think they will take you in the society we live in?

You are a good doctor specializing in obstetrics, but that alone isn't enough. You also need a good start to develop connections, acquire a prosperous clientele, open a clinic . . . You know better than I what a well-appointed obstetrical clinic costs . . . Or perhaps you prefer to remain a poor, unknown doctor who takes his clientele to clinics belonging to other people . . . Why? To keep your independence perhaps . . . But you can keep your independence more easily, Makis, when you live comfortably."

She fell silent and waited. But he did not say anything this time either. However, her experienced eye observed that her words did not miss their mark.

"Let's make ourselves clear, as you like to, Makis," she said. "I don't suppose that you plan to stay unmarried."

"Of course not."

"Good. What do you think of Tereza, aside from her social position and her fortune?"

"How do I know? . . . from the short time I have known her, she seems a lovable girl."

"I, on the other hand, know her well, and I assure you she is an exceptional girl. But let's leave my opinion out of it. Your opinion is enough for me. Well? . . ."

Makis remained thoughtful for a while.

"That's not the only thing that will motivate a person," he said at last. "There are a great many other considerations: the environment that one lives in, his perception of things, the way he sees life . . . There is also the way an acquaintanceship develops . . . a mutual attraction . . . How shall I put it . . . One does not marry just by . . . calculation."

"You talked about mutual attraction. Right. Without that a marriage is a mistake. But for your part you find Tereza lovable, yes?"

Makis smiled. Yes, he said with a nod of his head.

"Everything else you said," continued Merope, "is both right and wrong. It depends on the circumstances that govern our lives. I don't need to tell you of the circumstances in our country.

She saw him reflecting and sensed that it were best to leave the conversation where it was for the time being.

Except that she added, "Think about it, my child."

That night Makis decided on his trip.

177

He was very busy on the day he returned from his trip. He had to be briefed on the patients he had left in the hands of a colleague; he had to visit some of them and take care of matters that had piled up in his absence. He hadn't time to think about anything else.

But in the evening, when he set out to visit Aunt Merope, he began to reflect on what he would say to her if she questioned him.

But she said not a word on the subject. She only said that the Mentrinos family was inviting him to an informal party at their house the evening after next. It was not the first time.

At the Mentrinos party a very proper boredom prevailed, as usual, founded on the quiet conversations about small details that never touched on the subject lying behind them. Otherwise, the guests, persons of higher qualifications and important positions, knew the art of making you feel comfortable on these occasions by moving on as soon as their importance showed through their good manners.

Makis was flattered in spite of himself when Mr. Pantazaris spoke to him with enough familiarity to say, "I didn't understand a bit of it, my dear fellow."

The discussion had been about the exhibition by the well-known artist Kamberos, which Pantazaris opened officially two days earlier at the Hilton. In his brief remarks he had praised Kamberos's original technique and nonrepresentational art in general, in terms that would be repeated in the morning newspapers.

Klimentis had set the discussion in motion. He had just entered the spacious salon and, when he had greeted people left and right, headed for the corner were Pantazaris, Makis, and Mentrinos were standing.

"Costas, we didn't know that you were so well informed about abstract art and had such high regard for it!" he said with a comical expression of admiration.

Pantazaris then responded to Klimentis's teasing, but addressed himself to Makis as if confessing especially to him.

"It's a shortcoming of mine, I admit it. Eulogies are usually a matter of politeness imposed by one's position. But there are others who, knowing no more than I do, pay high prices for abstract art."

It was known that Mrs. Klimentis, who liked to pass as a modern art fancier, bought a picture from Kamberos's exhibition for her own rich collection.

Makis, who liked art and could appreciate it without bothering with schools and fashions, found Kamberos a good artist in his genre. For a moment he was itching to discuss the subject, to find out whether there was any measure of personal judgment behind the jokes and teasing. But he restrained himself. They'll take me for some pedant who doesn't know anything about good manners, he thought.

Besides, Pantazaris did not give him a chance. He turned to Klimentis and, taking his arm, asked, "How is the high rise going? Are the apartments renting?"

At the same time Aunt Merope came up and took Makis by the hand.

"Come and meet Grandma Tereza," she said.

That was what the circle of intimate friends respectfully and fondly called Mentrinos's ancient mother. And they would enthrone her, always and everywhere, out in front, like a living coat of arms, to remind them of the glory of their position and the good old days. In all other respects, she was a very polite granny who lived the part of great lady with sincerity, perhaps because she was the only one who continued to believe in it with absolute certainty.

Makis felt some displeasure as he followed Aunt Merope for this introduction, which in some way seemed to have taken on a formal character.

The old lady was sunk into her easy chair amid the folds of a knitted cover spread across her knees. She was wearing a beautiful old-fashioned outfit, and her completely white hair had been carefully done.

"I've heard many good things about you, Mr. Karavazis," she said to Makis, extending her thin hand to him. And she looked at him searchingly. In contrast to her pleasant smile, her faded blue eyes recalled the stern gaze of Mentrinos.

Makis was at a loss. What was he to say to her?

But luckily her maid arrived just then to help her up and away. Grandma Tereza rarely appeared in the salon when there was company, and then only for a short time.

The young Tereza, however, did not resemble her father. She was tall and thin, with olive skin and thick, wavy hair and the eyes of a doe, like her mother.

Makis observed her now and then out of the corner of his eye as she chatted or helped Mrs. Mentrinos and Marcella, the younger sister, serve the guests drinks and hors d'oeuvres of various kinds from an overloaded table on wheels. He found her lovable indeed, in spite of the studied woman-of-the-world pose he would occasionally see in her movement and expression.

The relationship between them did not go beyond a formal friendship.

"How was your trip, Mr. Karavazis?" she asked as she was filling his plate.

Her comfortable manner, the abandonment of any trace of pretense, convinced him that she had no idea about the plans of his aunt and her parents.

"Very well, Miss Tereza," he answered, as he watched the movements of her hands. Her hands were very delicate.

Nevertheless, his good mood did not last all evening. How many hours must he struggle to take part in that colorless chatter among people comfortable in their security, their prosperity, and their little round convictions. He was bored. He felt that he was outside the circle and they inside, fenced in, not so much by their wealth or what they called their social position, nor by the personal character, whether good or bad, of each one individually, as by the identical way in which they all looked at life and at themselves in the midst of life.

He had no reason to doubt that they thought highly of him. And hour after hour in this very comfortable climate of life he was willy-nilly joining in their way of thinking, and he had the pleasant feeling that he was on the way up. But once again something awakening in him said no, that he had only been captivated, that he was tumbling downward.

After eleven o'clock that night, when he was returning from the party, his wavering back and forth had ceased of itself. Without even having thought why, he was certain that he could not satisfy Aunt Merope's wish. She was seated next to him now in the car.

They spoke of one thing and another, but never broached the matter in the short distance to her house.

"Good night, Makis," she said as she got out of the car.

"Good night, Aunt Merope."

This discreet manner of hers set him to thinking: how could he tell her his decision without causing her grief? That's all that bothered him right now. She was so good to him.

DISAGREEMENT

The difference between a person's longing to live
better and his longing to be *better is irreconcilable
in a society in which the worst people are ensured
the good things of life.*

Maxim Gorky

WITH THE SHIFT of Public Services to new offices, the
tenor of Phoebus Karelas's life changed. In some way his
spiritual horizons seemed to have broadened after the move
from the barracks of colonial government to the newly-built
complex of the independent republic.

And so he went through a period of high spirits, possessed by feelings that combined change with expectation.
Something like the flavor of new life was bound up with
this spaciousness, the newly-tiled floors, the modern office
furniture, and the big windows with aluminum frames.

It was an interlude that did not last long—only as long
as it took for the everydayness to cover everything with its
haze, long enough for the hallways and bathrooms to lose
their fresh, scrubbed look.

Little by little the feeling of change faded. Life in the
offices returned to what it was before, bearing the seal of
employee indolence, the general indifference towards anything not of personal interest. The only difference was a
spirit of expectation, which for some replaced the old spirit
of subjection and flattery as the way to success.

And Phoebus found himself wavering again between
feelings of superiority, which he thought he should have as
an intellectual, and uncertainty, which he had whether he
would or not. He doubted whether his intellectual interests should support dreams of success different from those
pursued by everyone else. Whether he should look upon
them as so limited by their one and only thought: how to
guarantee themselves a position of comfort and prestige
more advantageous than that of their neighbors. And at the
same time compelled by an unexplainable feeling of inferiority before them, to envy their talent for grasping and ac-

cept their indifference to his literary proficiency as if he were to blame for something.

O.K. for the others. But Mr. Landos?

Mr. Landos was his department head.

When he had begun pursuing his interests in literature, he had been impressed by some of Landos's articles about the new trends in Europe and by his translations of foreign poets, Eliot in particular. Later on Landos stopped appearing in the journals, even though his name was respectfully preserved among those few who were interested and those who pretended to be interested in writing.

When he secured a position in the service and was placed in Landos's department—he had by then become chief—Phoebus was happy in the thought of having the opportunity to be close to his idol and to chat with him. But he found himself instead in the presence of an impeccable, capable official, politely demanding of his associates and sheltered behind the tactful way he had of keeping everyone at a distance. His pallid face and indifferent expression betrayed fatigue and boredom. Phoebus respected him even more. Nevertheless Landos did not respond to Phoebus's attempts to seek out his opinion on this or that literary topic.

He combed his thick hair carefully, tied his tie attentively (at the end of the month he would definitely purchase a wider tie) and set out for the office earlier than usual.

At the corner kiosk he got the morning paper and opened it to the weekly Literary Page. He jumped. Parayalis's column was devoted to his collection of poems, his second, which had been published the previous month. He went and sat down in the first coffee shop on his route
. . .

Though it seemed superficial and spotty, Parayalis's review was quite favorable. With obscure words and unusual figures of speech, he conveyed the impression of thoughtful recognition of talent in the young poet.

He entered the office singing softly.

Niki, Landos's private secretary, who was putting on her lipstick using the mirror in her compact, seemed surprised and smiled at him. Then she uncovered her typewriter and sat down. On the wall next to her hung a photo of Tom Jones the size of a postcard.

Phoebus put the newspaper on his desk deliberately folded open to the Literary Page and got ready to continue examining the duplicates beginning where he had left off the day before.

Soon Mitellides arrived, and after him Kaouros.

They were four all together in the spacious room with the metal desks, cupboards, and file cabinets of various types. The door labeled "Department Chief" was shut, but they knew that Landos had been in his office for a long time.

The coffee man came by, too, and took their orders. Each one was busy with the documents he had in front of him, and Niki was typing when the door opened and Landos came out carrying a large, tightly written sheet of paper, which he handed to Phoebus.

"Please fill in the file numbers where there are references and give it to Niki to type up," he said. Then he turned to Niki.

"I'll be in the director's office," he said and left.

He seemed not to have noticed the Literary Page and the title of the book which Phoebus had inscribed for him only a few days earlier.

Mitellides took a form for soccer wagers out of his drawer and concentrated on filling it out. Kaouros went out to the telephone booth in the hallway. He avoided using the office phone for personal business affairs. Phoebus picked up the Parayalis article and read it again.

§

An hour later, when Landos returned, they were all hunched over their documents again.

Soon a slender young woman came into the room. Without being especially beautiful, she drew attention with her simple, tasteful way of dressing and that confident feminine grace that the easy-living daughters of the aristocracy usually have.

As soon as Phoebus saw her he got up from his chair. She gave his hand a squeeze.

"Thank you, Mr. Karelas, for sending me your book."

Her eye fell upon the Literary Page.

"I also read Parayalis's critique. Very nice."

She turned to Niki and said, "May I see Mr. Landos? Tell him it's Mrs. Miskoundas."

Niki pressed the button on the little device in front of her, leaned over it, and said, "Mrs. Miskoundas."

In a few moments the door opened and Landos came out, a polite smile on his face.

"What a pleasant surprise," he said flatly in greeting. He stepped aside to allow her to go first into his office.

Mrs. Theoloyides-Miskoundas had published, shortly before Phoebus, a deluxe edition of a collection of her own poems. Her marriage, just last year—a brilliant marriage according to the perception of the wealthy—gave her, among other things, the satisfaction of inscribing her book with her double name.

Phoebus found that she had talent, except that she squandered her time socializing and did not apply herself to her poetry as much as she needed to. Moreover, he had learned that the publication of his book had annoyed her, because she regarded it as a rival for the prize. It was well-known that she was eager for her own book to get the prize, and, since she knew many people, she worked to guarantee support from persons whose opinions count in literary circles. They were saying that she had even persuaded Mourides to postpone till next year the publication of a collection of poems that he had ready to go.

Her visit lasted for some time. When she came out, she greeted Phoebus again. Landos saw her as far as the hallway.

Shortly the sound of a departing automobile was heard from under the window.

Phoebus tried to retrieve his good mood, but he could not. Without knowing why, he had even lost interest in continuing the audit. He flipped through the copies, but his mind was wandering. Until it was quitting time.

His house was a twenty minute walk from the office. It was a golden day. But how he would have liked to have a car waiting for him in the Personnel Parking Lot like so many others did! . . . A sports car, two-seated, cherry-red; he preferred dark red! . . . He was walking along in distraction, seeing it in his imagination as others passed him by in their cars.

A SONG FOR AUNT CHRYSTALLOU

My heart is steadfast, O God,
my heart is steadfast.
I will sing and raise a psalm.
David, Psalm 57

BUT YOU, Aunt Chrystallou, preserved the dreams in our hearts.

Not that you were dreamy—anything but. I've seen you dealing sagely with your difficult life, observing people and their deeds without self-deception. But in some way, which was your own secret, that solid wisdom of yours embraced the whole truth—the naked truth of the ordinary and that other truth that speaks in dreams and fairy tales.

You were so small, darling, that anyone not knowing you would think you fragile. But in the same way that the vast song of the cicada comes from so tiny a creature, your own tiny existence radiated all the patience, the unshakable power of our people.

Whenever my restless young soul was oppressed by one or another small torture, I remember finding support in your clear eyes, so unbelievably childlike in the wrinkles that framed them.

You would hear me out attentively as I unwound my emotional nebulae and my exasperations (with life, because it did not keep the promises I imagined that it had made; with people, because they were not the way I expected them to be . . .). You heard me out with humility before all my eloquence and knowledge! You didn't know anything. Nothing but the few great truths which only the heart can comprehend—directly. And you did not imagine that it was precisely these truths I found in your glance, in your determined integrity, in your readiness to forgive our errors without wounding us with a display of long-suffering. You were only sorry for the errors of other people. And you were ashamed of their shamelessness.

In our family circle we youngsters adored you. And the grown-ups loved you, too, but I must admit that their love was touched with a condescension that spoiled it. And there were times when they would fret and stew because you were determined to wear your kerchief and did not appear to be impressed by our lifestyle and our new social position. They imagined that they were better than you. (But were they certain? or was it just that their condescension towards you helped them prop up their conceit?)

And even with their supposedly affectionate teasing they were attempting to show how naive you had always been and therefore how much better they, the brainy ones, were than you.

You would hear them out, nod your head: yes, so it is, and laugh along with them, content to see us enjoying ourselves. But when they made these jokes in front of visitors, you would struggle to conceal your agitation and smile as though you were to blame.

This humility of yours enraged me. It was the only trait of your character that I condemned. To blame for what? Your guilelessness?

In the village old and young still preserve the memory of your goodness. The liveliest memories were kept by the young who were children when their mothers would run to you whenever they needed advice or help. You knew how to calm their hearts and get them through dangerous moments of anger or despair. And you knew the remedies for the children's indispositions and small hurts; bathing blurred eyes with elder medicine, giving them mint tea to drink and applying hot bran plasters when they had the belly-ache, putting on the cupping-glasses followed by a good rubdown with olive-oil when they had caught cold, cleaning wounds with alcohol after giving them a handful of raisins to head off the screams.

(All the mothers in those days knew all that, you'd tell me. Not all. There were also young mothers who got confused and needed help. There were also those who trusted Chrystallou better than themselves. There was always some one of them who would send word or come to find her, dragging the wounded, crying youngster by the hand.)

§

Heaven bless us, we who want to save civilisation. We had better make up our minds what of it we want to save.
D. H. Lawrence, *Aaron's Rod*

When they tried to transplant you from your village to the City, you got scared; you thought for once about yourself and you tried to protect yourself.

Your husband Kyriakos had been dead for years. Your children had resettled, one here, one there. Everyone thought you lived a solitary and indolent life in your empty house. How were they to know that you were as busy as ever and with as many friends, since the flame of your love was such that it did not require the physical presence of loved ones to keep on living. And how were they to know that you were not alone even at night, when, wide awake, you would hold merry converse with the shades of your dead, who would come forth into the small circle of lamp-light and bid you come to them to the sacred ground. And you would smile and wait patiently for your time.

But you ceased thinking of yourself when Kostakis, your oldest son, who was married in the City, said to you that, aside from his concern for your staying by yourself, he needed you at home as well to help your daughter-in-law.

You lived your last years in the City, quite alone in a world that you could not understand; nor did it bother to understand you, wrapped up as it was in wallet-pride and affluence—its new conquests.

Nevertheless, you did not sink into the mire. You put yourself again in touch with the earth, seeing to it that the courtyard in the City house was green. And you poured your overflow of affection upon the chestnut brown head of Kristiana. You had a special weakness for her, perhaps because she was the first of your many grandchildren. Also perhaps because, as a budding young girl now, she strongly resembled the Chrystalla that you once were. And she even had your name.

191

Don't deny that you were hurt when you heard them call her by a new, foreign name. Did they not like the name that mirrored you and the other Chrystallas before you? Without knowing how or why, you felt that a name did not come from nowhere. It has roots. It is laden with memories. Without knowing how or why, you felt that this new practice of casting aside whatever is ours in favor of aping all sorts of imported gimmicks is like not wanting to know where we come from—how, then, are we to know where we are going?

You were not so prudish as to be bothered by the daring attire. You knew that this was not what brought about any fundamental change—the girls of each generation have their own ways of driving the boys crazy. The ones nowadays preferred to cast off the heavy adornments of your era and adorn themselves with their own bodies. This is better. And besides, your little granddaughter was beautiful.

Your uneasiness came from something else, which you could not get straight in your thoughts, but you sensed it behind the foreign-bred foolishness that you saw guiding our life and thought, like something powerful and treacherous, undermining the foundations.

§

My heart decided to sing a song about you and I got carried away and idealized you, as I did once before in my prime.

I forgot my years and my present good sense, which tells me that the perfection we yearn for is not to be found in you or in anyone else.

Nevertheless, even now that I have learned to look soberly at life and at humanity, I sense that you stand above the confusion that we are embroiled in. I sense that your life, like anyone else's, might have had weaknesses and ennuis, yet it stood solidly because it was rooted in something true and necessary and real. It is that foundation of life that we lack. Not the same as yours—life has left that behind— but something like it which springs from yesterday and leads us into tomorrow.

VIGNETTES

1

IN RECENT TIMES the poet would come frequently to our house. Always when the sun was about to set.

He would sit on the veranda to have a cup of coffee and gaze at Pentadactylos. He loved Pentadactylos. He made much of it, especially when it rose silent and powerful in the purple dusk.

He was very tired, disappointed I would have said, if I hadn't known that all that was trifling and false around us wounded him but did not shatter the foundations of his life and work. And it was one of the beauties of his spiritual courage that he found support in the small joys of life—such as those peaceful hours on the veranda—and saw them as a poet would for their true value.

"How beautiful, how good life could be in our country!" he said.

In his pained look I saw, like a revelation, a concentrated expression of everything he stored up for us in the forest of his verses.

Time has passed since then. The poet rests in the soil of his country.

But every time I chance to be on the veranda at dusk, I see that look of his abiding there, existing of itself, facing Pentadactylos.

2

He fixed his coffee, and, just as he was, in his pajamas, un-washed, he went out into the courtyard. He sat down on a stool, placed his steaming cup on the threshold step, and lit his first cigarette.

He was always a morning person. He liked this early hour, even when he could sleep well. At that time he would wake up easily and sit weaving dreams that suited the magic of the new day. But now he is not weaving anything. He is just quiet, letting his mind wander in a jumble of reveries and concerns.

The lemon tree was motionless in the dim light. Suddenly the topmost branches turned gold at the touch of the sun's rays coming from behind the roof of the house next door. All at once everything was joyful . . .

And memory called forth the image of Anita . . . She was charmingly serious when she made her severe critique of my lyric verses. She wanted poetry to be deployed for revolution . . . On this point she was in agreement with Stamatis, the dark gypsy, the Bohemian of the group . . . The two of them were completely different people, blond, laughing Anita and sullen Stamatis. But we loved them as if they were an inseparable duo, and we allowed them to be our leaders. We made dreams and found ways to make them real in conversation and song . . . And you, my singer Xanthos, what has become of your guitar and your love for humanity . . .

The cat sidled up quietly, curled up on the ground and remained motionless, her slanted eyes half closed, as if in some unexplainable way she were taking part in his reverie—he seemed to see something of the sort in her green eyes when she turned and looked at him . . .

Later, Stamatis was seized by a mad longing to escape. He would go to the seashore and stand for hours looking at the steamships arrayed out at sea. And afterwards when he came to our gathering, he would sit without saying a word. Until he finally succeeded in saving up his fare and left. One cloudy morning when the sea was dull and the mole reeked of seaweed, carob, and wine . . .

He heard his wife washing, then pottering about the kitchen as she fixed Themoula's milk. And the image of Themoula fluttered into his mind, as if the time would come when she, too, would be defending a poetry deployed for her own ideals . . . He smiled. But the next moment he remembered that above all he must go get her a bed. Themoula is grow-ing up, already more than four years old; she needs to be comfortable when she sleeps . . .

The thought annoyed him that he would have to ask for an advance on his wages. Thoukides would once again go through his usual routine to point out what a great favor he was asking, then play the fatherly man in charge, the skin-flint. But he saw no other way, so he would ask for an ad-vance, indeed today. And he would buy the rose-colored bed with the swallows on it, the one he had noticed the other day with his wife at Houvaris's . . .

3

Come to think of it, whatever happened to Xanthos's guitar, now that he has become a reputable citizen? Do you sup-pose that he remembers—and which chords does memory touch in him?—that he was once the singer in the group? Who can know? Who can know the shadowy roads in the heart of man? Can anyone possibly know what goes on in one's own heart?

You see only that the once slender young man—who used to show so much feeling when he sang and shared the plans closest to his heart, such as we all used to make back then—is this slight gentleman with the little pot belly, short legs, and plump hands, who just went into the church, threw his coin into the candle box, lit his candle, looked at his gold wrist watch out of habit, and took his seat in one of the pews reserved for dignitaries, the one closest to the chanter on the left.

He is wearing an expression of satisfied devotion. And though he is standing on his feet normally, for some reason unknown to me he gives the impression that he is standing on tiptoe in order to appear taller. Every now and then he accompanies the chanter beautifully. This then is his regu-lar place in the pew, I said to myself. And I confirmed it when the time came and he recited the Apostle's Creed as if he were a member of the president's staff whose turn had come to speak.

We came across one another at the exit. Then something happened that I didn't expect. For one split second, quick as lightening, I saw, in his blue eyes and in the way he smiled at me, the Xanthos of old. As if his old smile, forgotten behind his present face, was revealed to me.

4

He sat dazed before the blank paper and tried to concentrate, to find some thread of argument that would enable him to articulate the substance in the nebulae that his future work was coming to. But the persistent buzzing of the fly would not permit him to do so.

Clinging to the glass of the closed window, it struggled, beating its wings, to get through. Outside, a bright sun was calling, and the fly could not understand what was hindering its flight.

Then it stopped trying, walked about here and there on the unaccountably solid surface, rubbed its wings with its two hind legs, then its head with its two front ones, and, finally, stood motionless, as though in reflection—having come to terms with it.

So thought the man, who was watching it and, in some strange way, living out its struggle as if it were a reflection of his own inability to understand the rough edges of reality and come to terms with them.

But within a short time the winged mite took off around the room again and suddenly, with fresh resolution, rushed at the window and collided frightfully against the invisible wall and began once more thrashing its wings with gallant obstinacy.

The man rose, opened the other windowpane and blew on the fly, sending it on outside.

He closed the window and tarried there, looking out wistfully.

5

As the young maid stooped to serve the sweets and coffee on the tray, Kyria Polymnia observed that Father Gervasius's gaze clung hungrily to the girl's ample breast, then drifted probingly downward. . . .

He should be ashamed, thought she in confusion. But the pious smile she wore remained intact.

Kyria Polymnia has defined her role as president of the Philanthropic Society to suit herself and embodies it to perfection. Middle-aged, corpulent, with a small, pale face and double chin, she shows by her way of sighing and raising her eyes to the ceiling that she is gifted with all virtues but one: the capability of reflection, for which she substitutes an enormous capability for virtuous cunning.

Nevertheless, Father Gervasius, who did not care what might be concealed behind Kyria Polymnia's smile, recovered his most reverend expression, ate the sweets and had a swallow of water, after first turning to her to say "cheers!"

Then, drinking his coffee, he informed her of the status of the Vernakidis separation.

But this discussion, although interesting, was only preliminary, as good manners demand.

Madam President was listening, occasionally adding a "tsk . . . tsk . . . tsk" to show how sorry she was, but she was awaiting the moment when the most reverend would speak of that which was the real reason for his visit. It wasn't, after all, his first. For six months now he had come regularly for the same purpose, beating about the bush in the same way, and broaching the topic with the same question.

"What do you think of the Company's latest offer, Kyria Polymnia?"

"Interesting, certainly," she will reply with a small sigh. "But . . . it's so difficult for me to leave my home . . . my comforts . . . I must think about it . . ."

"I understand your feelings. But out of sincere interest for so cherished a parishioner as yourself, I tell you it is an excellent opportunity . . ."

The topic is Kyria Polymnia's house, a one-family dwelling of the old days, with a large courtyard. It happened to be located along the new avenue, a hold-over confined by the many-storied buildings that during the last few years had been altering the appearance of the capital and the meaning of our lives.

From all this turmoil Kyria Polymnia understands one thing only. That from year to year, even from month to month, the house rises in value, imparting to her a greater and greater sense of security.

Father Gervasius's visit will not come to anything today, either. The matter will remain up in the air.

Kyria Polymnia will pretend that she is uncertain, but she will wait for the Company's next offer.

And Father Gervasius will tell the director of the Company—who had assigned him the task of mediator— that "the old lady is a tough nut to crack."

6

In our little place Papadiamantis's words "Little village, big malice" come true.

Without this being the general rule, you will see in many people an unexplainable maliciousness, an unexplainable envy for their neighbors.

Perhaps because we live so close to one another—and the walls of our houses are made of glass—we spend our time spying behind the shutters and cultivating petty rivalries. Until our hearts rot.

And in no few cases the Arabic fable comes true:

There was a good Moslem. And one night of nights there appeared before him an Angel, sent to tell him: "Allah has seen your reverence and to reward you he shall give you whatever you want. But he will give your neighbor the same twice over."

The man was perplexed. What should he ask for? And how valuable will any of God's gifts be if his neighbor gets double the amount?

He fell to his knees and beseeched the Angel to give him until the following night to think about it. And the Angel granted his wish.

The good Moslem thought earnestly and on the next night he was ready. When the Angel appeared, he bowed before him and said, "My request to Allah is that he put out one of my two eyes."

7

Of all the commendatory phrases woven by the party-boss for his audience, Leonis was especially impressed by the one called "Indomitable people!"

And during all this time Leonis listened like one magnetized to the fireworks that shot from the orator's mouth and swung about, lighting like fireflies the glowing strains about progress and prosperity and the demands of the people, meaning the demands of each one of us—and of Leonis, too, naturally.

Every now and then the orator would toss his head back, his eyes open wide, raise his voice even higher, and salute his audience with flattering epithets which made Leonis feel important. And indomitable.

Therefore he was fully satisfied when he left the gathering. Everything smiled at him: the bright spring day, the richly-laden shop windows, the folks circulating about the streets in holiday mood, the thought of the Sunday roast waiting for him at home . . .

How could they not humor him? Work at the shop is going well, land values in the area are rising. And since Leonis is a person highly regarded in business circles, the party-boss considers him important and denies him nothing.

8

The weather was persistently rainy all January. The village was sunk in mud. Then the sky cleared and the drenched plain turned green from end to end.

The only tree in the courtyard, a warped almond, aged before its time, succeeded in scattering some sparse flowers on the few living branches it still had, to sum up conclusively the message of the coming spring.

Old Kosmas made it to the threshold, looked at the smiling sky, the sun-drenched plain, and, with the help of his cane, went with dragging feet to the courtyard door, where he tarried for a moment waiting for Nikolis's tractor to pass. Just at that moment it had emerged from round the corner making a terrific racket.

But when he was in front of the courtyard gate, Nikolis stopped the tractor without shutting off the engine.

Kosmas was amazed every time he saw Nikolis on his tractor wearing that khaki cap with the tall peak. He looked like an attachment on the tractor.

"Good day, neighbor," shouted Nikolis loudly enough to be heard over the roar of the engine.

"Good day to you, too," answered Kosmas indifferently.

Nikolis gestured widely towards the plain.

"Smells like a good year, doesn't it?" he shouted.

"God willing," said Kosmas, and he turned as though annoyed back to the courtyard.

He walked very slowly towards the corner where an old cast-off cabriolet was rotting, its wheels half sunken in the mud.

He stood looking at it. His mind was swamped by his enthusiasm for the promise of the green plains and by his bitterness at not having a share in the harvest. Others were seeding his fields now. And Kosmas, a farmer for so many years, among the best in the village, was only waiting around for the rents.

"Just as well that I didn't listen to him when he told me to sell . . . He will pay off the debt some day . . ." He was talking to himself about his only son, who had talked his father into taking out a mortgage on his property, taken the money, and gone to the City. Now he is an entrepreneur. At least, that's how Kosmas tends to think of him: a gentleman forever busy with one thing or another, in a hurry, talking all the time, dealing with important people. He must be making a lot of money to be spending it so thoughtlessly.

Kosmas did not think that his son was wrong. For hours at a time he would wonder at his capabilities. But, then, to show such indifference for his land!—that was more than Kosmas could fathom.

In the midst of his confusion he could see the cabriolet take on its former beauty. Ah . . . if he could only hitch up Psari, his mare, again . . . and she could move along with that light-footed canter of hers . . . to take him back to his own times!

He cast his dim gaze at the main road beyond, where, there it is! the cabriolet flying along . . . But suddenly the image changed and in place of the cabriolet was the village bus taking the workers to the City, and another bus behind it . . . and behind them, one . . . two . . . more and more cars . . .

"How are we going to make it, Psari? The cars will trample us under," Kosmas said to himself and laughed bitterly.

9

On the way to see the exhibition, he recalled the dead artist's face.

They had joined with a few other friends and admirers of that genuine craftsman and had come up with the idea of the exhibition. And they had made every effort to draw together as many of his pictures as they could, so that his contribution to renovation would be apparent in its totality.

On the night before last he attended the opening over which the minister presided. It was a social event, adorned with eulogies, but unrelated, he thought, to that which impelled them to organize the exhibition.

"Naturally," he said to himself, "the opening has nothing to do with the substance. It's just a social formality, a necessary evil." And he decided to go again today.

As soon as he entered the Hall, he found himself in the atmosphere that he had looked forward to. Aesthetic joy and memories wrapped him up and carried him off . . . until he realized that he was the only one in the Hall. His pleasurable mood vanished, replaced by a bitter taste of desolation.

As he usually did in moments of indisposition, he roamed the city streets aimlessly, and then the outskirts, until without realizing it he was at the Hill of the Archangel. He went as far as the cliff and stood.

Beneath him spread the great croplands, and beyond, in the background, the city, wonderfully shining in the slanting rays of the afternoon sun.

He stood looking at the croplands. The trees planted in straight rows formed a picture of harmony and order that affected him. His mind calmed. Then he noticed, floating out over the city, one . . . two . . . three . . . and more kites.

201

He contemplated the children clinging onto the ends of the strings, their minds swimming up to the sky . . .

"There's still hope," he said. And he felt like Antaeus did when he touched Mother Earth.

10

When the seeker after the ideal was assured that he would find it neither in his friends nor in his adversaries, he retreated into himself.

In the beginning he found a sick pleasure stirring up his disappointment, in pretending that his aloneness was something unique. But for how long? He began to tire of it, to lose the feeling of righteous indignation that put him sweetly to sleep at night.

Now he could remain awake for hours, troubled by a dull nostalgia and sometimes sink into a state somewhere between sleep and wakefulness, living through nightmarish moments.

. . . As if he were walking along the shore of his island. The great sea shone, mirroring the morning rays of the sun. The peaceful plain rose undulant to the apron of the mountain, dimmed in the low-hanging frosts. And above, bathed in light, the green bulk of the mountain peak rose upright.

And as if all this beauty, which at another time enchanted him, were remote from him, and he could only feel everywhere the longed-for yet undesired presence of mankind, all proffering the hand of friendship and at the same time turning their backs on him. And he felt a mute sorrow, as if he were deprived of something without which the beauty of his island was losing all meaning.

His body would become as heavy as lead. His feet would sink deeper and deeper into the thick element that was in some strange way both wet sand and his own self.

Until he was no longer able to get free of it, and he remained rooted there to be torn between the truth that he saw with his eyes and the world of the imagination within him.

But when he awoke, he returned again to his stubborn determination for self-containment and refused to see the meaning of the dream. Even though he understood that in this way he would be tormented without hope of deliverance.

11

I don't know what made me think that I could come to our wooded mountains and find an escape from the racket and stink that are choking us in the cities. Perhaps it was the need for hope.

But when I was up here one Sunday to try to rediscover my old wanderings, I was disappointed. I sat at the edge of the road and laughed bitterly at my noble hopes, watching the hordes of the affluent, who adorn themselves with automobiles the way that savages adorn themselves with beads and feathers, chasing each other as though they were in a hurry to get somewhere, choking with their dust both the pines and my soul.

For a moment I heard from the depths of a ravine the cackling of a partridge. It seemed to me a cry of hopelessness emerging from the inmost reaches of the mountain.

The next moment a bus load of young voices and song came around the bend in the road. It parked near me at the brow of the ravine and discharged a colorful and noisy mob of boys and girls.

Perhaps it was a refreshing presence, but it did not touch me or put aside my bad mood or my critical attitude towards whatever I saw as the triflings of youth: the crazy dress, the careless manners that looked to me like rejection and nothing more.

I was about to get up and leave when I spotted Kristiana among them. She saw me, too, and came cheerfully running over to me. She was lovely in her wide, mottled slacks, red vest, and brown hair blowing in the wind.

I loved this child. And I knew that I was her favorite uncle. But of late I had been in a quandary: how much had I created for her to think about when she was young so that she could form her own opinions, and why was I unable to understand now what she thought about by herself without considering my opinion? It was as if I were on one shore and she on the other with the rest of the children of her era, following paths that had no meaning for me.

She was excited and in a hurry.

"We're taking a walk in the woods as far as the waterfall," she said. And she ran back to her group.

Without my knowing it some of her high spirits rubbed off onto me.

I was watching now in a different mood as the swarm of youngsters scattered and moved off triumphantly through the woods, boys and girls mixed together, running around and hooting, some couples arm in arm. . . .

As Kristiana moved further off, she turned and waved goodbye, her hand raised high.

I don't know why her greeting brought to mind her grandmother, whom she resembled so much, in spite of the change in name and much else. It was as though Aunt Chrystallou's wisdom had blown across my mind, dissolving doubts and fears—wisdom straight from the heart.

How, I thought, do you expect children to sit obediently in the cage where their parents are settled and complacent. How do you expect them not to obey the drives that compel them first to break through the iron gates?

From the other slope I again heard the partridge cackling. This time it was a message of hope coming from the revolutionary new generation.

TIMES OF SUFFERING

FRENZY

ON MY WAY to work yesterday morning I stopped by Thomas's kiosk, as I did every morning, to pick up my newspaper and to ask my usual question.

"What's new, Kyr Thomas?"

Thomas had his own way of looking at the news of the day. A genuine common person, good-hearted but full of cunning, he had seen much in his sixty years, the last twenty moored at this neighborhood kiosk at the edge of Nicosia on the Famagusta road. We, his neighbors and regular customers, used to call him the station master, because buses and taxis on the Famagusta line would regularly stop here at his kiosk to pick up their last riders, if there were any.

He had his own way, too, of commenting on the news. Realistic and practical, this almost unlettered man noted the actualities behind the frenetic and contradictory headlines and commented on them with a humor that left nothing unscathed.

But recently Thomas's spontaneous humor had taken on a tragicomic tone. It is the only way left for him to comment, without making a liar of himself, on the news that pummeled us like a hurricane and drowned us—along with the bombing raids—on the news that drowns us even today in the abyss of pain and uncertainty in which we find ourselves, with the Turkish invader lurking but a short distance from our neighborhood behind his lines, which divide our island in two.

Yesterday morning, then, when I picked up my newspaper and asked him my usual question, Thomas looked at me sadly and pointed out with his glance a woman standing next to his kiosk where the passengers to Famagusta used to stand.

"See her?" he said. "She's been waiting there for two hours now."

I had not noticed her because she was standing not on the curb, but almost in the middle of the street. She stood there unnaturally still. From where I was I could not see her face, but only her back. Her tall, slender frame, the cut of her gray hair, the suit she wore, untidy but of good quality, the black leather purse she held all revealed that she belonged to a prosperous family.

"She's waiting for a taxi for Famagusta," continued Thomas.

I shuddered.

"For Famagusta?"

"Yes. At first, when she had waited for some time for nothing, she came and asked me why the taxis were so late. I thought she was kidding. But when I noticed the look on her face, I knew that she was not all there. ' There is no taxi to Famagusta any more, ma'am,' I said to her. 'How can that be? ' she said to me. 'I've taken the taxi from here many times. I must go home, sir. How am I supposed to get there, walk? . . .' I tried to explain, but she wouldn't listen. She stands there and waits just as you see her."

At that moment a car came speeding down the road. The driver honked at her to move aside. The woman did not stir from her place, but only started to raise her hand to signal him to stop. Either because he did not realize her intent or because he was not disposed to stop for her, the driver swerved suddenly to keep from hitting her and continued on his way.

Her hand stopped in mid-motion, then lowered. She indicated her impatience with a shrug of the shoulders and resumed her motionless posture.

"She's liable to get hit by some car," said Thomas.

"You had better phone the police," I said. "She's probably staying with some friend or relative and they'll be looking for her by now."

I left without turning to look at her face. For some reason I imagined that my curiosity would offend her.

November 1974

PERSEVERANCE

WITH HIS STAFF under his left arm as a prop, old Zenios the shepherd was standing and watching the child who was running up the slope.

The dog next to him looked now towards the child, now at the shepherd as if he were looking for an explanation for the unusual presence of the child. The animal was jumpy anyway from the number of unusual occurrences today: the thunderclaps, heard for the first time in the middle of summer under a perfectly clear sky; the unexplained rattling sound that broke out time after time from the reaches of Pentadactylos; the screaming birds that sliced through the sky pitilessly; the hubbub that came from the village; and now the child running in mid-afternoon, when everything should be quiet and sleepy. And, not being able to take any more of it, he lifted his head, stretched out his neck, and let out a howl.

"Sh!" ordered the shepherd.

The dog looked sullen, lay down, and buried his muzzle between his forelegs, glancing sidelong at his master.

"*Pappou!* . . . *pappou!*" called the child as he came running.

The dog wagged his tail, sweeping the ground, seeming to recognize a good sign in this familiar voice.

"What is it, lad?" asked the old man.

The child now stood in front of him.

"They're leaving, *pappou* . . . they're leaving . . . the whole village. Uncle Pieros came in the car to get us, too . . . Mother said you should come . . . we're waiting . . . before the Turks arrive, she says . . ." said the child, catching his breath, then started playing with the dog, who had gotten up.

The old man stood looking towards the village. He was struggling to put his thoughts into a semblance of order, to find some reason for all this, but he could not. He turned and looked at his flock. Forty ewes, all resting in a group, hunkering down under the heat, with their muzzles touching the ground, and one ram with curving horns.

"I'm staying here," he said, without taking his eyes off the herd.

"The Turks will come, *pappou*," said the child.

"And then? . . . So what? . . ." said the old man, but he was not confident. In his mind the word Turk now meant something else than the Turks from his village. It meant something coming from far away, loaded with dark and murky fears.

"Have we perhaps annoyed the Turks?" he added to calm himself.

He turned and placed his hand on the child's head.

"Go on now", he said; "they'll be waiting for you. Tell them I'm staying. What would I do with these animals? And why would the Turks harm me? . . . You go ahead, and God be with you."

The child ran down the hill towards the village. The dog followed him a ways, then came back. But he soon jumped up, bristling, and began growling as he looked at the opposite slope of the mountain, where some creeping monsters were rumbling towards the village amid great racket, raising clouds of dust.

The old shepherd cried out a signal, whirled his staff and moved towards the folds before his usual time. With the help of his dog he whistled the reluctant herd into motion.

He brought them down behind the tableland and put them in a dry riverbed, leaving them to graze under cover until evening, when he would pen them up. His pens were on the next rise; a bit beyond them were Halil's pens.

He sat down on the ground. His mind was wind-driven on a sea of confusion. And he felt that this whole peaceful land, his land—himself—was wind-driven on the same sea, with him and within him, as if it were a place inseparable from himself.

The sun was about to set when the bells of Halil's arriving herd jarred him from his thoughts.

He got up. It was quiet now. Everything seemed peaceful. Nothing distinguished this pleasant evening from so many others. Zenios calmed down. It was like a bad dream and it passed.

Soon the bells of his own herd were responding to those of Halil's herd to perform the age-old and always new melody of the Cypriot evening.

In the summer, when they penned the sheep high in the foothills of the mountain range, Zenios and Halil had always had an agreement that one would spend the night in the village and the other would guard the neighboring pens alone.

Tonight Halil decided to go to the village.

"You had better stay up here," he said to Zenios, "till I go see what's happening. I'll send my son Naim to tell you the news and bring you bread."

"I have bread."

"For good or ill I'll send you some anyway," said Halil. He seemed uneasy.

Naim arrived late at night. He was not bringing any bread. He only said, "My father sent me to tell you not to go out to the pasture until he gets here." He spoke quickly and left.

Zenios noted that when he arrived and now as he was leaving, his steps were scarcely to be heard. That meant he was traveling with great caution.

Near sunup Halil returned, dejected, to bring bread and news: the Turkish army had entered the village. The Christians had got out in time, except for old Christophas, who had to look after his old bedridden wife.

The two of them sat on the parapet. Halil remained for a long time bowed and silent, puffing forcefully on his cigarette. Then he reached over and put his hand on Zenios's knee.

"You should stay up here," he said. "Your people have left . . . And we'll watch the flocks together."

He sat bent over a while longer, then added, "The infidels are ransacking your houses."

211

They watched their flocks together for three days, wrapped in uncertainty. Zenios was frightened after all that he heard had taken place in his village and in the neighboring villages; Halil was uneasy to the point that, on the third night during their conversation on the parapet, he said:

"Zenios, you'd better shift over to the other side until things calm down. It keeps getting worse here. Yesterday we learned that they arrested Agapios and took his herd away from him."

Zenios had already made up his mind.

The next night he wrapped the bell clappers in rags so they couldn't be heard, and set out.

"Till we meet again, Halil," he said to his friend, crossing himself.

"Safe trip," answered Halil.

§

In the calm August night under the dim light of the stars trembling there on high, the herd moved in unbelievable silence, like a company of ghosts, bleached of color.

Only occasionally, when the leader chanced to stray, did Zenios make hushed reproaches and strike his staff to the ground, but only enough to restore order to the march.

The dog, who was afraid, slunk along with its tail between its legs and replied with a choked, scarcely audible bark to the barks of other dogs challenging from afar.

Zenios had been informed by Naim regarding the positions occupied by the Turkish army and accordingly planned his route, which would proceed southward, in a way that would lead for the most part through lowlands that would afford protection, first in the dry riverbed of Phylerkos until it drew close to Kythrea, and afterwards, when he would have passed Tymbou in the dry bed of the Yalias as far as Dali, out of the Turkish-held areas. Only in one stretch, from where he would leave Kythrea and pick up the Yalias, would he be forced to cross an open field and run a greater risk. He planned to do that stretch before the moon came out. Then he reckoned that by daylight he would be in Dali.

He walked at his usual loping pace, which had measured off this land so many, many times. It was as if he were find-

212

ing again in each step the traces of his countless earlier footprints binding him to his roots.

Without making a detailed reckoning, without clearly defined bitterness or fear, he was calmly sorrowful and at the same time wide awake, eyes and ears alert, to search out the darkness that lurked about him.

His ageless soul was communing without words with the ground he walked upon, with the isolated, uncultivated trees that emerged dimly here and there, raising their gnarled arms like outcries behind the embankment; with the aroma of thyme; with the mystical whispers of the night—and he felt them all to be as he was himself, sorrowful but steadfast.

But when he was in the field, exposed, and he needed to be even more careful, he put aside his introspection and grief. He set his mind to one matter alone: how to protect his possessions and his own life; how to lay out a route far from any place where there was so much as a hint of danger.

As he had reckoned, the light of the moon found him in the dry bed of the Yalias, leaving behind him along the way the places held by the Turks. The tension in his mind eased; he did not pick up the bitter thoughts again. Now he was moving along lightheartedly and took to studying the lands around Dali, those he knew to be good for pasture, weighing the ups and downs of each.

He arrived in Dali at dawn.

He rested his flock under the bridge so they would be in the shade when the sun came out; then he stretched out on the ground with his *vourka* for a pillow.

Both he and his animals needed a rest.

UNCERTAINTY

TWO MONTHS is a short time. But it can also be an infinity. It all depends on what you've *lived* through during that time.

For Paraschos the span of time that separates that ill-fated day in July and now, the end of September, is an abyss.

On the far side of the abyss he was a young man with a heart of gold, as his friends would confirm. Now, on this side, he is a tormented foot-soldier, who has, in place of a heart, a knot of powerless rage, and he troops through the fields where thousands of homeless islanders are scattered and asks for his family—whether anyone has seen them.

The island stopped being sunny. The fields stopped being redolent of the peaceful human labor that had made Paraschos's heart golden and impelled him to take his guitar down from its hook.

Now and then, willy-nilly, he recalls wistfully those songs with his friends. But instead of bringing him peace, he is tyrannized even more. A bitter mockery breaks forth from within, and he wants to spew out whatever reminds him of kindness. He wants to hate only to hate, without being sure whom—the villains who set this evil business afoot? . . . the Turk, who brought on the calamity? . . . whom? . . . There are moments when he wants to hate himself.

Until the day he ran into old Zenios, the shepherd, his fellow villager, whom he found sitting under a crab apple tree. His flock was grazing beyond. When he spotted Paraschos, he got up, looking at him as though he were expecting him.

"My parents?" asked Paraschos.

215

"They stayed in the village. Your mother was sick in bed. How could the old man leave her alone?"

"Have you heard any thing about Vathoula?" asked Paraschos, his heart in his mouth.

The old man bowed his head.

"She and her mother were on their way to Anoyia. They were caught there. They didn't get out in time," he said, in the way he would speak of a calamity . . .

"I have a message for you," he said after a pause.

"From who?" asked Paraschos.

"From Naim."

"?!"

"He said to tell you when I saw you that he wanted to see you, but that no one else should hear of it."

Paraschos said nothing.

"He said to tell you," continued the old man, "that if you want to, too, go some night to Ai Lias and light a fire, and on the next night at eleven you would meet at the rock of Farangas."

Paraschos was shaken. Without wishing it, a wave of tenderness engulfed him.

"He said you were not to tell anyone . . ." repeated the old man, and, as if finding his mission completed, he sat back down under the crab tree.

Paraschos stood there with his head bowed searching his memory for the time that he played war games with the other village children, roaming the mountain-side and the gullies. It was part of the game for two or three of them to climb way up the slope through rough places to get to the peak, where the chapel of Ai Lias was located, there to light a fire to inform their comrades that pirate ships had appeared and were approaching. Whereupon all of them together would commence fighting a great war with wooden guns and swords in defense of their country. Naim and two other Turkish children were among them.

Now the peak of Ai Lias lies on this side of, and the rock of Farangas on, the line that separates us from the places that the Turkish invading army overran.

Since then Paraschos and Naim had been friends. But now? . . . What intentions does Naim have now? . . . Do you suppose he is setting a trap for me? . . .

§

He went into the night with great caution. As he approached the rock of Farangas, he was bothered by the thought that what he was doing was crazy—but that thought was dismissed by the same determination that spurred him yesterday to come up to Ai Lias and light the fire.

It was a starry night, one of those pensive, honey-sweet nights that make it seem that pain on earth did not exist. But its magic did not touch Paraschos. It did not break through the barrier of expectation and suspicion that knotted around him.

When finally the familiar hulk of the rock appeared in the silver light, Paraschos hit the ground face first, took out his pistol, and crept along the gully to the edge of the slope, where he took cover behind an outcrop. He stayed there for a while listening attentively to the silence. Then he called softly.

"Naim."

"Is that you, Paraschos?" came the voice of Naim.

"It's me . . . Are you alone? . . ."

"Yes . . . You? . . ."

"I'm alone," answered Paraschos.

Soon he saw Naim emerge from behind a rock, take three steps, hesitate, stop . . . He held something in his left arm, hugging it to him like a baby, but Paraschos could not make out what it was. In his other hand he, too, was carrying a pistol.

Paraschos got up, went forward a few paces, but his suspicions held him back. He stopped, holding the pistol out in front of him, searching the flanks of the ravine behind Naim.

The other dropped the object he had been carrying. Paraschos recognized the guitar from the sound it made when it struck the ground. He let down the hand holding the pistol, but raised it again when Naim shouted angrily.

"You came armed? . . . You came here to kill me? . . . Good thing I suspected it . . ."

217

He jumped back again behind the rock.

"Move back, *giaour*, before I shoot!" he shouted.

Paraschos was back hiding again already in his previous spot. A rage took possession of him.

"Dog!" he shouted.

As if he found relief in this curse, he began thinking more coolly. He knew he was in a difficult position, isolated here in the middle. Even if Naim was indeed alone, the first pistol shots would surely bring the Turks running and they would catch him like a rat in a trap.

He crept back a good distance, got on his feet and left at a swift pace.

He had a mad desire to cry. But instead of crying he laughed scornfully.

PERSEVERANCE II

STYLLIS made the beginning.

He went one morning to Skala, and when he returned at noon he brought with him, loaded on the bus, four joists and a few boards. In his basket he had a saw, an adze, and a sackful of nails. He got off at the point of the public highway, which had become the bus stop for the encampment, removed his freight, and spent the rest of the day getting it piece by piece over to the encampment and piling it next to his tent.

To those who wanted to know he said that he was going to put up a coffee shop.

"A coffee shop?" They were surprised.

"Certainly. A coffee shop. I'm a cafe-keeper. What do you expect me to put up, a factory?"

Some of them liked the idea. It was something they really missed amid so many other deprivations.

"You *were* a cafe-keeper, Styllis," said old Toumazos bitterly. "But now you're a refugee. That is to say, nothing."

From the day that they had abandoned the village, old Toumazos scarcely ever opened his mouth. Previously an affable householder, he had shut himself up in a heartrending silence. For that reason the words he had just uttered set the others to thinking. Maybe he is right, they said to themselves.

But Styllis recovered first.

"Even as refugees we're still human beings, Uncle Toumazos," he said. "I'll set it up as best I can. And you should come to pass the time."

Old Toumazos did not reply. He left, dragging his step.

Within three days Styllis and two others, who offered to help, set up a vine-arbor, covered it with leafy branches which they had cut from the acacias, and fixed up some benches and four small tables.

Then Styllis struggled for hours till he succeeded in writing the word *Kafeneion* in blue letters on a long, narrow piece of board, which he then nailed to one of the struts of the arbor.

We can say, then, that Styllis was first to set an example, though such a thought never even crossed his mind. But if we want to be accurate with respect to examples, we must first mention the women, who, just like that, succeeded in setting up housekeeping in their tents, decorating the outsides with flowers and basil in tin cans. They were urged on by the need to water them to keep their spirits high.

At the same time the younger set got to their feet. They came and went, filled out applications, procured materials, set to work, and succeeded in putting up a barracks with a wide doorway but no door. On the lintel they affixed a wooden sign with the words "Youth Club" flowing in sea-green letters.

Then came Milia's turn.

Her brother Lambrianos was not in on this since he was getting ready to leave.

Old Toumazos, her father, had no objections.

"Do as you please, daughter," he said tiredly. "But what's the use of the sign? Everyone in the camp knows which tent is ours. And as for the girls, they're here gathered around you most of the time."

But the girls saw the matter differently, and an inexplicable fire played about their wits, which had been dimmed for so long. *Certainly* they needed the sign. Not in order to point out which was Milia's tent (not even in the village was the sign there to point out which house was Milia's and to declare her trade, as was the case for the signs on every store on the streets of the City). The sign would have a different meaning here, just as it did in the village. But here the meaning would be broader, to say that Milia, our own Milia, who had once decided to go to the City to learn the trade, was the first to become a hair-dresser in the village, and has now decided to take up her work again amidst the refugees.

That's about how the girls felt about it, and they naturally called on Andros to paint the new sign since he had
been so successful with the beautiful sign for the Youth
Club.

So now there was this oblong board with the words
"Milia's Beauty Shop" nailed to a tall pole hammered into
the ground next to the tent. It became a flag that unfolded
and flapped in the winds of adversity in its resolution to
shout out with seagreen letters on orange background that,
no, we are not giving up.

The girls also remembered their right to look after their
beauty. A detail, surely not small, but nevertheless a detail.

Souls began a revival, shaking off day by day the afflic-
tions that held them face to the ground, rising up and moving slowly up the slope. But there were also those unable to
do that, who remained crippled, gazing at their losses.

But when they mentioned the wedding reception, Old
Toumazos emerged briefly from his passive state.

"What do you want with a party, son, in the mess we are
in. And what about the bride's family. The brother is missing. No one knows whether he's dead or not or where he is
if he's alive . . . You should be bride and groom leaving for a
foreign land, to go seek a livelihood in Australia . . . A wedding party means a joyful party . . . Where do you see joy?"

Lambrianos tried to explain.

"It isn't for amusement that we have the party, father,
even though, come to think of it, I'd like my wedding with
Anna to be joyful, too. We want the party because it's the
custom, call it a complement of the ceremony. Let it be a
send-off, since we're going away."

The old man shut himself up again.

"O.K., my son, do as you see fit."

And so the wedding party was set up in Styllis's coffee
shop. Those invited were those who wished to come, as
long as they were all fellow villagers in the encampment.

They came from all the tents and brought whatever they
had available to sit on and whatever they had for food.

Gradually, with the help of the little drink provided by
the groom, they alleviated their worries by singing, their
mood a mixture of joy and grief. There was a trace of a

smile even on the lips of Old Toumazos when he lifted his glass for a toast. He drank his wine, wiped his mustache with the palm of his hand, and then rubbed his wrinkled forehead as if to erase his worries.

§

Lambrianos and Milia were at last alone in the tent.

The father had gone out to sit, as he often did, at the overlook on the far edge of the encampment. There he would gaze for hours out over the fields of his village, embrace the soil, which were turning green after the heavy rains, and inhale the aroma of the freshly watered earth. Those heavy rains, which fell this year like a mockery after two years of drought, made his pain even more unbearable.

Milia was sitting outside on the bench with two friends. They were amusing themselves by throwing crumbs to the pigeons, which came up close, pecked at the crumbs, and danced in tiny little steps. When Lambrianos came, he greeted them with a "hello, girls" and went into the tent with no further remark—the girls understood. They exchanged meaningful glances with Milia and left.

At this hour of the afternoon the tent was still a beauty salon, furnished with a chair and a mirror upon a small, narrow table piled with scissors, combs, and a variety of small bottles. The three mattresses, rolled up in a line in the corner and covered with a throw, was the couch.

They sat down on this couch. Lambrianos was quiet for a while; then he lit a cigarette.

"Milia, I'm thinking about your staying by yourself with the old man in his present state," he finally said. "Be patient until I can get on my feet. I won't forget either of you."

With no intentions of doing so, Milia had been nursing a secret bitterness recently about her brother's departure. She struggled to resist it, to see that Lambrianos's decision to marry and emigrate was not his own wish. He had been engaged to Anna for two years. And one of Anna's uncles, well established in Australia, had written to invite them to join him as soon as he had learned of the catastrophe. It was sensible, then, she said to herself, to accept the invitation. Otherwise, what would they do to make a living.

Nevertheless, she did not succeed in dismissing her bitterness. She was not even able to feel joy at her brother's wedding. The best she could do was to show a happy face. And now she sat hunched over, silent, struggling. What was she to tell him that would not offend him?

"Father's condition troubles me," she said at last. "How long can he go on like that, saying not a word all day long and talking in his sleep all night."

"I'm asking you to hang on, Milia," said Lambrianos.

Milia did not answer.

Then her ear suddenly caught a strange sound, something like a sob, coming from Labrianos's throat. She raised her head and saw his pale, drawn features, waiting. Her bitterness immediately dissolved. Her other self stood resolutely tall.

"I'll make it, Lambrianos; you can count on it. I must. We must all make it," she said, looking at him with a courageous smile.

Lambrianos's face lit up.

They spoke no more about the matter. They knew there was no need to. They only lived the moment, one of those moments of determination, which without our wanting it or realizing it, abides rooted within us.

SOCIAL GATHERING

FOR THE ENTIRE past week the trial gave the newspapers daily opportunity to attract the attention of the public with gigantic headlines and sensational coverage. It became the chief topic of conversation in the salons. The social position of the murder victim and the accused, their lavish lifestyles, the rumors of great excess that would be uncovered to the discredit of the defendant, and especially the savage way in which the crime was committed, the horrifying—heartrending to many sensitive souls—details reported by the coroner displaced the normal subjects and spurred discussions to fever pitch, an agreeable fever, I might say.

Of course, there were those in the world of the salons who were not carried away by this or any other current, those who were unconcerned with anything but their personal prosperity in its tender correlation with the prosperity of their offspring.

Mrs. Fouskalidou, for example, was concerned these days with her ten-year-old daughter's recent success in the recital at the Sylvia Ballet School. She was eager to talk about this subject, and, aware of the manner in which proper social conversation proceeded, she awaited the opportune moment. But when she realized that the general discussion tonight, too, would be revolving around the trial, she artfully cornered Mrs. Koumbi and Tolis and initiated a private conversation with them, by posing the question of which school of ballet was best nowadays, that is, the most aristocratic and expensive.

"Sylvia's, unquestionably," opined Tolis, adjusting the knot of his violet tie with two fingers of his left hand, a gesture he frequently made. And the way he did it with his white, well-groomed hand, adorned with a solid gold wristwatch and a heavy ring, also gold, of course, on his middle finger, revealed an almost feminine coquettishness.

Young Tolis was the great worry of his wealthy father, who could not manage to put him on the straight path—that is, the path of his own business concerns—and saw young Tolis preferring women companions. On the other hand, his mother took pride in watching him excel in the salons with his fine clothing, his aristocratic impudence, and his authoritative knowledge of everything related to art.

"My dear Tolis, I'm glad we are of the same opinion," said Mrs. Fouskalidou. "My daughter Vouvoula also goes there. And you should see how she has progressed in only a year! The day before yesterday at the school recital she impressed them all . . ."

"She's certainly charming, your daughter," Mrs. Koumbi hastened to say, who could stand neither Mrs. Fouskalidou nor her daughter.

And to change the subject, she interjected, as if just then noticing, "Well, look at that! Erasmia wearing the same orange outfit she had on at the Kareklarides party, the day before yesterday!" She pointed with her glance at Mrs. Velonidou, who was seated a bit farther down with another small group next to the decorative marble fireplace. Just then she was reaching for a martini from a tray borne about like the Holy Gifts by a waiter in white coat and black bow tie.

Mrs. Velonidou held one of the foremost places among the ladies who "knew how to dress" and regarded it as a matter of personal pride not to appear more than four times—and never twice successively—in the same outfit. But it was well known that she had decided to disregard this important principle to show that she was a participant in the Cyprus drama and in the measures of frugality imposed by circumstances. (Her consolation on this occasion was that the orange proved to match perfectly with her brown hair, the wheat color of her skin, and her green eyes.)

Taking the cue from Mrs. Velonidou's decision, Mrs. Koumbi would praise her noble sentiments, especially when speaking with people who would convey her words to Erasmia. Naturally, she had her reasons: the magnate Velonides kept close relationships with English businesses and banks. His adversaries here in the marketplace regarded him as a powerful and dangerous rival and let off their steam by laughing at his weakness for—and his *blind* trust in, they would add with a grin—his charming wife, who was much younger than he. It is on her intervention that Mrs. Koumbi rested her hopes of obtaining references from Velonides that would be useful in securing work for her son in London, where he now was, having completed three years of studies at the Norman School of Economics and Management. That was Mrs. Koumbi's great concern, her agony I should say: that her Dimis find work in London, to escape having to return to Cyprus, where the child would be obliged to do military service when it was so unstable and dangerous in today's circumstances.

Those by the fireplace talked about the latest car models in general and the beautiful and powerful new Jarry in particular. Mr. Pitsis recently purchased one to replace his older model, which he traded in.

Mr. Pitsis, a thirty-year-old with athletic build and sunburnt face, had two weaknesses: women and cars. And somehow he brought the two together. His success with women he owed primarily to his personal charm. But his openhanded way of life and especially his lavish care for his automobile contributed to a certain extent. In his worship of the latter he saw to it that he always had the latest, the perfect model, for which he would turn in his previous one, no longer perfect, as we know, after a year or at most two years of use.

After Mrs. Velonidou had drunk her martini in tiny, tiny sips, she stood for a moment, her hand adrift, not sure where to put the empty glass. At that time Mr. Pitsis—who had been standing opposite her, hands akimbo, giving information about the virtues of the new Jarry and at the same time devouring her with his gaze, receiving a smile from time to time as a reward and as a promise—seized the opportunity to move swiftly to her side and take the glass and place it on the marble fireplace, caressing her hand on the sly as he did so.

But Mr. Velonides was not as blind as his sarcastic antagonists thought. He was seated with three of them who exchanged views and information either for mutual advantage or for setting traps for one another. From there he followed with sidelong glances the carrying-on of his wife and Pitsis, and he was getting angry, as is natural for a family man when he sees someone encroaching on his personal property. I am quite certain that something like jealousy was coming over the short, stout fellow, but he did not show it, nor did he appear to notice anything but the subject under discussion.

The subject was whether in today's up-turning economy the construction of new hotel units in the free area of the island offered prospects of investment satisfactory enough to retrieve the capital, or at least some of it, of those who had had the foresight to remove theirs at the first opportunity after the Turkish invasion. Naturally, the discussion was theoretical, and none of the four participants gave the slightest clue that his own capital might be under consideration. Velonides was as usual seated in the depths of an armchair with his short legs scarcely reaching the rug and with his stomach thrusting out. He was smoking his cigar and asserting that he could see the prospects as very good, which made Mr. Tsouriou, one of the four, suspect that Velonides, with these optimistic views of his, was attempting to prod the others to make the experiment so that later he would have surer ground should he decide to do so himself. Tsouriou knew perfectly well that the wily Velonides was not wont to depend upon hypotheses.

The four tycoons had isolated themselves in a corner to discuss their own matters, which they found more interesting than the trial. Not that they were ignoring it or thought it not worth their time to read whatever the morning paper reported about it and comment upon it like everyone else. It was just that, like capable entrepreneurs, they were gifted with a talent for applying whatever thought and passion they had to the pursuit of profit, relegating to the realm of occasional attention whatever else happened around them and chanced to impinge upon their lives.

Since his wife had been set aside in this manner, then, it would be an exaggeration to say that Velonides' pique at her game with Pitsis was very serious. For all his feelings had been engaged in the game he himself was playing with the other three sharks in his group. It was, then, only a fleeting upset that did not reach the point of roiling the tepid feelings of love he had for his own special expensively kept little wife. His sentiments, so householderly, led him, as is natural, to a sense of security, which the malevolence of his rivals chose to see as blindness.

A number of other small groups of this sort, of people who shared interests or were simply disposed to gossip among themselves about the others in attendance, had retreated to various enclaves in the large salon of the Paradakises' house.

The house, a modern single-family dwelling with a large garden, was in the most aristocratic area of the capital, an area which, after the Turkish invasion, was located near the line where the Turks had halted and set up their defense. The Paradakises, as is well known, spent large sums for building, decorating, and furnishing it and had every reason to be proud.

Especially impressive was the great salon with its two crystalline crown-shaped chandeliers, the cherry curtains with golden fringes, the Persian carpets, the ebony furniture with bright tapestries in the uniform old turn of the century style, brought from Italy, and the walls decorated with three expensive modern abstract paintings strikingly out of keeping with the rest of the luxury. The central heating, providing a delightful warmth, completed an atmosphere of fine living, especially appealing because of the storm raging outside just then.

Next to the large salon was a smaller one with green tables. Around one of them three men and two women were seated already, preferring to start right away with a hand of rummy.

But most of the company was in the large salon gathered in a circle around the lady of the house.

Mrs. Paradakis could, at fifty, be a beautiful, attractive woman, if she would consciously highlight what remained of her original beauty, especially her figure, which was still slender and svelte, and if she did not cancel out these charms by her mania for looking young in dress and manners. Her hair, dyed golden brown and tended by the best hair-dresser, her bright *imprimé* dress, which left her thin arms bare to the shoulder, her make-up, applied by the most famous beauty specialist, had an effect opposite to what she thought. It made her look older than her age. Nevertheless, she was quite sure of herself and accepted in her own way her reputation as a very chic lady.

She was sitting with her legs crossed smoking continuously and listening to Phardilis the lawyer explain to the gathering the point made by the foreign expert's statement about the blood spots found on the jacket of the defendant.

"As you see," concluded Mr. Phardilis, "the expert gave convincing proof of his opinion that the bloodstains were fresh, which weakens the defendant's case."

These details about the blood disturbed Mrs. Samaropoulou so much that she took a small box from her purse, removed a small pink pill, and swallowed it down with a draught of orangeade from the glass sitting on the table next to her. For all her stoutness, Mrs. Samaropoulou had very delicate nerves. The pill calmed her down.

"I am curious to see," Mrs. Paradaki said in her rough voice, "what the famous Lipton will say in his defense; they brought him in from London . . ."

"For a princely fee," completed Phardilis.

"Is it proof, then, that the blood ran at the time the murderer struck his victim?" Mrs. Samaropoulou wanted to know about the blood.

But before Phardilis had a chance to answer, Alexis's arrival brought everything to a halt. He entered the salon late as usual, stood at the edge of the circle, mopped the raindrops from his hair with his handkerchief, and, facing his hostess, who was scolding him from across the room with a shake of her head, spread his arms and bowed in appeal for pardon for being late.

Scion of one of the old wealthy families of the land, Alexis found himself, by tradition and acquired habits, in the circles of the mosaic whose desire is to be known as "the beautiful people" and to be presented as a special social group, with no common label of recognition for its membership other than the illusion of exclusiveness which opulence depends on. Most within this mosaic were the nouveaux riches, who looked upon Alexis with that feeling of inferiority mixed with arrogance that all these people feel in the presence of the old establishment. Moreover, they looked at him with the compassion and condescension they would display toward a good but simple child, and agreed that poor old Alexis was a lovable guy. His pale features, the way he looked at you when he spoke, with an expression of trust in his bright, blue-gray eyes, made him likable. But his careless attire, the strange remarks he was wont to make when others were conversing about matters that interest them, justified his label: poor fellow.

"What terrible weather!" said Alexis, as if addressing everyone as well as himself. "And just think of those out there living in tents!"

Mrs. Paradaki raised her eyebrows, but immediately changed her mind.

"Poor people," she said sympathetically.

"Which poor people, then!" Alexis barked. "The refugees? . . . The rest of us, you mean, who are left out of it?" And with a wide sweep of his hand he drew a semicircle in the air indicating the immediate surroundings.

He seemed upset. From the depths of his eyes there darted a gleam at variance with their usual calm.

The others were quiet, thereby signaling their agreement. But the silence soon began to grow heavy. And, besides, what good was it? . . .

"Couldn't the blood have dripped on him later, when he found the corpse, as he says?" Mrs. Samaropoulou wondered again.

"But we said that the expert showed that the blood was *fresh*, that is, still *warm*," answered Phardilis as one would reply to a person who does not understand what is being said.

Alexis moved away. He began wandering about the salon here and there quietly greeting whoever happened to greet him, approaching now one group, now another. But he seemed not to notice what they were saying; he was only absorbed in his own thoughts.

The others were not surprised. They were quite used to his distractions.

231

At one point there appeared before him the waiter with a tray. Alexis took a small glass of cognac, drank it off in one gulp, and smiled at the waiter as he thanked him.

Some time later, when the discussion had turned to cars, the question arose as to when the first cars had come to Cyprus.

"Let's ask Alexis," someone said. "He usually knows such details about the history of the country."

They looked for him, but he had left.

No one could say when.

HIS LAST THOUGHT

HE HAD PLANNED to visit Andros's parents. He saw it as an obligation to them and to the memory of his dead friend. But the days went by and he never got around to going. Since everything they had shared for so long had shattered within him, what was he to say to them? What would he say to Andros's father, who would certainly provoke discussion, as he always did and perhaps even more now, if all the things they say are true about the way he exploded when he learned of his son's death, the way he keeps on celebrating the coup d'etat and cursing those he considers responsible for the unjust killing of his son? Didn't he understand the bitter truth that we were the ones responsible? We, who went out to kill? The others were striking at us in self-defense . . .

But on the other hand, not to go to see them? to forget the years during which he made no distinction between their house and his own? . . . Perhaps Kyr Dimitris does not understand a few things, but after all what did I understand when I was in agreement with him? . . . Even now what would I have understood if I had not taken part . . .

Lambrianos was tortured with this, especially at night. A dark, strong young man, squirming like a worm, sleepless, his thoughts wandering through a mass of disconnected considerations which, wherever they start, would always end up with the same feeling of guilt, striking like a knife . . . An undefined longing was now coming over him for something, he knew not what, that would relieve him of it . . . If he could at least sleep . . .

He felt again that unbearable tension across his mind and along his body, the mad compulsion to scream, checked

233

only by the fear of frightening the others asleep in the house.

Then came the release, the contrition, the desire to cry . . . He remained motionless as he was, lying on his back in bed looking into the darkness . . . He rolled over on his right side, turned on the lamp on his nightstand, and looked at his watch: three a.m. He turned out the light and stayed there on his side until he wearied and slowly sank into a troubled sleep . . .

He dreamed that he was in his military uniform, wearing massive boots, heavy as lead, and, though it was difficult for him to lift his feet, he was trampling upon himself . . .

He awoke disturbed.

The room was flooded with a gentle light shining through the shutters.

He looked at his watch again: a little after six.

He heard his mother pottering about the kitchen and his brother washing and loudly blowing his nose.

He got up, went to the window and opened it. The golden light, the morning freshness eased his troubled mind.

Out over the courtyards and the rooftops of the Nicosia suburb covering the horizon, rose the great eucalyptus tree, an entire evocative world, so familiar to him since childhood, yet so self-sufficient.

He calmed down somewhat, found the will again to put his thoughts in order, to clarify finally to what extent this guilt torturing him was justified. He had been part of a betrayal, a crime, yes, but not willfully. He never even imagined it. On the contrary, he believed that he was heeding the voice of his ideal. Only at the moment when the troubles broke out, and he found himself in the midst of a fray in which kids from his own land who might have been his brothers were killing one another, only then did he wake up to the fact that something dirty had to be behind the whole business. It was a flash of suspicion that stunned his mind and would not be driven out. Nor could he examine it very well amidst the uproar he was in. But the certainties that he had wholeheartedly embraced up till the moment he had set out with his platoon in obedience to orders, in the belief that he was doing his duty, lost the solidity they once had.

234

As if in a nightmare, he carried out orders mechanically, took cover, shot at random, until suddenly everything stopped and he saw his commanding officer strutting around talking about success. He felt nauseated.

He tried to find Andros, who was in the same platoon, but they told him that he had been killed and showed him a human shape on the ground covered with a filthy blanket.

He approached, lifted the edge of the blanket, and looked at the marble face of his friend. A lump in his throat was choking him, but he clenched his teeth stubbornly to keep from breaking into sobs in front of the others.

§

Next came the great catastrophe, the invasion of the Turkish army, which devastated land and people.

Lambrianos went through difficult days, his thoughts tyrannized by questions, his heart riveted by this feeling of guilt—in spite of his finding it unjustifiable during the rare moments when he could think calmly. We allowed our inmost thirst for the ideal to get trapped in the deceptive signals set up for us by those who know the art of proclaiming truths adulterated in a way that strips them of their integrity. They become the counterfeit checks for tricksters to pass so they can succeed in their unacknowledged purposes. And in the hearts of those of us who are without guile, they become the seductions to bring us here where they have brought us . . . He felt his bond with Andros strengthen in another dimension, in which the journey they had shared till his death now took on a suggestion of complicity.

As he was getting dressed, he decided today was the day to see Andros's parents. The decision to do so had matured unexpectedly in his mind and he stopped wavering about it.

§

His heart jumped as he came upon the lane on the far side of his neighborhood, the stone house, its tile roof, its shutters painted indigo, the palm tree in the courtyard . . . How many memories, Lord! from our childhood, and then our school years—study, scandals, dreams, long-range plans, secret meetings and missions, from the time of the uprising, with the gripping sensation of danger . . . and Andros's presence living everywhere . . .

Kyria Panayota was sweeping the courtyard.

She was astonished to see Lambrianos. She dropped the broom, spread her arms, and kissed him. But she did not utter a word. She was choking. Only a silent wail arose within.

Lambrianos was at a loss. What could he say to her? What could there be other than empty words before this pain? . . . He remained looking at her until she recovered somewhat.

"Come inside, Lambrianos," she said quietly and went staggering into the house as though she were dizzy. Lambrianos followed her.

When they reached the hall, Kyria Panayota called, "Dimitris, Lambrianos is here."

Almost immediately a door opened and a tall, solid, heavy man appeared. He was younger than his wife, around fifty.

Harshness was chiseled on his face as he looked with fixed gaze upon Lambrianos, causing him to wonder what Kyr Dimitris could possibly have against him. But this lasted for only a moment. Then his face softened, took on an expression of controlled grief, and he shook hands with Lambrianos.

They sat around the small table, and when Kyr Dimitris had lit a cigarette and took a first long draw on it, he said:

"So they succeeded in killing your friend, the villains."

Lambrianos did not answer, but, then, the other was not expecting an answer. With a jerk he knocked off the cigarette ash and continued angrily:

"They murdered my son . . . Why? . . . I'll tell you why: because he was a pure patriot. Your patriotism, your adherence to national ideals, that was your crime."

Our crime was something else, thought Lambrianos, but he did not speak. How could he array the thoughts that tormented him against the outburst of a blindly embittered man?

"They were not happy with going their own way and throwing the contest; they got to the point of killing us . . . But now that their star has set, the ones responsible must be sought out and punished . . ."

He continued to talk with greater and greater passion, beating against "enemies of the nation and criminals," but Lambrianos stopped paying any attention to his words. He had heard them often before. Except that now he realized that this enraged man was not getting words from within himself; he was parroting what others told him. Nevertheless, although he had come prepared for it, the fact that Kyr Dimitris's opinion and biases had not changed in any respect seemed strange to him. Strange that he had understood nothing, that he put the responsibility for all the suffering right where he was now putting the responsibility for his son's death and the country's catastrophe—on those same people whom in a vague, authoritative way he labeled as "enemies of the nation!" . . . But it may be that the need he has to reduce his pain has now exaggerated his biases, so that he is whipped about by his madness and breaks into prolonged utterances of it. Consequently, he is whipped about by it even more, so that he willingly commits himself to these two mutually supportive drives, finding a kind of escape in them . . . Be that as it may, an impassable desert now separates us, concluded Lambrianos.

Kyria Panayota was seated leaning forward with her distorted arthritic hands resting in the folds of her apron. She turned her face now towards her husband, now towards Lambrianos, her expression full of grief and unrest.

Lambrianos observed in her expression the indefinable beauty of the sufferer, and a wave of compassion and love welled up within him. Finally, rising, he said, "It's time for me to go."

Kyr Dimitris rose also, extending his hand to Lambrianos.

"You still have to take revenge for the death of your friend," he said.

Kyria Panayota saw Lambrianos to the fence gate in the courtyard.

"Godspeed, my child." she said quietly. *"I Panagia mazi sou."*

Lambrianos took her hand and, impelled by a sudden urge, bowed and kissed it.

He knew that he was telling her goodbye.

VIGNETTES

1

WITH HEART AND SOUL I listen night and day to your rending, my homeland, creating within me a surge that impels me to mold it into words of lamentation and hope. I feel it as an urge and as a mission.

But my self-confidence is moderated when I see Nikolis coming out at dawn from his refugee tent to go to his little field he succeeded in renting and working with a borrowed tractor to grow tobacco.

In the village he was well-off as a tobacco grower. I knew him to be dedicated to his work and his household, an even-keeled person, but closed up and somewhat self-interested.

He confronted calamity and uprootedness with clenched teeth. Without delay he took care of the details of arranging a comfortable enough place for himself and his family. Then he moved adroitly about one place and another, and now he is starting up from nothing to cultivate tobacco on strange ground in a place where this crop is unknown.

I am not able to say how Nikolis hears inwardly the rending that shocks my own spiritual existence. But I can say that his courageous obstinacy and his productive activity are what we need now to get on our feet and hold out.

My own contribution will, of course, be different. I only hope that it will be equal value to what Nikolis offers, perhaps without his realizing it.

2

Weavers as capable as Katelou were few in this area, but for embroidering on the loom, there was none to compare with

239

her. In traditional designs and colors she embroidered her own golden dreams.

The dreams she had when she was still a girl.

The years rolled by. Katelou—now a grandmother—did not stop working at her loom whenever she could find time amid all her everyday chores. But she no longer embroidered dreams—everyday toils covered them over—she only embroidered her life. Nevertheless, from the designs and colors of tradition Katelou derived the assurance one finds in creating beauty with one's hands. And she found that her life might have been difficult, but it was good.

When the barbarians broke in and she found herself uprooted from her soil and from her life, feeling like a hurt and useless being, Katelou knew deep down that if she at least had her loom she would find some consolation.

Then well-meaning folks were found who saw to it that this consolation was provided for the weavers among the refugees. And Katelou ceased feeling useless when she was enabled to embroider her sorrow into the designs and colors of tradition.

3

He could not shut his eyes all night long, hounded by tormenting thoughts: should we leave? . . . should we stay? . . .

But when morning came, he was impelled by long-acquired, everyday habits. He got up, went out into the courtyard, picked up the basket and shinnied up the fig tree to cut some fresh figs for breakfast. And when he breathed in the pungent odor of the fig tree, he stopped thinking and felt as if life continued the same as before the misfortune.

Suddenly voices were heard, then the trampling of feet . . . and more voices . . . and more . . . and cars starting up . . . The village was humming, but he kept on picking the early figs, one by one.

Even when his wife emerged from the house, in a state, the little boy in her arms and the girl clinging fearfully on to her dress, he continued, with unaccountable stubbornness, to hunt through the foliage for a ripe fig.

But he recovered himself when he heard his wife's voice.

240

"Good Lord, Mihalis! . . . Can't you hear what's going on? . . . The Turks are coming . . ."

He came down from the fig tree.

He stood a moment, rattled, undecided. Is he to abandon his house, his possessions, everything else just like that and leave? And go where? . . . And there was something else deeper that was eating him: to run away? . . . Is that manly? . . .

"Let's go, Mihalis . . . Think of the children . . ." his wife implored.

He saw her protecting the child in her arms; he saw his daughter look at him wildly, seeking help . . . His hesitations vanished.

How can you stand up like a man, he thought, before an armed, cowardly, and rapacious enemy? In this case being a man is just the opposite, to bear the pain of uprooting.

He smiled at the girl and gave her the basket of figs. And she immediately became calm.

"Relax, Katerina," he said to his wife. "Hurry up and get ready to leave."

4

Back when Yannakos was living well in his village, he saw with his mind's eye that happiness was always somewhere else, away from his own surroundings.

Even beauty, which he thought of as an inseparable part of happiness, he had no eye for in his beautiful village. He only saw it—and hankered after it—elsewhere, now here, now there, but especially on the mountain, where they would go from time to time on an outing during the summer.

(This is the way we all are. We look from afar at a house in the meadow. Its beauty charms us, and we consider its inhabitants fortunate. And we do not see our own house in the same way, neither the beauty it might have nor the good times we have under its roof. The routines, the worries, the toils of everyday wrap us in a fog that does not leave us an opening to see out of.)

But now that the calamity has uprooted him from his village, and he found refuge in the mountain, in a cottage

241

kindly offered, Yannakos has an eye for nothing but his mental picture of his village, the beauty, and the happiness that he lost.

5

Alarmed by the fear that passed through the crowd at the news that the Turks were on the way, Paraskevou followed along with the others, placed herself in the hands of those who helped her scramble into the truck, and, before she had a chance to realize how and why, she was left looking at the village they were leaving behind. The truck was last in the procession of refugees, following after the bus and the cars.

When they finally stopped at a woods and they helped her get out of the truck, she felt lost somewhere in the void, incapable of thought.

The others scattered. Each family picked out one of the pines, piled at its roots the small possessions they had time to take with them on their flight. They were chatting.

She realized then that she was completely alone, and she was frightened.

She had never felt loneliness or fear for as long as she had lived in her village and in her courtyard. Even though there, too, she lived all alone, since Elias, her only son—the only bond she had to life—had joined the army.

6

Her loneliness in the refugee camp, the fear, the uncertainty about the fate of her son—the only support left to her—became a whirlpool that grabbed at her and spun her about, drawing her into its depths, into hopelessness.

But Paraskevou resisted being hauled under. With the quiet courage which she had learned to battle against the torments of her difficult life, she battled the current now, too, strongly supported by her old, deeply rooted devotion to work and housekeeping. By finding herself occupied all day long with some task for herself or for the others around her, she could relax.

The order and decorum that she took care to create out of nothing in her tent reflected in her heart and expelled hopelessness, expelled from the word "missing" any meaning except the vague assumption that her Elias must be somewhere, either in hiding or in prison. She was sure of it. She could see him dressed in his uniform running and hiding. . . hear him cry out for help . . . and there were moments when she would reach out and take him by the hand as she used to do when he was a child . . . And she faulted herself bitterly for senselessly fleeing from the village without taking anything with her, not even a change of underwear for the boy if nothing else, and now where would she find a change of clean clothes to give him when he comes . . .

7

A small dog, a neglected half-breed cross between a shepherd and a hound, was the only animal from the village in the refugee camp.

In the village he didn't belong to anyone, now wandering about and snuffling through the garbage, now following the children at a safe distance until he was sure of their intentions: whether they would pelt him with stones or call him over to play with them.

It was one of the times he was playing with the children when the black day came and they fled from the village. When the children heard the anxious cries, they ran and got on the bus. The dog thought this was part of the game, hopped in after them, and crouched under a seat.

Now, in the encampment, he continues as he did before: sometimes wandering about, slinking and uneasy, among the tents; sometimes playing with the children.

But at night he is not at ease as he used to be, when he would go to Arestis's stable and curl up next to the cow, feeling companionship and replying with a soft sigh whenever he heard her move and snort.

Now at night he roams inconsolably in the encampment, yowling pitifully, in search of his lost companion.

8

I remember the cemetery of my village and hold in my mind the image of it, laden with a vague, complex, and overpowering sense of holiness, made out of memories.

As young children we looked at it with the same superficial reverence with which we regarded the church—a reverence that did not impede our shooting with our slingshots at the sparrows in its cypress trees. But it made us tremble lest we tread on a grave.

Later, in the poetic years of youth, we saw it as a visible expression of our emotional world: a place of refuge and peace, an Ark alone in the field, where our roots and our dreams were preserved in the shadows of its crosses.

Later still, in our mature years, it became a link to bind the toils and concerns of everyday with that ineffable something else that protects us from cynicism.

And all this in a synthesis, to constitute the foundation of our hearts and our earthly souls.

The barbarians came and sewed ruination, pillaged, raped, because they were slaves of their drive for rapine and bestiality.

But the village cemetery had nothing to carry off or despoil. Lord, what compelled them to desecrate the village cemetery?

9

The hardships and humiliation suffered throughout his captivity wearied Christos so much in body and soul that he involuntarily fell into a state of indifference. He was aware of the dangers of it. He attempted to shake off this creeping lethargy, but he could not.

Even now, on the bus taking him and his companions back, he was looking out the window, like one in a torpor, almost unmoved, at the familiar places in Nicosia smiling at him under the bright light.

But when the bus arrived at its destination and stopped amid a noisy crowd, his mind at once came awake and realizing fully what was happening.

Shaken, he saw the women crowded around out front, each one holding out a photograph, questioning in supplication those on the bus. At first he wondered what was going on. But he soon caught on, though he could not make out their words, which were drowned out by the shouts and cries of those who recognized someone on the bus.

For a moment his attention was caught by one of the photos in particular, the face of a young man who reminded him of Sotiris, the joined brows, the bold look. . . . But on closer look, he saw that it was only a vague resemblance. It was not Sotiris. No.

"Have you seen him anywhere? . . . ," he heard an impatient voice accost him from behind the photograph, a spark of hopeless expectation in the young woman's eyes.

He looked again at the photograph. No. He was sure.

"Have you seen him anywhere? . . . ," he heard the voice again, this time heartrending.

"No," Christos shook his head and felt indescribable grief as he looked at those eyes riveted on him, darkening and fading out.

10

Contrary to the opinion of his parents, who regarded his decision to take work as a day laborer as the utmost degradation, the crowning of their misfortune, Renos looked at it cheerfully as a deed of daring, perhaps the first of his life.

Gifted with intelligence as he was, he had been taught from childhood to live in the manner of the upper classes, to be surrounded by pampering and praise for his good grades at school, to see now and tomorrow as a well-spread rug. It was natural for him, then, with the calcified certainties he had acquired at school and home, to lay out a solitary, level route upon which to walk smoothly from success to success up to his graduate degree in economics.

(But that did not corrupt his heart, as one might expect. It did not have a chance to. The hearts of youth can be lulled to sleep when guided by the certainties we mentioned, but they stay strong as long as their first youth lasts.)

The calamity found him at the beginning of his apprenticeship in his father's enterprises. It caught him unexpect-

245

edly, as a downpour out of a clear sky; it scattered the paper wrappings that had protected him in his false middle-class urban life and left him unprotected within a hideous reality.

He shared the grief of his parents and their circle during their nightmarish flight from all that their lives had been founded upon, and during their first days of life in exile.

But as those bitter days passed, which he lived through not as his own personal suffering, but as a fate common to a great many others, the withered half-truths which had kept him entrapped in a world of superficial reality began to break down and finally vanish. And then appeared before him another truth, deep and unexplored, one held in common by all his countrymen: these here and now of the calamity, but also those of the past and future. Out of the ground, out of the ancient buildings which he knew only as revered ruins from times past and dead, he was now hearing a different message, something like maternal instinct seeking help, which dug to the depths of his world within and rearranged radically his psychological makeup and critical faculties.

Naturally, he did not cease to consider his necessity to find some way, no matter how temporary, to earn a living in the difficult circumstances he and his parents found themselves. And when he heard about a job in inventory at the loading docks at good pay, he took it without hesitation.

11

When I turned the corner I caught sight of him some distance away coming in my direction. He went along the wall with short, hesitant steps, stopping in front of each shop, proffering something like a pile of papers that he held in his right hand, then moving on his way. He did not see me in the bustle of the street.

I knew him when he was different, when he walked with his head held high, a tough old fellow, a hospitable host in his village, where I went every now and then on business.

246

After the disaster I often thought of him and others I knew from the area where the Turkish invader now treads. I remembered them as they were when I met them. I would not have imagined that they could change so much in so brief a time. I would just say to myself, "Where do you suppose so-and-so is?" about one or the other of them.

I stopped at the corner and watched him.

When he came closer and saw me, he quickly pushed the hand with the papers into his pocket. But before he could do that I saw that it was lottery tickets.

I pretended that I had just then seen him.

"*Ora kali*," I said, "how's it going?"

"O.K., I guess," he answered quietly.

He tried, successfully, to straighten up and smile at me, but he showed no interest in continuing the conversation.

I realized that I had to let him go for the time being. I just said to him:

"I'd like you to drop by my office some day for a chat. I'm still at the same place. You know where it is."

12

She entered the doctor's waiting room, glanced around at those seated, and went dragging her feet to sit next to another middle-aged woman, who was as poorly dressed as she was.

With both hands she adjusted her dress, fixed her kerchief, and remained hunched over, looking at the floor with an expression of pain and endurance on her hollow face.

"Is the doctor in?" she turned to ask her neighbor.

"Yes," answered the other, and shortly asked, "Where you from?"

"Ais Yorkis."

"Refugee?"

"Refugees," she sighed.

Some of them looked at her with compassion, but she seemed not to notice.

She stayed hunched over for some time. Then she raised her head. Opposite her was the large window and beyond its closed glass was the cloudy autumn sky.

Her eyes sparkled.

247

"Our olives will be ready for harvest now," she said as if talking to herself.

13

But let us not forget the words of the immortal Makriyannis: "Man is both for good and evil."

Along with good intentions and hope, fatigue lies se - cretly in wait within us, along with the temptation to forget, to watch out for the easy way.

Even the greatest misfortune turns to monotony when enough time goes by. The pain, unbearable at the start, the indignation, the determined demand for rights that have been trampled down may then give way to a mood of melan- cholic perseverance that bores secretly within. This is not far distant from habit, from acclimation to misfortune, a condition worse than the misfortune itself.

ADDENDUM

The following stories, not included in the original edition of *Times Immovable,* were reviewed by the author for inclusion in the Greek edition of *Tetralogy of the Times* published by the Bank of Cyprus Cultural Foundation.

MELANI

WITHIN THE LAST few years the large village has become a small town.

An expanse of green once used to surround the single, somnolent shopping district. The green was colorfully dotted with little country houses each with its courtyard and fence. But one area after another became crowded with sections of town, between which there remain for potential profit shapeless areas of land divided into lots. A heterogeneous, discontinuous totality taking on shape. "The town of the future," the local weekly once wrote, among other such bombast. And ever since all sensible folk on every occasion sip up that beautiful summing-up of their sudden prosperity, abandoning nostalgic memories of the good old days to a few dreamers.

Nevertheless, if the good old days passed into the realm of idealized memories, their traces have not yet disappeared. Crammed in among the fanciful structures of the new town, or isolated out in the expanse of the building lots, they persist in maintaining their arches and aged walls upright in spite of the newly established street plan: sad remnants, two-storied mansions with tumbledown wooden balconies and charming inside courtyards, or simple brick cottages hiding for protection behind the remains of a fence.

Such is Melani's little house. It stands by itself, wedged between the new structures along the shore road, a stranger amid so much change all around it; well-preserved, nevertheless, with its indigo windows, immovable in time, housing an immovable being: Melani.

Immovable being! . . . How might an outsider know how wildly disturbing for Melani the apparently motionless interval was that separated her from the beautiful Melanitsa!

251

There were storms that she tamed by her minute everyday attention to housework and to the needlework by which she made her living, until she became the spinster she is today, a creature hermetically sealed, addicted by her small mania for order and cleanliness, one of those squeaky-clean little women who are graced with the ability to walk through the mud without getting any of it on her shoes.

But now the storms have been relegated to the mists of the past. And one day comes and passes by like the others in a senseless, busy fussiness that did not vary even the other day when she received the telegram nor today either when the postman brought her the letter. Except that her heart was somehow liberated and she trembled like a bird that was used to its cage and is not sure whether it wants to fly again.

When the light faded, she stopped sewing. She got up, put her work table in order, and went out into the courtyard. She stood there for a short time looking at the sea, listening to the song of the evening. She felt memories flutter within her, but put them aside. She watered her plants, closed the shutters, went into the house, turned on the light, and sat down at the table, bolt upright, her palms on her knees; a black-clad, inviolable, ecstatic figure.

The letter was on the table. She reached over and picked it up, unfolded it, and read it again. Her sister-in-law had written her from overseas to confirm the message of the telegraph of a few days before: the death of Kleitos, Melani's brother.

". . . during recent months he felt some twinges in his heart on his way to work . . . the doctors said he needed rest and change . . . suddenly he had an attack and was dead in a few hours . . . Now the child and I have no support . . . we're in God's hands and yours . . . I send you kisses, your sister, Annika."

Melani smiled bitterly. She had not met her nor had ever thought of her as a sister, the woman Kleitos had married overseas. Kleitos had written her about it, and in that letter next to "Your brother Kleitos" the sister-in-law had set her name. And Melani was enraged and did not reply.

There ended the dreams that she and Kleitos had made, and the promise that he would sponsor her so she could join him as soon as he had settled in a job. Melani waited; she waited for five whole years. She worked with her needle and waited; she paid off the mortgage and waited . . .

They had grown tired, Melanitsa of waiting for a marriage that never happened and Kleitos of chasing elusive hopes. They decided that their boredom with the island was to blame, and they were taken with a strange yearning for life abroad.

So brother and sister sat down and laid out a definite plan. They would mortgage the house to pay for the fare and Kleitos would go abroad first. Afterwards they would meet in the great country they had made the homeland of their fantasy. And they built their happiness, built it with their fantasy upon the promises of the "Emigration Agency."

But Kleitos—or life—did not keep the promise. In the beginning he wrote regularly. His letters spoke of the difficulties of life but also of his determination to make their "plan" work. And Melani's hopes soared. Then his letters became less frequent and conveyed only weariness, fuzziness, longing for the island sun, and a feeling of loneliness that dripped uneasiness into Melani's heart. Then suddenly he wrote that he had got married. ". . . how much could I stand of the bachelor's life . . ." And Melani, in exasperation, refused to answer. She had been doubly excluded from that time on and her soul withered. Nor did he write again in the five years that followed. And during all that time, as if from an instinct for self-preservation, Melani stubbornly drove her memories away.

But the telegraph, and now this letter, weakened Melani's resistance; she felt strangely liberated when the memories flooded the house and confronted her again with the day that Kleitos departed.

§

The hours kept passing by and Melani sat there, head bowed, listening to a longing that had been stirring within her all these days: for Kleitos's child to come fill the void

253

left by so many things gone before she could catch them! She saw in her mind's eye the child she did not know filling the house and her own emptiness with his presence, and she came to a decision. She got up, opened a drawer, took out paper and pen, placed them on the table, and before she began writing, listened to the roar of the sea.

"Dear sister Annika . . . my house is your house . . . bring the child and make yourself at home . . ."

For the first time in a long while Melani smiled that night in her sleep.

Nevertheless, during the days that followed she passed into her busy lethargy. Her care in housekeeping, her persistent attention to her thousand little routines did not leave room for the magic of expectation. Only during the motionless nighttime hours did a trace of hope tremble within her, but it was nothing certain.

A month had gone by when a telegram from Annika arrived to put the seal of certainty upon the vague thought of change in Melani's life. They would arrive, it said, on such-and-such a day on such-and-such a ship. Melani shuddered a bit and wanted to believe that it was because she would be seeing Kleitos's child. "Lord, how I will love him!" And she set about straightening up the room for the child and the "other" woman, the room Kleitos had grown up in.

She opened up the linen chest and from its unused stores, redolent of cedar, she drew double-ply bedding, sheets, her finest *taista*, bright-colored curtains and, with lips tightly shut, in a state of excitement, she got everything ready. Ah! Melani would offer faultless hospitality.

The evening before, she had sent for Theoris, the driver. And he arrived already informed about the trip to the harbor where the ship would arrive next morning. You see, everybody had been made aware of all the details, and the neighbors, who mocked the spinster for her odd behavior and loved her for her industry, now would talk about her decision.

"I'll come by for you at dawn," said Theoris.

254

But Melani decided that, no, she would not go with him. The trip would take two hours, both ways, and she gets car sick. She had better stay here.

"As you like," said Theoris, downing in one gulp the cognac she had offered him on a tray. "I'll take care of it myself. Lots of luck with your new arrivals."

Melani remained pensive.

It was almost noon when Melani, her ear long since on the alert, recognized Theoris's horn and came to the threshold.

Annika got out of the car first, a pale, unimpressive woman in black. And after her a bashful youngster with tousled hair and huge eyes. He had hold of his mother's skirt and looked around indecisively. Melani observed that the child was neglected.

"Welcome," she said.

The two women exchanged a hesitant kiss.

Then Melani stooped over and picked up the child, petted him, and began making baby talk to him. But when she sensed those great eyes searching her own, she was twinged by a guilty feeling that she was not telling the truth.

In the meantime Theoris had unloaded the luggage, two worn suitcases and a large bundle.

Annika, who was not expecting such hospitality and a separate room, stumbled over her words as she tried to express her gratitude. At one point she reached out and took Melani's hand and was about to draw it to her lips. But Melani caught her in time and suddenly withdrew her hand.

In the evening, when she was shut away alone in her room, some incoherent worries came niggling in her mind and she could not expel them. She felt deprived and out of sorts.

She spent a sleepless night, tormented as before by that fierce disturbance that she thought she had got over.

A LIFE

SUDDENLY the sound of the church bell settled over the party. The dancers listened questioningly. Dong! . . . An evocative bronze groan that spoke to their souls with simple and abiding patterns of all the emotions in the life of the village, be it joy or sadness, or that vague and devout exultation of the humble towards some kind of redemption.

The sound covered the revelry of the partiers with a flutter of expectancy. But one peal, by itself, may not mean anything.—Sometimes the little kids get brave and go haul on the bell rope, then scatter and hide in fear of what they have done.—The lightfooted dancers continued their high-spirited rhythms. The partiers toasted by touching glasses. Panayis, in high spirits, set up the cry, "Eeeeh!"

But, dong! . . . the peal was heard again, calm, other-worldly, beckoning. Now there was no room for doubt. It was the funereal, single stroke of death. All at once silence fell on the coffee shop. The partiers looked at one another. Which house might it be? . . . And their thoughts turned to Vassiliki.

Dong! . . . came again the sound, huge in the silence.

Kouvaros carefully laid his lute on the table and said thoughtfully, "It must be poor Vassiliki . . . Praise be to God . . ." And he crossed himself.

No one answered. Some got up and left.

Prokopis, who was sitting among the householders, kept his eyes on the ground for a long time. He started to speak, changed his mind, raised his head, muttered something between his teeth, leaned on his cane, and got up. He was a middle-aged gentleman, tall, austere, with whitish blond mustache and thin, uncombed hair. He was wearing *vrakes* and heavy boots.

A woman went by in haste down the slope.

"Who?" someone from the parapet of the coffee shop asked with a gesture.

"Vassiliki," she said without slowing her step.

Prokopis left the coffee shop and started up the slope. He took long, measured, steady strides, as the men of the mountains do. His steps and his cane struck heavily on the cobblestones. He headed up the slope, though the death-marked house was in the lower neighborhood. That's where Prokopis was going, because Vassiliki was a relative of his. But he wanted to take the long way around. He would leave the village and take the downslope outside the orchards. To clear his head a little. There wasn't any rush. Not any more . . . Vassiliki is at rest and will wait . . .

But was her life, her tortured life, ever anything but an endless waiting? Vassiliki was always waiting. Why? . . . Do we know what we are waiting for? . . . We're just waiting . . . all of us. Waiting for something vague and beautiful, a consolation, some indefinable ideal of peace, a joy that does not come but is supposed to come some day . . . This waiting that has no form, nor any occasion, somehow throws light on the darkness and softens our hearts.

But there are creatures who have upon them a deeper seal of endless and hopeless waiting. Creatures, separated off, as on the rim, deprived to a greater degree than others of the small joys, the support, the self-deceptions, which are the elements of a common lot. Tragic figures who are found standing outside the common lot. Such was the grievous and powerful figure of Vassiliki.

She was one of those exceptional women who, if life happens to give them a purpose, will enter the front lines to shore up a household, to give life to a struggle, to lead a village. But for whom, and when, does life, the endless toil we call life, open such roads in these mountain villages? But even in this dog's life of ours some creature is there by your side, husband, child, parent, to taste the bread you've kneaded, to put on the clothes you've mended, to receive the bitter offering of your sweat, and warm your heart with silent presence, at night, under the same roof with you. Vassiliki, brave soul, found herself very early deprived of all these consolations.

258

They married her off when she was fifteen. Yes. Fifteen. That's the way the groom wanted her, since she happened to be poor and he established, widowed and almost forty. A young woman would warm up his bed and his torpid heart.

In her linen chest where her modest dowry was stored, she had taken care to hide—at the very bottom where they wouldn't show—her dolls, two of them which she had made herself out of rags. And she loved them. When she was first married, she would go longingly to the linen chest every time she was alone in the new and strange house. She would open it and haul the dolls out of hiding, then shut the chest and spread it nicely again with its ornamental coverlet, and set the dolls on it, leaning them against the wall. All at once a warmth would sweeten the cold atmosphere. The unfamiliar and dumb objects surrounding her would bow and speak with compassion to her. The bride would smile. And the dolls, breaking out in laughter, stretching their arms out to her, would look at her lovingly with their non-existent, large eyes.

Other times she would go lean into the great empty jar and call softly so she could close her eyes and listen to the echo returning muffled and huge from the bottom of the earth. She would rise up with her face flushed and look fearfully around. Although she had taken care and assured herself that there wasn't a creature around to see her, the thought that there might be paralyzed her. What if this unheard-of game were heard in the village! That Vassiliki, a married woman, plays like a silly kid! Alas, Vassiliki. Where would you go to hide from slander! But she saw that she was alone and was reassured. The baskets all in a row, the plough from its corner, the smoky beams in the ceiling, all looked at her and smiled.

This strange isolation in the unknown of her new life, the incoherent and unanswerable questions she would ask herself, the disappointment and the vague hopes, lasted for several months. She lived in confusion within a dream fantasy. Sometimes she would secretly cry and other times she would secretly laugh. Until the day when she felt within her vitals the movement of the child. All at once everything was cleared up. Not, of course, that everything took on meaning. What meaning can life have in a backwards village? It was only that the incoherent questions ceased, as did the fantasies that did not take shape. Now the fantasies had quietly come to earth and waited, gently attached to one definite form. The world became simple and tamed, and it took the place of that magic, the superb and tormenting expectation which welled up from her fantasy. Vassiliki became serene. Her face, her arms, her breast began to fill out like a fruit ripening.

She gave birth to a boy. As happens with every special event, the neighborhood was in a stir, and the courtyard of Palities turned into a meeting place for the women, who came and went busily and officiously to make inquiries, give advice, and lend a hand. Vassiliki's birth-pangs and her restrained outcries became matters of common interest, though, to be sure, the lives of everyone in our villages are matters of common interest. And when she was delivered of it, the kerchief-wrapped figures, gathered in the courtyard like an ancient chorus, spread their arms in prayer, raised their eyes to heaven, and refolded their arms over their bellies with a sigh: "I glorify you, my God." And Palities, who had seen no child from his first wife, disconcerted everyone when he made a show of his emotions, sobbing like a child. Nevertheless Palities was a harsh man. He soon put his heart under wraps again and took care to put on his usual expression when he went in to see the new mother.

"Poor thing," said the old women of the neighborhood when the years had passed. "That was the only joy that Vassiliki ever had in her life. Afterwards it was bitterness and nothing else," and they would shake their heads with compassion.

Perhaps it was not her only joy—how would the old women know of the fairies, the dolls, the golden dreams— but it was her last.

The following year Palities died suddenly, brought down by sunstroke. When the child reached his fifth year, death took him, too.

"God gave her one consolation, then took that away from her, too," said the old women conclusively, bowing their heads before the inscrutable will.

But just as they could not know the bright flame of her joy, they could not imagine the breadth of her pain, either.

How could they conceive of what a brave-hearted woman like Vassiliki had invested in the curly head of a child. She had double-locked her soul and strangled the tormenting enticements of her body. She had inherited vineyards, you see, from Palities. And his relatives scrutinized the widow's life tirelessly and cruelly.

But Vassiliki did not bend the knee to them. She gritted her teeth, wrapped her head in a kerchief, and managed her household with good sense and industry. So success-fully that the living she inherited from Palities increased with the years. Thin, black-draped, and key-toting, she traversed the empty house tirelessly, or took the path into the field, the garden, the vineyard, to oversee the workers, to arrange every job herself, to bargain with buyer or seller, according to the situation, an equal among equals no matter whom, self-sufficient and cunning.

This life lasted for twenty years.

At first the villagers praised her courage and industry. But as the years passed by and she continued to travel her difficult road unbending and disdainful, they began looking at her with some apprehension.

"Enough, Vassiliki," the old women would say. "Have pity on yourself. Adopt a daughter to help you, so you will have companionship, too."

But she cut them short.

"Why? Don't you think I'm capable of running my own household?"

The neighbor women wagged their heads and muttered behind her back.

"Why is she being so close-fisted? My Lord! A dried-out wretch with neither child nor dog!"

How could these good folks understand? How could they understand the hell of desperation?

In time her figure and large dark eyes took on a pas-sionate, hard edge.

And with that she accepted, too, upright and unbending, the great ill fortune that plagued her for three years before sending her to the grave.

There was not a creature around to tell of her pain. How could that be! There were, you could say, both relatives and neighbor women willing to listen and come to her aid. But locking up her soul had become a second nature, which prevailed. And for that matter, is there any relative or neighbor really your own? No. Not your own. Vassiliki did not have a family. Nor did she long for any.

They vaguely knew that Vassiliki had a lump on her breast. She went from time to time to the doctor in the City.

"Get well soon, Vassiliki . . . Put an emollient on it, to open it up . . . ," chattered the woman next to her on the bus on the way back to the village.

Vassiliki smiled, but made no answer. She was looking beyond, at the peaks of the mountains. Only her eyes, which became more and more hollow and shining, revealed her quiet torment.

Nevertheless, she stood on her feet almost to the end. Only during the last two months did she take to her bed. And then the neighbor women again took hold of her courtyard and house, well-intentioned, with no discretion, eager to share her sorrows. Vassiliki surrendered without a word. The pain, now in charge, was galloping through her innards.

§

"Do you remember, Prokopis?" Prokopis heard an inner voice as he walked down the slope outside Palities's garden.

The garden was surrounded by a fence of reeds. And it was behind this very barricade that he had kissed Vassiliki one evening long ago. One single, unforgettable kiss. Oh! how that evening came rushing back now, with all its fragrance, like a wind in his chest, exciting him!

A year had passed since Palities's death, and Vassiliki . . . Oh! how Prokopis remembered her as she was back then! The sight of her left him breathless . . . He was also twenty . . . That evening he happened to be alone with her here, quite unexpectedly . . . All his blood had risen and was pounding wildly in his temples . . . He took her in his arms and felt her trembling like a bird from head to foot . . . He kissed her on the mouth and sensed that she was yielding to him . . . But all at once she shuddered in panic, pushed him brusquely away, and burst onto the road, running in flight towards the village. Prokopis was left behind like one turned to stone. He did not even try to follow her. He headed for the gorge as if trying to hide.

For a long time Vassiliki avoided him. And when un-avoidably they happened to be together, she never, abso-lutely never, indicated that she remembered that occur-rence. Once or twice when Prokopis attempted to remind her with the silent language of the eyes, she did not re-spond. Until finally there came moments when Prokopis wondered whether such a thing had actually happened or whether it was his imagination.

§

The courtyard door was wide open, as was the house door at the far end of the courtyard.

Back straight and under control, Prokopis passed among the people in the courtyard and went into the house. There under the trembling light of the candles, he beheld a flesh-less face framed in a tight kerchief, eyes shut, unbelievably hollow, very dark.

His lips began to tremble. He turned about and went out into the courtyard.

At that moment the priest appeared in the courtyard door. The shawl-draped myrrh-bearers, who were gathered in the courtyard like an ancient chorus, freed their hands, which had been clasped over their bellies, each raised the right one and with broad movements crossed themselves.

THE PRIDE OF THE POOR MAN

ON ONE SIDE of the square in the public garden, the marble bust of the Poet upon its tall plinth gazed drowsily and sorrowfully at the long line of dusty little pine trees and beyond them at the entrance of the garden.

It was afternoon. The sun was still high, but under its slanting rays the shadows of the trees had begun to lengthen, offering some consolation to the place, which was wilting under the searing heat, the blinding light, the dust. The cicadas persisted in their attempt to convert heat into sound. Every now and then for some unknown reason they fell silent. But before long they would take up their deafening hymn again, all together, triumphantly.

The little round cistern in the middle of the square was dry, and the bottom of it was full of the scales of dried-up mold.

All around the square the little benches waited expectantly, half of them in the sun, half in the shade, an unrefreshing shade, clear and mottled with bright, trembling blotches.

A little old man came hobbling along, leaning on his cane. He sat down on one of the benches. A little girl of about six was following him. She was slender and blond, wearing a faded red apron. Her pale face would have been unremarkable had not her large, gray-green, long-lashed eyes lighted it with a fresh glow.

The old man shared with the girl that indefinable resemblance that closely related people sometimes do when they are separated by a great many years. His half-closed gray eyes took on a tender expression when they turned to the youngster. He was wearing trousers of locally-made cotton and a heavy khaki shirt with pockets.

The little girl sat on the bench, too, at the other end, crossed her arms over her apron, and looked around her, swinging her legs.

A sparrow alighted from the pine, bounced two or three times like a ball, took a very hasty dust bath in the fine, warm dirt, and, phrr, took off again. The other sparrows in the tree took off, too, following the first.

"Go play, Maritsa," said the old man.

The little girl got down off the bench, went and leaned over the cistern, and tried to imagine it full of water, but got tired of it. She went to the swings and began swinging without enthusiasm until the moment she saw a beautiful, colorful group coming along the pines: an elegant lady with a little girl and behind them a young servant girl carrying a green oil-cloth bag.

The girl was a bit older than Maritsa. She was dressed in blue, with white anklets and white slippers. Her face, aglow from scrubbing, her jet black hair, polished with combing, revealed the great care with which this beloved creature was surrounded. She was walking along very properly, pushing a doll buggy with a red awning and nickel fixtures.

Maritsa stopped swinging her legs and watched as though hypnotized.

The lady went over and sat on a bench. She allowed some time to pass before she nodded to the young servant girl, who was standing indecisively, to sit down, too.

Like a mother, uttering sweet words, the little girl arranged the doll's bedding in the buggy. But when she became aware of the presence of Maritsa, who, charmed but diffident, had approached and stopped at some distance, the little mommy became more deliberate in her role-playing. She took the doll in her arms and rocked it, casting sidelong glances at the other girl, who came a bit nearer.

"Maritsa," said the old man softly.

Maritsa seemed not to hear.

The elegant lady turned and looked at the old man as if she were measuring the distance between her bench and his. Then she turned to the children.

"Lila, play with the little girl," she said with the patronizing tone of those who, from their exalted position, set an example of forbearance.

But the children found their own way to get together and play. Except that Maritsa gave way and played the role of the poor friend, as though it were natural, while Lila charmingly took on an air of importance and gave orders. "Help me bathe the baby—take it out for a stroll in the buggy—be careful not to let it get uncovered and catch cold."

The old man was watching and seemed to be getting more and more upset.

"Maritsa," he said again more loudly.

Maritsa turned and looked at him beseechingly, as if to say: I heard you, grandfather, but what can I do? It's so beautiful to be able to hold this wonderful doll in my arms and to push this buggy!

The old man bowed his head as though ashamed on behalf of his little darling.

The elegant lady paid no attention to him, but only said something to the servant girl, who took a thermos jug and a parcel wrapped in waxed paper from the bag she was holding. She opened the parcel on the bench and placed the thermos next to it.

"Come, Lila, and eat your sandwich," she said, and added in a tone of compassion, "Lila, let's give the little girl a sandwich, too. Come, little girl."

Maritsa, who was just then pushing the buggy, paused confused, ready to give in to this new temptation.

The old man could take no more.

"Maritsa! Come here!" he ordered.

The youngster realized that this time she had to obey. She left the buggy and came with bowed head.

The elegant lady shrugged.

The old man, stoop-shouldered till then, straightened up, stretched out his hand and caressed the little girl's head. She raised her beautiful eyes and, as if in understanding, smiled at him. I have no complaint, grandfather; no, I have no complaint, said her smile.

"It's time to go, my child," said the old man and rose, leaning again on his cane and, limping as he had come, moved towards the exit, holding the little girl's hand.

They left the garden, crossed the main road, and went up a lane that led to their neighborhood.

On the corner was a kiosk. One of those poor kiosks which one finds in small provincial towns and which cause one to wonder why they are there at all and what they are waiting for in the middle of the wasteland.

The old man stopped in front of the kiosk, hung his cane on his left arm, stuck two fingers of his right hand into the small pocket of his trousers, and took out a few coins.

"*Kalos to* Mastro Savva," the kiosk owner said to him from inside and reached out to give him a pack of cigarettes.

"Hello, Photis," responded the old man. "No, I don't want cigarettes today."

He turned to the youngster and caressed her head again.

"Would you like a chocolate bar, Maritsa?"

Joyous surprise flashed in the child's large eyes. Yes, she nodded twice.

"Give us a chocolate bar, Photis."

He paid, took a chocolate bar wrapped in red and silver paper from Photis and offered it to the little girl. Then he sighed with relief as if he had rid himself of some inner burden.

The little girl was happy.

GLOSSARY

carina: term of endearment (pretty; lovely)

giaour: one outside the Moslem faith; an infidel

kafeneion: coffee shop

kalos to: a welcoming greeting

koboloyi: a string of beads

koulourakia: cookies

koulouras: a vendor of fresh sesame bread rolls

kykas: a kind of tropical plant

Kyr: abbreviation of *Kyrios* (Mr.) often used as a title with first names

Kyria: Mrs., used also with first names

levendi mou: a term of affection and pride (my prince; my strong young man)

lountza: dried pork marinated in wine and coriander

Mastro: used, like *Kyr*, as a title with men's first names

meze: appetizers; tidbits; snacks

ora kali: a greeting

ouzo: a kind of aperitif with licorice taste

palia: old things

Panagia—I Panagia mazi sou: common *bon voyage* greeting, even for short trips (the Madonna be with you) *papadia:* a priest's wife

pappou: grandfather

poveretta: poor woman; poor little woman

pyrofani: light used by fishermen to attract fish

soutzoukakia: oblong-shaped meatballs with garlic

taista: a special kind of reinforced (double-woven and therefore treasured) fabric

tavli: backgammon

trayaska: a kind of coat

tyropita: cheese pie (pl. *tyropites*)

vourka: shepherd's bag, made of sheepskin

vraka: large black men's trousers or breaches (pl. *vrakes*)

ya hara: joyous Greek greeting upon arriving or leaving

ABOUT THE TRANSLATORS

DONALD E. MARTIN teaches Greek and English at Rockford College. He has also taught at the University of Cyprus. Educated in the classics (University of Cincinnati), his involvement with modern Greek letters began with a fellowship to the University of Thessaloniki (1966-67). He is the recipient of the Armand G. Erpf Award, given by the Translation Center at Columbia University, for his English translation of the novel *Leonis* by George Theotokas.

SOTERIOS G. STAVROU was born in Cyprus and educated in the United States in English literature and history (Augsburg College) and in ancient history and the classics (University of Minnesota). He is currently teaching modern Greek at the University of Minnesota. His translations of Greek literature into English include *The Free Spirit* by George Theotokas.

NOSTOS BOOKS ON
MODERN GREEK HISTORY AND CULTURE

Theofanis G. Stavrou, *general editor*
University of Minnesota

1. Yannis Ritsos, *Eighteen Short Songs of the Bitter Motherland.* Translated from Greek by Amy Mims with illustrations by the poet. Edited with an introduction by Theofanis G. Stavrou. $15.00 cloth. Out of Print.
2. Kimon Friar, *The Spiritual Odyssey of Nikos Kazantzakis.* Edited with an introduction by Theofanis G. Stavrou. $10.00 cloth.
3. Kostas Kindinis, *Poems: Reinvestigations and Descent from the Cross.* Translated from Modern Greek with a preface by Kimon Friar. $10.00 cloth.
4. Andonis Decavalles, *Pandelis Prevelakis and the Value of a Heritage.* Including *Rethymno as a Style of Life* by Pandelis Prevelakis, translated from Greek by Jean H. Woodhead. Edited with an introduction by Theofanis G. Stavrou. $10.00 cloth.
5. John Anton, *Critical Humanism as a Philosophy of Culture: The Case of E. P. Papanoutsos.* Edited with an introduction by Theofanis G. Stavrou. $10.00 cloth.
6. Ioanna Tsatsos, *My Brother George Seferis.* Translated from the original Greek by Jean Demos with a preface by Eugene Current-Garcia. $20.00 cloth.
7. Donald C. Swanson, *Vocabulary of Modern Spoken Greek (English-Greek and Greek-English).* $15.00 cloth.
8. Nikos Kazantzakis, *Two Plays—Sodom and Gomorrah* and *Comedy: A Tragedy in One Act.* Translated from Greek with an introduction to *Sodom and Gomorrah* by Kimon Friar. Including an introduction to *Comedy: A Tragedy in One Act* by Karl Kerényi, translated by Peter Bien. $20.00 cloth.
9. George Thaniel, *Homage to Byzantium. The Life and Work of Nikos Gabriel Pentzikis.* $20.00 cloth.